The Good Boy

The Good Boy

The Good Boy

A Novel

Stella Hayward

AVON

An Imprint of HarperCollins*Publishers*

HarperCollins books may be purchased for educational, business, or sales promotional use. For information, please email the Special Markets Department at SPsales@harpercollins.com.

FIRST EDITION

Interior text design by Diahann Sturge-Campbell

Gold Retriever illustration © panaceaart/Stock.Adobe.com

Library of Congress Cataloging-in-Publication Data has been applied for.

ISBN 978-0-06-341688-8

$PrintCode

For real-life Rory, who was a very good boy

Chapter One

I'M GOING TO TELL YOU A STORY that you are not going to believe. And that's okay, you don't have to. I can hardly believe it
myself. So, treat it like a fairy tale, or a fable. Take it with a pinch
of salt. Doesn't matter to me either way, because I know it's true.
It's happening to me, after all.

The real beginning of the story started about ten years ago,
when I thought I was one person but then suddenly became
another—you don't need to know about that for now.

Just come with me to yesterday evening, on the night before
my thirtieth birthday. Imagine you are on the back of a gull and
you are flying over the North Yorkshire moors, which are covered
in purple and golden heather. The North Sea is on your left: a blue
and sparkling wide-open horizon that promises to take you anywhere you want to go—but you are coming to see me. From a
distance you see all the little houses of the seaside town of Scarborough lined up in neat little rows like row upon row of a string
of pearls, and at least a dozen church spires reaching for the sky.
You whoosh around the ruins of the castle on a hill and swoop
down into the curl of busy South Bay, where the Ferris wheel
turns on the seafront and colored lights are looped between the
lampposts like it's Christmas all year-round.

The streets are crowded with holidaymakers, their overtired children and dogs in tow. The once great Grand Hotel sits proudly above the casinos and amusement arcades like a stately old lady who found herself at a rave by accident. If you take a left by the statue of Queen Victoria and then another at the crossroads, you will arrive at Scarborough's premiere (and only) Mexican restaurant, where I am having birthday-eve dinner with my loud, annoying, beautiful family. Hop off the back of that imaginary bird and come inside, where it's noisy and warm. Just like any other normal Friday night. At least that's what I had thought.

There's music pumping from a speaker positioned just above our table. I am six margaritas in and the fairy lights that crisscross the ceiling have all gone a bit floaty as if they might actually have wings. Sure, I am a bit tipsy, but, hey, it is almost my birthday, after all, and I will be thirty and a proper grown-up. Maybe even old enough for my parents to stop treating me like I am five, and not capable of knowing what I'm doing or why. This happens to be true, but there's no way I'm going to admit that to them.

My mum and dad are so in love, genuinely and enduringly, that it makes you question everything, but most specifically, Am I the third wheel at my own birthday dinner?

(Oh, and I'm the younger, dark-haired woman at the table: dark eyes, short, sitting opposite the parental pheromone fireworks display, wondering how long I have to wait until I can go home to my dog, and if I can escape before the sparkler-packed dessert arrives and the singing commences.)

But I won't be the first person that you notice. It won't even be my parents' ostentatious bliss that catches your eye. No, the first person you will notice is my grandmother, Nanna Maria, as she likes to be known in the Maltese matriarchal tradition. You will notice that there is nothing remotely nanna-ish about her, as she sits at the head of the table flirting with a young waiter who, make no mistake, flirts right back.

Impressive cleavage, jet-black hair, a laugh like a sailor's, and an accent that becomes more Maltese the more she drinks—that's the version of Nanna Maria at my birthday dinner: sexy, sultry, and queen of all she surveys. Though, as I will later find out, she contains multitudes.

Most of my friends, who I'll be having a birthday-night celebration with tomorrow, are in full panic about turning thirty. Behaving like it's some kind of deadline to have your life together by.

Not me; I learned early on that this is it. Life is hard, you get into debt, and then you die. Having dreams are just a gateway to disappointment. Once I used to dream about being the next Vivienne Westwood. Now I realize that big ambitions only lead to big fails. That might make me sound miserable, but I'm not. I'm fine because I'm resigned, and that's a whole different ball game. Every now and then my friends and family will encourage me to dream big and reach for the stars. I always tell them I'm in my chill era. Where enough is literally enough.

Unfortunately, everyone I love cannot get their heads around the fact that I am okay with this. Especially not my nan, who also happens to be my boss.

I complain often and loudly about working for Nanna Maria in her seafront fortune-telling parlor, but everyone knows I don't really mean it. I love Nanna Maria and the weird, never-the-same-two-days-in-a-row job I do running the behind-the-scenes show while she dishes out prophecies to passersby or summons up spirits from the netherworld for only £15.99 per twenty minutes.

Every day might be different, but it's different in exactly the same way, and that's how I like it—me rolling my eyes at all the gullible fools who part with their cash for some of Nanna Maria's wisdom. Well, look who's laughing now.

Nanna Maria finally releases the waiter from the thralldom of her bosom and summons me to her side with a crook of her perfectly manicured finger. It's time for the annual birthday interrogation, which, like death and taxes, is one of the only things in my family's life that cannot be avoided.

Benefiting from regular unsolicited advice from Nanna Maria is a daily occurrence (Why do you only wear black? It drains you! Are you at a funeral? Are you mourning the death of your youth?), but on birthdays her teachings are always loaded with extra drama and some sort of made-up pseudo-magic nonsense laced with superstition and ancient family tradition for good measure. Nanna Maria, encouraged by my mother, maintains the belief that the women in our family are descendants of the powerful priestesses of ancient Malta, imbued with a magic older than time. Which, if that was the case, you might think she'd use to solve the world's problems instead of telling Lorna from Scunthorpe that Elvis is not the man for her.

Anyway, I knew she would have something a bit woo and a bit crazy to tell me. After all, what seaside mystic worth their salt wouldn't? Even so, I had no idea how strange, weird, and wonderful things were about to get.

"It's not too late, you know?" Nanna Maria tells me, instructing me to turn my chair with a whirl of her forefinger so that we are sitting knee to knee. All I want is to get this part over and done with ASAP. Don't get me wrong—Nanna Maria is maybe the most magnificent woman I know next to my mum, who is wonderful for all sorts of other reasons. But when you feel like you are at the opposite end of that scale, it can be a bit intimidating to get her quite so full-frontal, if you catch my drift. Also, I know full well that the clock is counting down to the ignominy of "Happy Birthday" and time is running out to exit the premises before it is too late. Nanna Maria has other ideas. Of course she does.

"I said it's not too late, Eugenie," she repeats, taking my hand as if she were about to read my palm, which she definitely is.

"No thanks, Nanna," I tell her, gently withdrawing my hand. "You know I don't want to know my future. I like to find out stuff on a need-to-know basis."

"You are never any fun." Nanna Maria sighs. "Give me your hand, Genie. I promise not to read your palm. Can't an old woman hold the hand of her only granddaughter before it's too late?"

Nanna has been threatening her imminent death since I was a toddler. In fact, I think my earliest memory is of Nanna replying to my cheerful "See you tomorrow!" with her trademark melodramatic "God willing!" You'd think she would have had a better handle on the situation, you know, considering she's a psychic and all that.

"Of course you can, Nanna," I say, returning my hand to her, which she immediately turns over and scrutinizes fiercely before looking at me and shrugging.

"Nanna!" I try not to behave like a sulking teenager, really, I do, but it's hard when your family treats you like you are one.

"If you don't want to know, you don't want to know," she says infuriatingly. "All I will say is that there are interesting times ahead."

"Well, that could mean anything," I tell her.

"You know you don't have to believe in something for it to be real, don't you? You are like those flat-Earthers, denying what is right in front of you."

"I am not," I protest. "I believe in science and reason . . ."

"You know science is simply man's best guess at trying to know the unknowable, and the thing about the unknowable is that—"

"You can't ever know everything," I finish for her with an adolescent sigh.

"Unless you are me," she says. "So, listen to me when I tell you that—"

"It's not too late, I know." I order another margarita, though I suspect that drinking it will make it very hard to leave without assistance. "I know it's not too late. I have never thought it was too late. I'm not sitting at home every night wringing my hands worrying about things being too late. I'm just living my life, and it's *fine*. I'm *fine*."

"Fine!" Never one to miss an opportunity for drama, Nanna Maria clasps her hand to her bosom. "When did young people decide that *fine* is an acceptable state of being?" Her flashing dark eyes fix on mine. "You only live once on this celestial plane, my darling girl. Yes, you faced a great sadness, too early in your young life. But don't just mark time until the end. You must grasp every second!"

"Must I?" I ask gently. "Sounds exhausting. Nanna, please stop worrying about me. I am okay, honestly, I am. You don't have to give me the pep talk. You could give me a birthday present, though. Remember how I asked for vouchers?"

"*Pfft*, I'm not going to give you vouchers!" She waves her hand as if batting away a fly. "Vouchers are so dull. How can a gift ever be a piece of paper, or worse, a link! What joy can be found in a link?"

"It doesn't matter." I kiss her on both cheeks, taking her hands in mine. "I love you, Nanna. Thank you for coming to my birthday dinner." I look over at Mum and Dad fondly. Almost everyone I really care about is here and I know that I am really lucky to have them rooting for me. Two more cocktails and I might even tell them.

"You are the best grandmother there is, you know," I tell Nanna Maria, before I go back to my seat. "Even if you do weirdly hate the idea of vouchers."

"I know," Nanna says. "But wait a moment, don't go! I do have a gift for you. Something very special."

Looking around, I peer under the table. I can't see anything present-shaped. Which, I realize with a sinking feeling, means that Nanna Maria's gift is something crazy and made-up, like a—

"It is a wish," Nanna Maria tells me very gravely. "I am gifting you a wish."

"Oh . . . good," I say. "Does it have an exchange policy?"

"Listen carefully." Nanna Maria sways in very close and speaks into my ear. "Ours is an ancient family with mystic powers built into our very DNA . . ."

"Yep." I scratch my ear, hoping the table next door is having too good a time to be listening in.

"Once every decade it is within our ancestral powers to gift a wish to those we love. It is an ancient and mighty magic passed down through the female line of our family since the dawn of time."

"Righto," I say, giving her a thumbs-up. "Excellent."

"My grandmother granted me such a wish, and I met your dear departed grandfather. And my mother bestowed her wish upon your mother." Nanna Maria narrows her eyes at my father. "I'm not sure what she used it for, but she seems happy enough so far."

"Nanna, they have been married for thirty-one years," I remind her.

"Anyway, the wish has rules—very serious rules—and it is very important that you pay attention to them because any cock-ups and you are in big trouble. So, are you listening carefully?"

The sooner I let her get on with it the sooner I can go home and pass out in front of the TV, I reason.

"What are the rules, Nanna?" I ask her.

"Once bestowed, the wish must be made precisely at the stroke of midnight."

"So, in about forty-seven minutes, then?" I say, looking at my watch. "Siri, set an alarm for midnight!"

Nanna Maria nods approvingly.

"Use your wish wisely and thoughtfully, for you can be granted only one."

She darts another look at my dad, who is singing something by Harry Styles into Mum's ear.

"Once the wish is made it is one hundred percent irreversible, so do not get it wrong."

"Yay," I say, a bit lost for words. "Thanks for that, Nanna. Lovely. I'll treasure it."

"Are you clear on the rules, my child?" she asks me. "It is very important that you follow the rules."

"Yes, Nanna," I assure her, although I have already forgotten the rules as soon as I see the sparkler-laden dessert approaching.

Unfortunately, it's about forty minutes too early for me to wish the ground would open up and swallow me whole.

"Any chance you won't do your opera-singing harmonizing this year?" I beg.

"Of course not," Nanna Maria says, clearing her throat. "Why deprive all these fine people of my talents."

"I might just duck out now because I've left Rory at home on his own all evening and he'll be crossing all his legs . . ."

Nanna Maria leans forward and kisses me gently right in the center of my forehead.

"You will stay and you will listen to me sing," she says in exactly the same way a mafia boss might discuss sleeping with the fishes. The dessert is placed before me. I try not to look directly at it in case I go blind. "And you know I love your dog. He is always my employee of the month. But I do wish he wasn't the only man in your life."

"He loves you too," I say, as I try to stave off the singing one last time. "Is that it for the wish, then? No incantation or bloodletting or some sort of ritualistic interpretive dance?"

"My dear Genie," Nanna Maria says as she pats the back of my hand. "What greater magic is there than the gift of love?"

Singing ensues.

Chapter Two

I T'S NEARLY MIDNIGHT when I get home, tired, tipsy, and looking forward to seeing my best friend in the whole wide world. I'm almost home free, free to take my bra off and sling it over the back of the sofa, eat crisps even though I am already stuffed to the gills, and pass out in front of the TV with my dog snoring blissfully next to me.

However, there is a short but, as it will later turn out, pivotal intermission, in which my old friend and the literal boy next door comes out of his house at ten minutes to midnight to say hi.

"Eugenie," he says, as he opens his door, a bottle of beer in hand. He is casually attired in joggers and white T-shirt and brown bare feet. He raises the beer to me, with a lopsided smile, and I am forced to concede once again that he is objectively quite attractive. Somehow at exactly the same time as being a total nerd-ass loser. He's also one of my favorite people.

"Happy almost birthday."

"Milesington," I reply. "Have you been waiting by your window all night for me to come home?"

His actual name is Miles, but when he moved in with his gran fifteen years ago, we all teased him for being from London and therefore posh (even though he came from a Hackney high-rise).

Then when he found out what Genie was short for, he teased me for being named after a princess (even though I am actually named after my great-great-grandmother, who apparently was also a magical priestess). So ever since, whenever he calls me by my unabridged name, I call him Milesington. Because, you know. That's what old friends do, right? Have silly in-jokes. And that took much longer to explain than it should have.

"Yeah, I've had my nose pressed up against the window hoping to catch a glimpse of you," he says dryly. "Birthday dinner go okay?"

"As okay as dinner with my family can ever go," I say. "Which is to say a sort of mix of warm fuzzy love, anxiety, inadequacy, and bad jokes. What about you? It's Friday night. Why aren't you on a date?"

"I'm saving myself for you," Miles tells me, before adding, "For your birthday tomorrow. Now we're all getting on, I can only manage one big night a week. But I'm looking forward to it. The old squad back together again, at the club. Having it large."

"I was thinking more like a quiet and early one," I say. "Just thinking about going to a club makes me feel tired. Anyway, I gotta go in. I am drunk and I want to hug my dog. Laters."

"Wait!" Miles reaches into the potted rosebush outside his front door and brings out a birthday gift, wrapped in brown paper bags from the gift shop of the museum where he works. "I wanted to give you your present. So you'll have something to open when you wake up."

"Milesington!" I cry, delighted. "Thank you!" I shake it and it rattles a bit.

"No rock this year," I say. You might think, Why would it ever be rocks? and the answer is because Miles is a geologist and he really likes rocks. I have a collection of several "interesting" rocks he has given me over the years.

"Can I open it now?" I plead.

"No." He smiles. "No. Tomorrow. Not now."

"Thank you." I rock forward and hug him, finding myself leaning into him a little more than I anticipated, so that my soft torso collides with his firm chest. We stand like that for a moment, until Miles awkwardly pats me on the back.

"Right, then," he says.

"I think I might need you to push me back into the standing position," I say. "I'm a bit squiffy."

"I got that." Gently he puts his hands under my elbows and returns me to a near-vertical position. "Sounds like Rory has had enough of waiting for you."

My dog scratches and barks on the other side of the door.

"Yeah, I'm going in now. Night, night, night, night."

I sway against my front door. It seems that my ankles are by far the most drunk part of me and standing up vertically is a considerable challenge. Meanwhile, Rory, who knows I am on the other side of the front door, has started barking like a maniac, wondering what the holdup is. Or the fall-down, in my case.

"Wait, before you go . . ." I lean back to look at Miles, who immediately looks at his feet. "The . . . the thing is that . . . that . . . Rory excavated another massive hole under the fence while you were out," he says. "So, there's that."

"I knew I shouldn't have let Dad put that bloody dog flap in," I say.

"Yeah, so I'm really worried it's stressing Matilda out," he says. "Cat therapy. It's expensive."

"How can you tell if she's stressed?" I ask. "Her face is always the same."

I look at his elderly gray cat, who is sitting on the sill of his living room window staring at me with yellow eyes that seem to glow in the dark. Matilda had lived next door for a good few years before Miles arrived and he inherited her when his gran died. It's possible she is the oldest and meanest cat on earth. Her demeanor is always the same: disdain bordering on sudden outbursts of unprovoked violence.

"It's safest just to always assume the worst with Matilda," Miles tells me. "Anyway, I promised Gran I'd take care of her, and she's basically all the family I've got now. That's all."

"Not all," I tell him. "You have me, the sister you never wanted! Anyway, I'll sort it. I'll give Rory a serious talking-to. But tomorrow, because you and Kelly are gonna make me go out again tomorrow and it takes effort, Milesington. It takes effort for a woman of my age and I need my sleep."

"Eugenie Wilson," he says, shaking his head. "You are only as old as you feel."

"Which is eighty-six," I say. "I'll see you tomorrow."

"Tomorrow," he says, standing there while it takes me several attempts to get my key in the lock. He's still there when I fall in through the front door. His face is still there even when I close the door, smiling at me with that sweet, rare smile.

Finally, I am home.

The upshot is that I go in through my front door a crucial ten minutes later than I otherwise would have done, which makes this whole thing Miles's fault, if you ask me. But I don't hold a grudge. That's a lie, by the way.

Ecstatic, Rory greets me as if I have just returned from a year-long journey in the Congo and not just popped out for dinner with the family, hurling his whole great waggy self at me as he woofs with unbridled joy and wiggles his butt, his tail thumping and whirling so fast that if we had lived in a cartoon he would probably have taken off like a helicopter.

"Hey, boy!" I hook my arms around his neck and slide down the wall to sit on the floor with him as he licks my ear. *"Who's a good boy? Hey? Who's a good boy? You are! You are! You are the bestest boy there is, yes, you are! Yes, you are! My little darling boy. Yes, you are!"*

Rory continues to dance around my feet as, remembering Miles's gift in my hand, I climb to standing, more than a little unsteady, Rory tripping and blocking me in turn as I basically tumble into the living room. Carrying it as if it might detonate I place Miles's lovely gift on the dining table and then flumph onto the sofa. Rory bounds up beside me, leans into me, and rolls his head back to gaze at me with adoring, mismatched eyes, one dark brown and one ice blue like the big goofy weirdo he is.

"I know, Rory," I tell him as I rub his tummy with one hand and reach for the remote control with the other. "This is not our usual Friday night of takeaway and telly, is it? I'm sorry, darling, I missed you too." I kiss him on the nose and turn on the TV. "Still time to watch something on catch-up, though, hey? No work tomorrow . . ."

The thing is, I'm thinking as I search for something mindless to watch, that Nanna Maria, Mum, and Dad can't stop worrying about me because they think I am lonely and sad. Nanna Maria and Mum found the love of their lives when they were twenty years old, and I am not even looking for a casual snog off Bumble—they just don't get it.

They just don't understand that I gave up on all that stuff a decade ago. It's not for me. I'm better off alone. I like my job, despite my boss being my clinically insane Nanna. I like my little house, I am grateful for my friends, and most of all I love my loopy, funny, crazy dog, Rory. And he loves me right back, unconditionally. As far as I'm concerned, I have everything I need and I'm at minimal risk of life-altering heartbreak and misery.

Just then the alarm goes off on my phone, and because I am tired and tipsy and I can't remember why I set it in the first place I turn it off.

"I wish you were a human, Rory," I say absently as I scratch his ears. "Then maybe my family would see they can stop worrying about me being lonely when really I am not lonely at all."

That was my first mistake, Reader. But it was not the last one. Oh no, not by a long, long, long, long way.

Chapter Three

SUNLIGHT SNEAKING IN through my not-quite-closed curtains wakes me slowly. Stretching into the luxurious expanse of my big empty bed I roll over onto my back and glance at my alarm clock. Past nine and Rory's not been in to wake me up, demanding breakfast! Happy birthday to me.

The tiny slice of blue sky I can see tells me it's a sunny day, and a sunny day in Scarborough is the best kind of day, especially when you are planning to spend it with mates. Lunch with Kelly at one and cocktails and dancing later with my mates tonight, because, though I am not a fan of going out, even I realize it is obligatory on a birthday, especially your own. It's not really for me, but for my friends. It's a public service. But before all of that Rory and I are going down to the beach, where I'll drink a coffee while I watch him run in and out of the waves, chasing tennis balls and getting soaked through. Springing out of bed, I get dressed in my signature black baggy clothes, while deliberately not looking at the rainbow of garments I designed and made years ago, which I keep but never wear. One emerald-green dress that is always especially hard to look at barely even catches my eye. I'm 100 percent confident that today is going to be a good day. A day full of friendship and fun. A perfect birthday day.

And then I find a naked man sleeping in my dog's bed.

Obviously, I scream; of course I do. And I mean *really* scream. Loud, shrill, bloodcurdling shrieks, but even then, in that first sixty seconds, I don't really feel afraid, which is weird, right? Screaming and wondering why I am not terrified at the same time. Shock, it's probably shock. Or adrenaline, or the brain's way of making things easier when you are about to die a terrible, violent death, and why am I thinking about this instead of putting more effort into screaming?

I put my all into it as I scramble for the nearest substitute weapon I can find, grabbing a frying pan. He must have got in through the stupid dog flap. As I shout for Rory I make a mental note to have a word with him over his guarding skills if I get out of this alive. Sure, the Sainsbury delivery guy is his best bud, but that is no reason to let in any old bloke with zero resistance. Back to the imminent threat. Oh yeah, and the screaming.

"What? What's going on!" The naked man leaps to his feet and I put the frying pan in front of my face to avoid seeing his man bits, because somehow that's scarier than him, oh, I don't know, killing me? Why is this so weird? And what is considered weird and not weird about a naked home invasion situation?

"What are you doing in my house!" I shout, trying to stay focused. "And why are you naked?"

"What do you mean, why am I naked? I am always naked!" he shouts back, voice deep and gruff. He sounds confused. Scared, even, like he's more afraid of me than I am of him. But he is not a spider, he is a six-foot-plus man with no pants on.

I take a breath behind my frying pan. Try not to panic. That's first. Second, talk in a calm, low voice. That's the advice the dog trainer gave me when Rory first came home from the rescue center, terrified of almost everything. It's maybe not entirely transferable to this situation but it's all I've got right now, and if it comes to it I can beat the crap out of him with my frying pan.

"Look," I say carefully, "I don't know how you've got into my house, mate, or why you are sleeping in my dog's bed, but . . ." A terrible thought occurs to me. My stomach plummets. Where *is* Rory? Diego the squeaky pigeon is still in his bed and Rory never goes anywhere without his best toy, Diego, especially not when he's upset.

"Where's my dog?" I ask him, not quite so calmly. "What have you done with my dog?"

"I *am* your dog," he says unhappily. "Why are you being so weird, Genie? This is very confusing. I don't like it and I haven't had breakfast yet, by the way, and it's nearly walk time."

The weird thing is, if my dog could talk then he would definitely say exactly that. Maybe this guy thinks he's a dog. Maybe he's having a psychotic breakdown. That's okay, it happens. Sometimes people's brains get overloaded with trauma and everything goes haywire. I learned that when . . . never mind. Rory will be okay. He has to be okay. I just need to help this poor man and then I'll find him, and we will both be okay.

"The thing is, you are not my dog, mate," I say gently from behind the safety of the frying pan.

"Why? What did I do wrong?" he says, sounding really upset. "Is it about your pointy shoe that I buried in the garden? Because the thing is, I didn't mean to chew it, it just sort of fell into my mouth . . ."

How does he know about my missing shoe?

"Look, I understand why you are freaking out," I say. "I am

too, a bit, but we will figure it out, okay? Only not with you in the all-together. There's a throw on the sofa. Why don't you cover yourself with that so I can put down this frying pan and we can talk? Is that okay?"

"S'pose," he says. "You should stop leaving your shoes just lying around, though."

I hear the sound of bare feet move from tiles to carpet, the sound of the springs squeaking in my secondhand sofa, and, hesitantly, I proceed toward the living room.

Peering over the rim of the pan I see the back of a blond head following my instructions. I lower the pan a little bit more to see muscular shoulders and arms and then raise it quickly again.

"Are you decent?" I ask after some moments of rustling.

"I think so," he says. Slowly I lower the pan. He has draped the throw entirely over his whole body, head and all, and is sitting on my sofa like a very awkward faux-fur ghost. Maybe he feels better that way—safer. Rory often burrows under the cushions and throw when he's worried. We've been working on his anxiety ever since I gave him his forever home. God, I hope he's okay.

"Feel better?" I ask the shape.

"Can I have Diego, please?" he asks. "I'd feel better if I had Diego."

How does this man know about Diego? There's a nagging thought at the back of my mind that I keep batting away because I'd rather not be sectioned on my birthday. I am Eugenie Wilson, the sensible and grounded one in the family. It's more important now than ever to keep it that way.

"How about we start with names. I'm Genie. What's your name?"

"I know who you are," he says, like I'm an idiot. "Are you okay, Genie? Would some chocolate help? Chocolate usually helps and we could watch *Dirty Dancing*."

"And you are?" I persist. There's a deep feeling of nausea in my gut, like I had a dirty burger on the way home last night, only I didn't.

"I'm Rory!" he insists. "I was called Rory by my first person, but . . . I don't like to think about him."

"The thing is," I tell the shape, "Rory is my dog. You are not a dog. You are a man who broke into my house and I don't know where my dog is . . . How do you know his name? Have you been stalking me?"

"I would never stalk you! You aren't a squirrel, and anyway, I protect you! Because I am your dog!" he all but howls. "I don't understand this. I don't like it and I haven't had breakfast and I need a pee. And a poop. You told me when I came to live here never to poop on the sofa again. You were very insistent! So can you just have a biscuit or something so we can get back to normal?"

There's a long moment in which my brain spins and spins but keeps coming back with an error message. It wouldn't be, it couldn't be. I take a breath. This is weird but I know that whoever is on my sofa won't hurt me. I just know it.

"Okay," I say, putting down the frying pan. "I am going to come over there and pull the blanket off just your head, okay, so we can talk face-to-face. Will that be okay?"

"Yeah," he says.

"I'm coming over now," I say, edging closer to him. "I'm going to lower the blanket a little bit now, okay? I'm not going to hurt you."

"I know," he says. "I trust you, Genie."

This. Is. Weird.

I lower the blanket. He looks at me and smiles cautiously.

"Breakfast?" he says hopefully.

He's about thirty-five-ish, I think; blond, shaggy hair and striking eyes. One brown and one blue, and . . . No. Fucking. Way.

"So could you tell me where my dog is?" I ask him, my voice trembling with the kind of terrifying fear a person only experiences when everything they think they know about the world is about to be turned on its head.

"I'm here," he says. "Can I go out for a pee now? Because this is weird and I don't like it, and you slept in. I mean, I'm house-trained, but I'm not *that* house-trained, know what I mean?"

"Rory is a golden retriever," I say. "You are a man."

"Don't be stupid." He laughs. His laugh surprises him. He frowns. Laughs. Frowns. Laughs again. Frowns again.

"Is this kennel cough?" he asks.

"Look, I want to help you, I do," I say. "But the thing is, I just woke up and there is a strange naked man on my sofa and my dog is missing, so if you could just tell me what you did with him, then—"

He gets up abruptly. The blanket falls to the floor. I grab a cushion to hide behind, obscuring his lower half. Slowly, as if he's not sure of his balance, he walks over to the full-length mirror that stands against the wall.

"There's a man in the house!" he shouts, spinning around in a circle. "Emergency! Emergency! There's a man where that other dog usually stands!"

"It's okay," I say. "That's your reflection. That's you. Move your arm around, see?"

He raises one arm and then stares, first in the mirror and then at the arm itself, back and forth. Then the other arm. He turns around, focused on his reflection, his eyes widening. And then back again. And again. At last he comes to a stop, holding his arms out stiffly.

"Genie, why have I turned into a person, please?"

"I . . ." No, this is a dream. I pinch myself hard. Still a naked man in my living room.

"No, no, no, no, nope," he says, disappearing into my bedroom and diving under the bed. Exactly what Rory does when he realizes he is going to the vet or the groomer, or Auntie Selena's with the mean poodle. Exactly what Rory does when he is scared.

But . . .

I slap myself around the face. *Ow.*

I know what you are thinking. You are thinking there is no way on God's green Earth that Nanna Maria actually granted me an actual wish yesterday that actually came true. And I definitely didn't very stupidly, accidentally use it right on the stroke of midnight with a throwaway comment, did I?

That's what you are thinking, right?

Well, you would be very surprised. I know I was. And now you are all caught up with the events as they happened.

Chapter Four

MY MIND IS IN MELTDOWN and there is a naked man who might be my dog under my bed. So, not knowing what to do about it, I walk out my front door in my nightshirt and bare feet because what the fuck is happening? I don't notice the rough paving stones under my feet as I pace up and down the street, or that I am muttering something incoherent under my breath, at least not until Miles appears.

"Eugenie, are you all right?" he asks, frowning. Miles often frowns. It's like his version of a resting bitch face. I'm not sure if he was born with that frown or if it just comes from moving from London to Scarborough at an impressionable age after losing his mum. But I hardly ever see him really smile, which is a shame, because at the risk of my sounding like an example of toxic femininity, he'd look so much prettier if he smiled. Still, Miles *is* my friend and right now I really need one of those.

"No, I do not think I am," I say as I stand on one leg and then the other. "I think I am having a breakdown . . . ?"

"What's happened?" he asks, dipping at the knees and taking hold of my shoulders. The touch is reassuring and distracting. Both good things. He fixes me with his kind brown eyes. "How can I help?"

"I don't think anyone can help," I reply, letting the top half of my torso lean into him.

"Genie, what is it?" Miles persists gently. He draws me into a hug. "When I saw you last night you were the same old Genie. What could have possibly gone so wrong since then?"

Hysterical laughter bubbles up from my stomach and bends me double, hands on knees, pissing myself. With laughter, I mean. I'm not quite at the incontinence stage yet. Though if things carry on like this it's not that far off.

Right now all I can do is laugh. Peeling away from Miles, I sit down on my step, my head between my knees, guffawing, and snorting and sobbing a bit.

"Eugenie?" Miles crouches next to me, one palm resting lightly on my shoulder. "Should I call your mum? Your nan? Kelly?"

"Ghostbusters?" I suggest, and then fall about laughing again. I'm glad I'm finding my own insanity amusing. But this is not fair to Miles, who is doing his best to take care of his hysterical friend. I take a few deep breaths and get a grip.

"I'm sorry, Miles. Something really, really stupid and unbelievable has happened," I say, shoulders shaking, eyes streaming with tears.

"What?" he asks, concerned. "Are you still drunk? Are you having a bad trip? Shall I make you some really strong coffee? I'll go and make you some coffee. Stay right there, and don't panic."

I start laughing again as he rushes into his house.

If what I think has happened has really happened, then I need to try and explain it to Miles, somehow. And it has really happened, right? This isn't one of those occasional awkward erotic dreams I have about bumping into Miles half dressed in a public environment that means I can't look him in the eye for the following forty-eight hours, is it? I don't think so; I usually have better underwear on in those.

I punch myself hard in the leg. It hurts.

This is not a dream: official.

And I left Rory all on his own.

Wincing, I get up, go inside, and close the front door behind me. I fetch Diego the squeaky pigeon from the kitchen and carry it into my bedroom.

"You okay, Rory?" I say to the gap under the bed.

"Not really," a voice comes back. "I want my fur back. I'm cold. The floor is scratchy. What's going on, Genie?"

"I think that maybe I accidentally made a wish that turned you into a human," I say. Saying it out loud makes it sound awfully real.

"Why did you do that?" Rory asks unhappily. "Am I not a good boy anymore?"

"No, you are . . ." I kneel down on the floor and push Diego under the bed. "You are a very good boy. You are *the* OG goodest boy in the world." Suddenly this feels very inappropriate. A hand comes into view, scoops Diego in. "The thing is, I just didn't really believe that Nanna Maria is magic."

"Of course she is magic," Rory says. "She's always saying she is magic! Why would she lie?"

"Rory . . . don't worry, we will fix this," I tell him.

"Good," he says. "I don't want to be a human, Genie. It's rubbish."

"I know, I know it is, trust me. We'll sort it out, okay?"

"Okay." There is a long pause. "Can I have breakfast now?"

"I need to find you some clothes," I say. Miles. I can ask Miles for clothes, which means I have to explain this whole thing in the next minute. The good news is he makes very strong coffee.

"Can I go in the garden, then, and do my business?" Rory asks. "It's a bit of an emergency."

"No!" I say. "Look, I'm going to pop next door to Miles's house—"

"Be careful of the murder cat."

"—and borrow something for you to wear. While I'm gone you can use the bathroom."

"What for?" Rory asks.

"For a pee and whatever else," I say awkwardly. "You can go in the loo . . . you know what the loo is, right?"

"Oh, the big bowl where I sometimes go for a drink," Rory says. "Wait—you pee in there? This is a very bad day."

There is a long sigh.

"Okay, Genie, I'll work it out," Rory says, stoic. I must remember that Rory needs me to take care of him just like I always have. That he might look like an adult man, but he is still a five-year-old pup who carries a squeaky pigeon. He's basically just a tall child. I need to focus on that. Just focus on that. Worrying about how reality has disintegrated around me can come later.

"Well done, Rory," I say. "It's going to be okay, I promise."

"I know, Genie," he says. "I know you'd never let me down. Love you."

"I . . ." I choke, "will be back in a second."

Chapter Five

"HERE." MILES IS STANDING on my doorstep holding a reusable coffee cup when I open the front door. I grab it gratefully. It says *Geologists rock* on the side but I am too traumatized by the collapse of reality to be able to tease him about his nerdery. "Get this down your neck. Black, no sugar, just how you like it. Mind you, it's really—"

"Thank you." I take a big gulp.

"Hot," he says. "So, what's this all about, then? Is it that you are old now?"

"Firstly, take that back," I tell him. I don't know how to explain what is going on to him. So, I decide to start from the middle. Seems logical. "I need to borrow some clothes, if that's okay? Not for me, you understand—for a man. He's . . ." I look Miles up and down. "He's a bit taller than you and quite broad-shouldered. Muscular." Though he is almost thirty Miles dresses like a pensioner who is about to go on *Countdown*. I think there is some kind of dress code for geologists that a secret underground organization, like a sort of nerd Illuminati, enforces, because I have visited Miles at the Rotunda Museum, where he chose to work for some reason, even though there are many museums all over the world that tried to give him a job, and the geologists all have the fashion sense of a duffle bag that's been put away wet. Even at this early stage I can't imagine human Rory being into this look at all. "I haven't really had a good look at the dude I need to lend them to yet, but he's very fit, so if you have some stretchy stuff, say joggers and a T-shirt, some socks and . . . I don't know what size feet he has but if you have some sliders maybe . . . ?" I look at his lace-up shoes and wonder if geologists know about sliders. "You know—like flip-flops?"

I drain the last of the coffee.

Miles's face falls and he takes back his coffee cup.

"You have had a one-night stand with a tall muscley man who you haven't really looked at properly and you want to borrow my clothes for your . . . whatever it is? How did you manage that, when you came home alone?"

His frown has deepened, his chin dropped.

"Miles!" I'm shocked. "Don't be so judgy. It's not cool."

"I'm not judgy," Miles says, "but I gave you your present and you went in and . . . What, did you go on Tinder drunk? Because if you . . ."

"If I what?" I ask him.

"It's none of my business," he says.

"You're right, it is none of your business. But *no*, I haven't had a 'one-night stand.' *Ew*."

The thought of being intimate with a stranger gives my queasy tummy an extra squeeze. And that Miles could misjudge who I am isn't a good feeling either. If a girl wants a fleeting encounter, good for her. But I am not that girl. I'm a girl who just wants a quiet life with her dog. Her DOG.

I still do not know how to explain this to Miles, so I go with the truth in the hopes that it still has at least some gravity in one small corner of the world.

"The thing is, Miles, my nanna granted me a wish for my birthday, and I didn't pay attention to the rules, so I accidentally turned my dog into a man."

Miles looks at me through his tortoiseshell glasses with his dark, serious eyes, and for a moment his frown is replaced with confusion and, yes, surprise, unsurprisingly.

"Eugenie, have you taken any narcotics?" he asks me very slowly and loudly, like I might be French or on narcotics.

"No!" I don't know how to make him believe this. "Look, you have known my nan a long time. What is the one thing she always tells people within eleven seconds of knowing them?"

"That she comes from a long line of magical women who possess the power to read fortunes and some other stuff," Miles says.

"Right. Well, turns out she isn't a total fantasist," I say. "I appreciate that what I just said sounds completely mad, I do. But the fact remains there is a naked man under my bed and I really do think he's my dog and I have to at least put clothes on him as a responsible pet owner. Although I'm not sure how that's going to go based on the whole drama when he had to wear the cone of shame for three days. Neither one of us is over that debacle yet."

Matilda chooses this moment to slink out of Miles's front door, weaving in and out of his legs and eyeing me with an expression that tells me she would like nothing more than to hook my eyeballs out with one of her long claws. Tempting, but too late. Everything I've seen today is burned into my retinas.

"There's a man in your flat and you don't know who he is?" Miles repeats the information as if he is trying to get it straight in his own head. "Why aren't you more afraid? We need to call the police, now!"

"No, I don't need the police," I say. "I just need something with an elasticated waist, honestly."

"You have an intruder in your house and you seem to be trying your best to make him feel at home. It doesn't make sense."

"Just friendly, I guess." I shrug. "I'm not scared, because its *Rory*. I'm serious, Miles! Can I borrow some clothes or what?"

Miles seems to give this quite a lot of thought. Or maybe his brain is just buffering.

"I know you've got joggers!" I say. "I've seen you jogging in them!"

He raises one dark eyebrow.

"By accident," I say. "I wasn't looking on purpose."

"Fine, wait a second." He goes back into his house and slams the door shut. On any other day, with any other person, I would take this as the internationally understood sign to piss off, but Miles isn't like most people. No matter what else is going on he always shows up for his mates.

As I wait Matilda stares up at me, probably planning on how to flay the skin from my face and drink my blood in a diabolical plot to restore her youth and beauty.

"Rory's turned into a human," I tell her. She regards me as if I am a perfect example of an idiot. She's not wrong.

"Right." Miles opens the door again. He has a carrier bag stuffed full of clothes. "Come on, then. We'll give him clothes and then we will call the police."

"Wait—you don't have to come into my house," I assure him. "I don't want Rory getting freaked out."

"You're worried about the strange naked man under your bed

getting freaked out? Sorry, not happening," Miles says firmly. "You are a woman and I am honor-bound to come with you and offer you protection."

"Fine. Well, they're your knickers, I suppose. Come on. But don't come running to me with your therapy bills."

"RORY, IT'S ME," I say outside the bathroom door. Miles waits by the front door. "You okay, b . . . b . . . feller?"

"Yeah, I worked out the big bowl thing, Genie," Rory says from the kitchen. "And I got food on my own!"

"You did what?"

We follow his voice into my small, open-plan kitchen–dining room. Rory has tipped his bag of kibble all over the floor and is on all fours, tucking in with typical Rory gusto. Thankfully he is still wearing the blanket draped over his back.

"Flip," Miles says.

"Right?"

"What's Miles doing here?" Rory sits up abruptly, gathering the blanket around him, and grabbing Diego so tightly to his chest that it squeaks. "Is the cat here? We cannot allow that cat on our property, Genie. One minute it's all *purr purr* and the next it's *death to my enemies*, and I am that cat's enemy, Genie!"

"Don't worry," I tell him quickly. "Matilda isn't here, and anyway, Miles has brought you some clothes to wear."

"Clothes?" Rory scowls. "Like that stupid costume you made me wear last Halloween?"

"Sort of, a bit," I say, thinking of the old shirt I ripped up, squirted with red paint and buttoned onto him, telling everyone he had come as a cheerful werewolf.

"I don't like clothes—they are uncomfortable."

"I know, but the thing is, while you look like . . ." I gesture at him, "*this*, you need to wear some human clothes, Rory. I'm sorry, but on the bright side you will be much less cold."

Miles sets down the carrier bag within reach of Rory before retreating.

"They smell of cat," Rory says unhappily. "All my friends will laugh at me."

"They are freshly laundered," Miles says, a bit touchy.

"Cat and lavender," Rory says. "I will never hear the end of this from Dozer."

"Dozer the English bulldog?" I ask him. "So, when you are down at the park playing with the other dogs, are you chatting?"

"Of course we're chatting." Rory is indignant. "We're not animals!"

"Okay, well . . . look, bud, you need to put the clothes on so that I can take you to see Nanna Maria and get this sorted, okay?"

"Okay," Rory says.

"Take the bag into the bathroom, then . . . I'll talk you through any issues you have through the door. Maybe Miles here can give you some man tips?"

I look at Miles, who seems to have frozen. Maybe I've broken him.

"Why can't you come in with me, Genie?" Rory asks. "You helped me get dressed at Halloween!"

"I know, but now that you are a man, it would be weird."

"It's not weird to dress me in a man's shirt when I'm a dog, but it is wrong to dress me in a man's shirt when I'm a man?" Rory asks.

"I know," I say, glancing at Miles, who has clearly gone to his safe place. "It doesn't make sense."

Rory grabs the handle of the bag with his mouth.

"Rory, wait." I crouch down and gently take the bag from between his teeth. "You have opposable thumbs now, see?" I lift up his hand, hooking the handle of the bag over his fingers, and close it. "You can carry stuff with your hands, open doors, push buttons, throw your own balls to fetch. The world is your oyster, pal."

Rory looks at the fridge.

"So, go and get dressed and shout if you need a hand, and then we can work out what to do next. While you're doing that I'll make you a proper breakfast."

"What, like sausages?" Rory asks.

"Sure, and toast and—"

"Spaghetti Bolognese?" Rory suggests hopefully, looking at the fridge again.

"I might have some bacon?" I offer. "Go on, Rory, off you go. Good lad."

"Okay, Genie," Rory says. As he takes the bag and straightens up slowly the blanket falls off him and I close my eyes just a fraction too late. "I'll go put clothes on. Love you."

"Thank you," I reply.

"I HAVE QUESTIONS," Miles says as Rory heads off to get dressed.

"No shit," I say.

"Has Rory had . . ." He winces as all men do when they tackle the topic. "You know, the snip?"

"Yes, as is standard from the rescue home," I say. "I am a responsible pet owner . . . was a responsible pet owner."

"Well then, have you had a look to see if, you know, that giant hunk of man has got . . . you know."

"Testicles?" I ask him. "No, Miles, I have not, and I am not planning to go anywhere near that bit of him, thank you very much.

That man is my dog. He is basically my child! I have to do my best to look after him until I can get him changed back into his dog body, and that's that. There will be no looking at boy parts or the absence of them. Unless you want to have a peek?"

"I do not," Miles says emphatically.

"Then we will be glossing over the whole issue from this moment forth, understood? That man in there, he's just a big kid. We need to protect him from everything and everyone."

"We?" Miles looks alarmed.

"You are honor-bound to help, remember?"

"Yeah, but I've . . ." Miles looks at the wall that separates my house from his. "This isn't my area of expertise, Genie. I was just trying to help you get a grip on reality. Because if your dog didn't have . . . you know . . ."

"Testicles." I roll my eyes.

"But if this individual does, then . . . you know."

"Oh, you are so right, why hadn't I thought of that," I say, oozing sarcasm. "If only the fact that he has identical mismatched eyes to Rory's, supreme fitness, and a mane of golden locks could be considered useful indicators."

"Point taken," Miles says. "Anyway, I'll guess you'll be wanting your nan, so . . ."

"No, uh-uh, nope," I say, shaking my head furiously.

"What do you mean?" he asks.

"You can't leave me here alone stuck in *Freaky Friday*, the canine version. Miles! It's my birthday! And you are Miles. Good old dependable Miles. One of the few people in my life I can really rely on. Please don't leave me, Miles. I need you."

Miles nods.

"Of course, I'm not going to leave you. I'm sorry. I was just caught off guard for a minute."

"I know, it's a lot."

"And then some, but you're right. Friends stick together."

"Genie!" Rory calls through the door. "Are these earholes in this neck thing?"

I think for a moment, my eyes fixed on Miles. "I think they are armholes in a T-shirt—like, you put your front paws through them. Your head through the small hole, got it?"

"Stupid clothes," Rory mumbles.

Please? I mouth to Miles, pressing my hands together in prayer.

"Fine," Miles says. "Fine. I'll go in there and show him how to put on trousers."

"Thank you." I sigh, leaning against the wall in relief. If Matilda turned into a human, I think I'd probably hide, legally change my identity, go into witness protection or something. But that's Miles for you, much nicer than me.

A few chaotic moments later Miles comes out again.

"Well?" I ask him.

"If we were in an episode of *Scooby-Doo* I would say that that guy is Rory. But as a man of science I would say it is simply not possible that the human in your bathroom is your dog," he says. "*Except*, I think that he might be."

"Here I am!" Rory appears, grinning, more or less dressed.

Miles's joggers come to just above his ankles and his T-shirt is very tight. It's like a Hemsworth brother went through the wash wearing his clothes and only the clothes shrank.

"I've got an idea that may resolve this once and for all," Miles says, somehow still here.

"Time machine?" I ask him. It doesn't seem outside the realm of possibility for Miles.

"Your garden?" Miles goes to the back door. I nod and stand aside as Rory scrambles past us both at speed in a bid to get outside first. Once we are there he runs to the end of my short and narrow garden and starts sniffing the perimeter excitedly.

"If this is method acting he needs an Oscar," I say.

Miles goes to the fence that divides our gardens and peers over it. Underneath it is the very conspicuous hole my single blue shoe is sticking out of.

"*Psp-psp-psp-psp*," Miles goes.

"What are you doing?" I ask him. "Are you calling your cat? Are you mad? Rory hates Matilda and she hates him, and now he can climb! There will be violence! And Rory will come off worst!"

"Act like it's the Ice Age and chill," Miles says.

"Are you being serious?" I ask him. He winks at me and I decide to forgive him for being Lord Lame of Lamesville, Arizona, because, well, he's here and he has a plan. Or at least he says he has.

"What we need to remember is that Matilda is like Moriarty to Rory's Watson. No real threat to her."

"What happened to Sherlock Holmes?" I ask, a bit offended.

"A dog can never be Sherlock Holmes," Miles says. "Too stupid and trusting. A fox, perhaps, but never a dog."

"Wait a minute—if Matilda is Moriarty and Rory is no threat to her, why did you come out of your house at almost midnight to tell me that Rory was upsetting Matilda, thus making me late and causing me to say stupid things about wishes at precisely the wrong moment?"

"Because," Miles huffs, "my Star Walk app told me I might see a meteor shower."

"It would be your nerdery that ruins reality," I say.

"And I wanted to give you your gift. Anyway," Miles continues, "We'll be able to learn a lot from how Rory responds to Matilda. Her opinion is the only one we can truly rely on here. She's the only one who is really objective. *Psp-psp-psp-psp.*"

Soon enough Matilda's gray head appears over the fence, then with one agile bound she hops onto the top of it and tiptoes elegantly along to where Miles is waiting.

"Hello there, Matilda," Miles says softly, looking at her fondly as she gently nudges her head into the palm of his hand. "How are you, old girl?

"Call him over," he whispers to me, but Rory is way ahead of him.

"Cat! That bloody cat is attacking!" Rory races almost up to the fence before stopping short of swiping distance. "Right— you, cat!" he shouts at the top of his voice. "You are very scary and I do not like you. Please get out of my garden now—please, you are making me look bad in front of Genie, cat! Also, please don't kill me! I will bring you kibble and leave it in the hole under the fence like we agreed!"

Matilda somehow sits down on top of the fence with the grace that only cats possess, and looks down her nose at him with the world-weary expression of a feline who has lived long enough not to be surprised by anything.

"Go on now, cat! I think there are some injured birds over there you can kill, or a mouse or something!" Rory continues to shout at her. "Please go away and stop looking at me. I don't like it! If anyone asks, I chased you away."

Miles stops stroking Matilda, who gives Rory one more glance and hops off the fence, presenting him with her cat butt as she goes.

"Sorted her right out," Rory says proudly, looking at me looking at him. "What?"

"It's just that I can understand what you are saying when you are barking now," I tell him apologetically.

"Oh well. That's reverse psychology, that's what that is. Let the murder cat think she's in charge, yeah? Clever, see?"

"Fetch!" I say, throwing a ball for Rory, who races after it.

"So?" I ask Miles. "What did Matilda's reaction tell you?"

"That your dog has somehow turned into a man," Miles says, his frown more frowny than ever. "Well. This is a conundrum."

"Bet your flipping life it is," I say.

Chapter Six

H OW CAN SHE NOT BE HERE?" I say, standing in front of Madam Maria's Magical Mystery Emporium, which is sandwiched between the Waxwork Museum of Horror on one side and Jenny's Slots and Amusements on the other. *Enter to discover what your future holds!* the peeling painted sign proclaims. *Spirits contacted, futures told, credit cards accepted.* "I know I've got the day off for my birthday but she hasn't, and it's Saturday, the busiest day of the week!"

"Give her a call?" Miles suggests, as we're engulfed by a stream of holidaymakers. "Perhaps from somewhere a bit less busy."

"There's nowhere less busy in Scarborough in August," I say, with a huff, before remembering that I'm really glad Miles is in this with me. I try again.

"Thanks, though, for coming with."

I'D HAD TO RESIST the urge to hug Miles, when, having just managed to persuade Rory to climb onto the back seat, and to sit still while I put a seat belt on him, I'd found Miles in the passenger seat. Even though he was wearing, and I kid you not, a pair of clip-on sunglasses over his regular glasses. The gorgeous dork.

"What are you doing?" I'd asked him. He'd shrugged.

"Well, you still haven't called in Kelly, so I figure I'm your next-in-line best friend. And about five minutes ago you were having a breakdown about the thought of me leaving you alone. So, I'm coming."

Here's the thing about me. I want people around, but I am always highly suspicious when they actively *want* to be around. And I don't mean I think they have an ulterior motive. Miles is so wholesome he makes the Dulux dog look sketchy. No, I mean that sometimes I think if a person is keen to hang out with me under any circumstances, then maybe there is something wrong with them. This is very broken thinking, I know that. But another thing about me is I prefer not to think for too long about the things about me that need fixing. So, I just brush it under the rug with all that other crap I keep there and decide to be grateful for small mercies.

"I thought you'd want out," I'd said. "I thought you wouldn't want to hang around the colossal mad mess that is my life."

"I'm not working today," Miles had said, as if it were no big deal. "And I thought that the dog might need a coach. You know, man coaching from a typical man."

He'd looked straight ahead as he made this suggestion, totally deadpan. With his clip-on shades.

"Good idea," I'd said, "do you know any?"

Miles smiles.

"The truth is I still owe you from back in the day when you took me under your wing."

"It was more like just hanging out," I remind him. "Like kids do."

"You invited me into you friend group, you made me laugh when I honestly thought I might not laugh again. And you always had my back. The last time you really needed your friends I was away at university and I couldn't do much to help. But now I can. So, man coach at your service, Eugenie Wilson."

I was trying to think of a way to say thank you, without crying or looking like I cared one way or the other, when Rory saved me the job.

"Why do humans talk so much?" he complained from the back seat. "And can I have the window rolled down so I can taste the day?"

"NANNA MARIA DOESN'T have a mobile," I tell Miles now. "She has always insisted that she will know if we need her and will phone us. Nanna Maria!" I call up to the heavens, or at least the top of the Ferris wheel. "It's me, Genie! Give me a call, please? Got a bit of a situation here!"

As I'm despairing out loud, I notice Rory drifting off toward a fish-and-chip shop.

"That looks nice," he says to a young woman in her twenties, hanging out with her friends and holding a bag of chips, awarding her a winning smile and a tilt of his head.

"Want one?" She giggles, fluttering her lashes.

"Yes, please," he says, opening his mouth. She laughs, drops a chip in his mouth, and smiles at him invitingly over her shoulder as she leaves, laughing with her delighted mate. Rory sees an elderly couple receive their lunch wrapped up in paper.

"That looks nice," he says, with the same winning smile.

"Sod off, you pervert," the old lady says.

"Rory, come here." I pat my thigh out of habit. "Just because I can't put you on a lead anymore doesn't mean you can go around begging for food. You are over six feet tall. People won't like it."

"I think that lady wants to give me some more, though," Rory says, pointing at the girl, who smiles and waves at him from the other side of the road.

"She wants to give you something . . . oh, dear god." A terrible thought strikes me. "Look, you are a really handsome dog who has turned into a really handsome man. That means that you must stay away at all costs from anyone who might fancy you." Rory cocks his head. "You don't want to make puppies. You are a dog, and it would be . . ." I gag by way of an explanation.

Rory gags back at me. Luckily the thought seems to appall him too.

"Genie's right," Miles says, as he makes the decision to lead us up the narrow flight of steps that took us off the main drag and onto the only slightly less busy street above it, right next to the taxidermy shop.

"Dead birds," Rory says approvingly.

"Rory," Miles tells him. "Here is your first lesson in being a human male. Women are very mysterious."

"Ugh." I roll my eyes. "Come on, Miles—that's not true. Women are people too, you know."

"It is true," Miles assures Rory. "They don't tell you what they are thinking, and you have to guess, and then when you get it wrong, because unlike Genie's gran you are not psychic, it's all your fault." He looks at me. "Although not Genie. Genie is actually quite simple to understand. But most women: mysterious."

"Are you sure they don't just want biscuits?" Rory asks.

"Hang on—why am I so simple to understand?" I ask.

"Well, you tend to say most of your inside thoughts out loud," Miles tells me.

"Oh."

"It's your best feature," Miles adds.

"Oh," I say. I'm fairly sure I am being insulted. "Well, if only more men could be loyal, open, and honest like dogs."

"Human communication is so complicated," Rory says, watching us, bemused. "I'm used to just sniffing a butt, and, bob's your uncle, I have a new best friend. No wonder humans are always smelling so stressed."

"Do not sniff anyone's butt, dog, human, or otherwise," I instruct him.

"Is there anywhere else where Nanna Maria might be?" Miles asks me. "A coven, perhaps, or a satanic cult?"

"Nanna Maria is many things," I say, "but she isn't a joiner. Maybe my mum will know? Come on, we can walk it from here—get Rory a bit of exercise."

"Are we going to Granny Rita's?" Rory hops along in excitement at the news. "Can I have a biscuit? Can I have two biscuits?"

"If Granny Rita has anything to do with it you will get the whole packet," I tell him.

Rory yips with joy, and other people who are not trapped inside this surreal nightmare don't give us a second glance. Because one of the good things about Scarborough in the summertime is that there is an awful lot of day drinking.

Chapter Seven

"HELLO, LOVE, HAPPY BIRTHDAY!" Mum says, opening the front door. She engulfs me in a big hug, and I lean into it hard. There is nothing like a hug from my mum; it's the safest place on Earth. She looks at Rory hopping from one foot to the other, then at Miles.

"Hello, Miles, love, how's it going at the museum?"

"Brilliant, we've been working on this new dinosaur footprint find in Cayton Bay, top secret obviously. Totally fascinating," Miles replies enthusiastically.

"Well then, Genie." Mum looks at me. "Don't just stand there, bring your fellas in."

"They are not my fellas," I say, ushering the men in before me.

"Hi, Granny Rita, I love you!" Rory says, hugging Mum so powerfully that she yelps, frowns, looks at me, and rolls her eyes. You are not telling me that Mum has worked this all out already in fifteen seconds flat?

"You cocked up the wish, did you?" Mum asks, as I nod at Miles to follow Rory into the kitchen, where he is sitting cross-legged on the floor pointing his whole body at the biscuit cupboard. Mum goes to the back door and opens it. I can see Dad at the bottom of the garden digging in his vegetable patch.

"Genie didn't follow the rules!" she calls down to him.

"No change there, then," he says, before waving me a cheery hello.

"Hi, Dad! Love you!" I close the back door and turn back to Mum. "You knew about the wish thing and you didn't warn me it was real?"

"Yes, dear, I knew about the wish thing," Mum says, eyeing Rory. "I'll be honest—I always thought it wasn't so much wishes coming true as nice coincidences. After all, Mum does like to be dramatic and mysterious. But I thought it was safer not to take a chance. Still, you wishing Rory was a human has cleared that up once and for all. Bit of a weird one, though, if you don't mind me saying?"

"Yes! I know!" I say. "It was an accident. I was just saying to Rory that if you thought he was a human you'd all stop worrying about me being lonely and sad—which I am not, by the way—and let me get on with my life. And it happened to be midnight. And then that happened."

I gesture at Rory, who is wiggling on his behind a little bit closer to the biscuit cupboard, looking at Mum hopefully, and then at the cupboard and back again.

"Granny Rita, I love you. Can I have a biscuit, please?" Rory asks.

"Oh, Genie," Mum sighs as she smiles at him, "what have you done?"

"I was not given the appropriate health and safety regulations!" I protest.

"Nanna Maria has been telling you for your whole life that she is magic, and that the women of our family are supposed to have magical powers. I heard her go through the rules of the wish with you. You didn't listen, did you?"

"I listened," I say with a shrug. "Just not to what she was saying."

"Human or dog biscuit for Rory?" Mum asks.

"Human, I suppose," I say.

"Rory," Mum tells him, "so you know that now you are human you can have a chocolate biscuit?"

"First strangers give me chips and now this! Maybe this isn't the worst day of my life!" Rory says, offering up a high five.

I taught him that trick.

"So, where is Nan?" I ask Mum as she hands me a cup of tea. "The shop's closed. She wasn't answering her flat bell." It has belatedly occurred to me, given her advanced years, that she might need her front door broken down, but Nanna Maria has always seemed invincible to me.

"She's had the day off for a tryst in Whitby, at the posh B and B she likes so much," Mum says. "I'm going down later to open up for a bit, do some tarot readings."

"What sort of a tryst?" I ask.

"The standard sort," Mum says, "lots of casual sex with a virtual stranger. Would you like a cup of tea?"

"Do you have anything stronger?" I ask.

"You are driving, madam," she says. "I'll make you a coffee. Tea for you, Miles? No milk, you're lactose intolerant."

"Yes, how did you know?" Miles asks.

"Well, I have known you for half your life, dear," Mum says, pursing her lips at me.

Rory has had four chocolate digestive biscuits and somehow managed to curl up his long limbs into a ball to fall asleep in my dad's chair. Mum gives Miles a cup of tea, smiling at him fondly.

"Look at you," she says to Miles. "Your gran would be so proud of you. All grown-up and tall and so handsome! And you're head geologist at the Rotunda Museum. Digging up dinosaurs and rocks. I'm proud of you too, Miles. You've come a long way since that shy skinny little kid that used to come round for his tea."

Back in the day, my house was our house. Mum and Dad's and mine. Mum and Miles's gran were really good friends, and Miles spent a lot of time in our house. Those were good days. It was overcrowded, and we never had much, but then again, we never went without. When I think about those days I am always smiling.

Then Dad won some money on the lottery after Mum randomly guessed the right numbers . . . (Goddamnit, why didn't I notice my family was magic?) Anyway, they weren't millionaires after that, but they won enough to buy a little place with a sea view, right under the castle, if they sold our old place. So, I got a mortgage and I bought the old house off them. I couldn't quite bear to let it go. It was the place I have felt happiest in my life, and I sort of believed that if I stayed there that feeling might come back again one day. And it does now and then; when Rory and I are chilling out on the sofa eating biscuits and watching David Attenborough, that's when it still feels the most like home.

But having human Rory's head in my lap is a whole different proposition and I am not here for it.

"There must be a cure or something," I say. "Apart from the whole chips and chocolate situation Rory hasn't shown any enthusiasm for life as a human. He's positively against it. And I'm not keen about having a . . . human as a pet. I mean the ethical considerations alone . . ."

"Your nanna explained the rules to you!" Mum says. "If you'd been listening, you would have realized that once the wish has been made it cannot be reversed under any circumstances. And that's not ideal, is it?"

"Yeah, but . . . not really, right?" I say. "There'll be a get-out clause, right? Kiss a frog or something?"

"Be very careful about what you wish for," Mum says infuriatingly, looking at Miles, who shrugs in commiseration.

"Yeah, okay, I didn't take it seriously. I've learned my lesson. I one hundred percent believe in the family magic now." I hold my hands up to illustrate my point. "So, Nanna Maria can reverse it, right?"

"No, darling, I don't think so. Mum has always said that it's ancient magic that stretches back to the dawn of time. I don't think there are any cheat codes." She looks at Rory, who snores and farts simultaneously. "You were a dog mum. Now it looks like you are a man mum."

"Excuse me?" I say.

"I know he's a great big lump of hot, sexy man," Mum says, rather terrifyingly, "but he is also your child now. You are the only parent he has ever known. The only kind one, anyway. You need to look after him. Teach him how to cope in the world now that his whole life has changed overnight. Help him learn how to be a human being. That's what mums do, darling. Though you are a work in progress."

"But . . . but . . . but . . . but . . . but . . . but . . . but . . . but . . ." That's it, I've finally broken.

"Would you like another biscuit, Miles?" Mum asks as I continue to malfunction.

"No, thank you, Rita," Miles says, patting his six-pack like he's got a dad bod, which he hasn't.

"Lovely manners you've got," Mum says.

"Thank you," Miles replies. "Mum always said manners maketh the man."

"I quite agree . . ." Mum nods. "I'm always saying that, aren't I?"

"THIS CANNOT BE HAPPENING TO ME!" I shout, standing up. Miles jumps and Rory sits up abruptly.

"Squirrels?" he asks anxiously.

"It's okay, Rory," I say. "Everything's fine. It's just me not handling this situation nearly as well as you are."

"What situation?" Rory asks. "Granny Rita, what situation?"

"The fact that you have a man's body now," Mum tells him gently.

"Oh yeah, not keen. Prefer peeing outside, actually. Which reminds me—can I go in your garden?"

"Best not, not when Grandpa is out there. He gets very precious about his courgettes. Bathroom's at the top of the stairs, pet," she tells him, adding, "You've got to learn."

"There has got to be a way to get out of this," I say once he's gone. "A tear in the time-space continuum, a time-travel machine, or a wizard. Or something. There has to be, Mum. Say that there is? Please?"

"This isn't like the time you had your nose pierced and it got infected and you had to let it close up," Mum tells me. "You've made your bed, Genie Wilson. Now you have to lie in it."

I gaze mournfully into my coffee.

"This is the first time in my life I don't want a lie-in."

"Don't worry, darling," Mum says, kissing me on the cheek. "Things have a habit of working themselves out for the best."

"What did you wish for?" I ask her suddenly. "When you got granted your wish by Great-Nanna Serfina? What did you wish for? Was it Dad?"

"No, you silly goose," Mum says, kissing me on my temple. "I'd been married to your dad for a year when I was granted my wish. I knew I wanted to be a mum more than anything, and so I wished for . . ."

"Was it me?" I ask her, wide-eyed in anticipation of a magical mother-daughter moment.

"No, I wished for money," she says. "You were on the way and I wanted enough for a deposit on the house."

"Oh," I say. "That was a sensible wish."

"I don't want to say I told you so, but . . ." Mum says.

I don't suppose now is a good time to start drink-driving, though it would seem on-trend for the quality of my life choices.

Chapter Eight

I KNOW MUM WAS ALL 'there is no cure,' but this is the twenty-first century. There has to be an answer to this," I say as we pull up outside my house, still disappointingly sober. "I mean, I can't just become a parent to a grown man overnight. I'm terrible with kids—all the children I know refuse to be babysat by me in case they don't survive the night."

"Also, I'm not into it," Rory says from the back seat. "This sitting up and wearing a seat belt and peeing in the sink—"

"Not the sink, Rory!"

"What's the difference, though?" he says. "They are basically the same thing. Anyway, I don't want to be your human son—it's embarrassing. I like being a dog. I am good at being a dog. Being your constant companion, guarding the house against dangers, ruling the park, holding dominion over all ducks and chasing tennis balls in the sea, eating cheese. I am good at that stuff. I want to go back to that being my stuff and not listening to you talking to me in the back of cars. I mean, look at Miles. He is the prisoner of a murder cat and obviously really lonely and sad. He'd probably rather be a dog too."

"I'm not lonely," Miles says, screwing up his face. "I get hundreds of offers for dates. Well, tens anyway. I am waiting for the girl I like to realize that she likes me back."

"What does that mean?" I ask him, willingly distracted. "Does that mean you have met her? Is it that girl at the museum, the new one you told us about? Do you fancy her, Miles? What's her name again?"

"Her name is Claudia," he says with a sigh.

"Claudia-from-work," I say. "And you like her, don't you? You like the new girl at work, don't you?"

"I do like Claudia-from-work, she is really nice, but not like that. But we are not going to talk about me right now," Miles tells me firmly. "We are going to deal with the very pressing situation at hand."

I had expected him to brush my suggestion of a crush off, but he did the opposite. He said he likes Claudia. He said "not like that" but we all know that when someone says that it means "exactly like that." So does that mean he likes her like he likes curry sauce on his fries or *likes* her, likes her? Gah! This is not the time to be thinking about this. Who Miles likes hasn't got anything to do with me anyway, except that I'd got used to him being mostly single with me.

"So, if this wish is a real phenomenon," Miles continues thoughtfully, "then it's illogical to assume that it can only be found in one location and within one unique strand of DNA."

"What?" I ask.

"Huh?" Rory says.

"I'm saying that if you made a wish that came true then there must be a tangible explanation other than 'magic.' Some sort of new branch of physics that we humans have yet to discover. And there must be other people with the knowledge and abilities to unravel this particular problem apart from your nanna Maria," Miles interprets for me. "Basically, you must be able to find someone else who can reverse the wish, if that is what has happened."

"Do you really think there is still room for doubt?" I ask him, nodding at Rory, who has dozed off sitting up and is drooling on the seat belt.

"No, but let's pretend there is, so we can keep ahold of our sanity."

"Fair enough," I say. After all, I'm still not keen on believing my eyes either. "But hopefully Nanna Maria will have finished having a sex assignation in Whitby tomorrow and I'll be able to talk to her first. I'm sure she will be able to sort it out if I grovel enough."

There is part of me that wants to apologize to Nanna Maria in person for failing her so badly. For failing to believe in the family legend, and more importantly, for not being part of it in the way the rest of my family is, with their lucky-in-love, always-landing-on-their-feet faith that magic is truly in the air if you are willing to look for it. However, there is a much bigger part of me that wants to go to the beach, stick my head in the sand, and wait for the tide to come in. And I would, but as Mum pointed out, I am a man mum now. Death by dog paddle is not an option.

My phone rings in my jeans pocket and I see my best friend's name. Oh, bloody heck.

"Shit, Kelly," I say, picking up. "OMG, I'm so sorry."

"Where the hell you been, Genie?" Kelly asks me. "I waited bloody ages outside the pub! I got your present and everything!"

"I know, I know," I say, looking desperately at Miles for suggestions of something to say.

"Tell Kelly the truth!" he urges.

"An amazing thing happened," I say as I look into his chocolate eyes. "Totally unexpected, but you'll never guess what—my cousin from Australia came over for a surprise visit."

Miles covers his face with his hands.

"What cousin from Australia?" Kelly asks suspiciously. "Genie, did you get laid and you're keeping it to yourself because you don't want to share the juicy details?"

"No. My cousin has come over from Australia for a surprise visit!" I try again.

"I've known you since we were nine and you've never mentioned an Australian cousin," she says.

"Because I never expected to meet him," I say. "Anyway, he's here, and guess what?" I force a fake laugh. "He's called Rory—how weird is that?"

"Right, I'm coming over to get to the bottom of this."

Kelly hangs up before I can try and stop her.

"Fuck," I say.

"Why didn't you just tell her what's happened?" Miles asks.

"Ok, you ring up Claudia and tell her that you are hanging out with a man who was previously a dog and see how that goes."

"That's different," Miles says. "Claudia is a colleague. Kelly has been your friend since you were little. She will have your back, if you let her. She will swear, demand vodka, and chain-smoke, but she will be there for you."

"Yeah, I know," I say. "I will tell her. I just need to find the right moment."

"So, you'll be okay if I leave you two to it? You won't try and keep pretending you have an Australian cousin called Rory?"

"'Spose," I say.

"Okay, I'll see you tonight, then."

I scramble out of my side of the car as he tries to leave.

"We can't go out now!" I say. "Or at least I can't. I have to stay in and disassociate."

"No, you don't," Miles says. "You'll just have one extra friend at the party. Now I'll give you and Kelly some space, and I *will* see you later."

"Why can't you let me have a breakdown, like a good friend would?" I call after him as he closes his front door in my face.

"Is someone coming to visit?" Rory asks sleepily when I open the car door. "Is it the Sainsbury's man? I'm starving."

"No, it's Auntie Kelly," I say.

"Oh, I like her—she always smells of cheese," Rory says.

"Do not tell her that," I say. "And also . . . do you think you can do an Australian accent?"

"SO, RORY?" I hear Kelly talking to my "cousin from Australia" as I boil the kettle. As I wait, I go over and over ways to explain the truth to her, each one sounding more ridiculous than the last. In the meantime, Kelly is falling deeper and deeper into my stupid lie.

"G'day," Rory says with more gravitas than Sir Ian McKellen performing *King Lear* in front of the king.

Kelly wants to crack open the bottle of Prosecco she's brought, and—I'll be honest—so do I, but it seems important to keep my wits about me just at the moment. Some people might say it's a bit like shutting the stable door after the horse has bolted, but those same people can sod off. "Australia, huh? I bet you surf, don't you? You look like you surf. Very powerful physique."

Kelly had looked Rory up and down the moment she set eyes on him, and it had been like pound signs pinging up in her eyes, but not pound signs—the signs you get for naked lust instead.

(Whatever they are—frankly, I don't want to know.) Either way it had been very disturbing.

"I swim a bit," Rory says. "I'm pretty good at it actually. Are you going to finish that sandwich?"

"So, do you live on the coast?" Kelly asks him, as he reaches over, takes the crust of the sandwich she has brought with her as a replacement birthday lunch, and shoves it all in his mouth at once. Kelly laughs in delight.

"I live by the seaside," Rory says, like it's obvious. I ditch the tea and open two cans of premixed G&Ts, tipping them into tumblers. Tea is not strong enough for this nightmare.

"Which part of the coast do you live on?" Kelly asks.

"The sort of roundy, pointy, yellowy bit," Rory says, nodding at two cream cakes she has put on the table. "Are you going to eat those? Because I'm allowed chocolate now I'm a man."

"Birthday gins! Yay!" I say, hoping to distract him as I hand Kelly a glass. "Quick gin, quick cake, and then, you know, I was thinking . . . now that Rory has turned up out of the blue I probably shouldn't go out tonight . . ."

"What?" Kelly snaps, narrowing her eyes. "What did you say?"

"I said that I'll probably give tonight a miss. You guys can go ahead, though . . ."

"Eugenie, do not dare to try and get out of our birthday night out," Kelly says, her eyes flashing. "We have been to that nightclub on our birthdays every year since we were sixteen years old and we are going to be there tonight. It's tradition! And what happens when you let traditions go?"

"Personal and social growth?" I answer weakly.

"Chaos," Kelly tells me. "Anarchy. Me having another night in with the kids while Dave shuts himself in the bedroom with his

Xbox. We are going out, and that's the end of it. You need a laugh more than most people I know. And you will bloody have one, whether you like it or not."

"Right," I say, knowing better than to try and argue with Kelly. "Well, I do need a drink, I suppose . . . Kelly, the thing is, you know how my nanna is always saying she is magic?"

"Genie, your nanna *is* magic," Kelly says. "Don't you remember when I was thirteen and flat as a pancake and I asked her to grant me bigger boobs?" She nods down at her ample cleavage. "My wish came true!"

"Are you sure that wasn't . . . puberty?"

"Yes." Kelly crosses her arm under her bosom as if to emphasize the point. Okay, well, fine.

"So last night Nanna granted me a birthday wish and I accidentally turned Rory my dog into Rory this man."

"WHAT THE FUCK?" Kelly stands up abruptly.

"Is that a yes or a no, re: the cream cakes?" Rory asks.

"You let me flirt with your dog?" Kelly glares at me. And this is why I love her. It's not that Rory is a human now. It's that she has been flirting with him. "Oh, I've got the ick. I'm going to throw up, Genie. I'm going to throw up!"

"I'm going to take that as yes." Rory helps himself to the cake.

"I THINK I MIGHT NEED COUNSELING," Kelly says, after I've told her the whole sorry story. She takes a big long swig of premixed gin. "Why didn't you wish for money, or . . . money?"

"Because I didn't know I lived in a Disney movie," I tell her.

"How could you not know your nan is magic?" Kelly asks. "Even my cousin Carole from the Penny Store knows your Nan is magic."

"Because I'm a realist," I tell her. "Or at least I was until I discovered reality is completely bullshit."

"Your nan is famous for miles around!" Kelly is taking longer to get over this than she did human Rory. "Your nan told Keith Cundale where his lost wedding ring was, to the square centimeter. On the beach, Genie."

"When you put it like that . . ."

"And you've always been a bit magic too," Kelly says. "Or you used to be, anyway. Until you repressed it. And got back in the magic closest."

"I have not," I protest. "I did not. There is no magic closet!"

"Oh, isn't there?" Kelly raises an eyebrow. "You always knew most of the answers on tests at school," Kelly says.

"That's called studying," I say.

"You are better at forecasting the weather than the Met Office. Just by looking at the sky!"

"That's the power of observation." I shrug.

"And when it was the kids' party, in the park, and it was raining, and they were crying, you looked at the sky and told the sun to come out, *and it did*."

"That was dumb luck. I'm not magic. Not even a little bit magic."

"Your art is magic, the landscape watercolors you used to make back before . . . well, you know. I'd look at them and I could hear the swish of the waves and the cry of the gulls. I could feel the spray of the sea."

"Was that the time I had an art exhibit by the literal sea?" I ask.

"I think you are magic, Genie," Rory says. "You made my life magical. Mostly."

Kelly looks at him fondly.

"So are you all right, then, Roar?" she asks. Rory now has cream on the end of his nose.

"Not really, Auntie Kelly," he says. "I mean, the food is good, but that's about it."

"Never mind, love," Kelly says. "You'll be all right. Your auntie Kel will help sort you out. And in the meantime you can come out with us tonight, have a few beers and drink away your troubles, in the time-honored human way!"

"No." I shake my head. "Nooooo. Not a good idea."

"Miles said you'd try this."

"You spoke to Miles? Did you already know about Rory?"

"No, 'course not. But he said that you'd try to get out of your birthday. But not tonight, Genie. I don't care if your dog is a man, we are going out. You are turning the big three-oh and I need a bloody decent flirt."

"What about your Dave?" I ask her. "You do remember that man you married, right? About ten years ago? You made me wear pastel? Made a promise to try not to snog anyone else?"

"Sod Dave," Kelly says, her bravado slipping. "I don't think he even knows I exist anymore."

Kelly had been low-key worrying about her and Dave for a while now. But it was a blip, it had to be, because Kelly and Dave have been together since they were ten and are forever, like Stonehenge or being on hold with the tax office.

"Things aren't really that bad, are they?" I ask her. Recently Dave had changed, Kelly said. He's distant a lot. Bought new underwear. Kelly's convinced he's having an affair, but she refuses either to ask him outright or snoop on him because, she says, she doesn't want to know.

"I've tried to get us back on track, Genie," Kelly tells me

gloomily, "but it's like he's checked out already. He never talks to me, doesn't even watch telly with me. Comes in from work, goes to the pub, goes to bed. And there I am just wanting to be noticed. I'm bloody pathetic."

"You aren't," I say. "There must be something else going on with him. Dave is crazy about you, Kels."

"Another woman." Kelly nods as if she has already made up her mind.

"No, no, I'm sure that's not it," I say. "For one thing, no one would fancy Dave except you."

"Just because you don't fancy him," Kelly says, "doesn't mean other women don't think he's a catch."

"Seriously, he is not a catch, but even if he was I'm sure he's not cheating on you, Kel," I try and reassure her.

"I hope you are right." Kelly sighs as she stands up. "Well, I'm not going to get my mustache waxed standing here, am I? We are still meeting at Spoons at eight, right? What's Rory going to wear? Not that, right? He looks like somebody inflated Miles."

"Spoons at eight," I say. "We'll be there. I can't make any promises on Rory's look."

"Okay, listen, Genie, Rory, this will be okay, okay?"

"Okay," Rory and I say as one. Rory seems reassured by Kelly's confidence, but I don't feel it at all.

I don't know what the solution to this predicament is, but I do know that this current arrangement is unsustainable. I've got work on Monday—what am I going to do with Rory then? What about Wednesdays and Thursdays when I take him to volunteer at the nursing home? I can't give them a huge great man in tiny trousers to stroke, can I? Though, actually, I think Mrs. Colton would probably go for that.

No, I need to find a way to get us both out of this mess. First thing tomorrow Nanna Maria is going to have to unhand her lover and give me answers.

As for tonight, well, it's my birthday and I do need a drink.

"Rory?" Rory is half asleep on the sofa, his legs in the air.

"Yeah?"

"You could stay home tonight, if you wanted? You don't have to come to the club. It will be loud, and hot, and full of people."

"I don't want to be home alone." Rory sits up. "I want to come with you. I always want to come with you. Don't leave me behind. Take me, I can protect you."

"I didn't know you hated me leaving you so much. I thought you knew that I always come home."

"But what if you don't?" Rory says. "What if the murder cat eats you and I starve to death? All alone. I don't even know how to work the telly. And what if the man from before comes back and tries to make me fight other dogs again?"

"I promise that won't happen. He is never ever coming back. Okay, we will all go out tonight. For an hour and then we can sneak home."

"Yes, together." Rory nods. "We have to stick together for safety."

Looking at him sitting there with his shoulders hunched, and such a worried expression, I wish I could just put my arms around him and kiss him on the top of his head. Ruffle his ears like I used to, and snuggle up under a blanket. I miss the Rory I know and love, almost as much as he does.

"Is there anything I can do to cheer you up a bit?" I ask.

"I could manage some cheese," Rory says, and I realize my Rory is still in there. And now he needs me more than ever.

Chapter Nine

WHAT HAPPENS IS what mostly always happens when a bunch of women with kids and husbands and magically recently transformed dogs, and Miles, get together for the first time in ages, which is six shots of tequila each, followed shortly by undignified mayhem. Rory stands next to Miles, hands over his ears and eyes wide with amazement at the scenes of Scarborough after dark but not alarmed, like I was worried he might be.

"Who is that handsome hunk of weirdo with Miles?" my friend Lucy asks me, raising a perfectly shaped come-hither brow at Rory.

"Hi, Lucy!" Rory shouts at her. "It's me, Rory. I'm not a dog anymore."

Lucy blinks rapidly. "I knew I shouldn't have played pill roulette with Carmen. I need to dance this off, stat."

We watch as Lucy grabs Carmen, who drags Kelly onto the dance floor.

"Maybe don't tell people that you are really a dog straight-away," I tell Rory after I've peeled one of his hands away from his ears. "It's a lot."

"It's always better to tell the truth, Genie," Rory shouts at me, "you taught me that."

"Did I?" I ask. "That does not sound like a me thing."

"Yes, that time when it was sunny and warm in October and you told Nanna Maria that you were sick, but actually you and me went to Filey to eat cakes and I had a dog ice cream on the beach, and then we bumped into one of Nanna Maria's *gentleman friends*," he repeats the phrase exactly as my dad always says it, with an air of shock and awe, "and you said crap, I should have just asked for a day off, it's always better to tell the truth—especially when your employer is the local femme fatale and has got the whole ice-cream-van industry eating out of her lap."

"I never thought you'd actually pay attention to my advice," I say into his ear.

"Sometimes you are quite wise," Rory tells me. "Even though you never listen to yourself." Rory frowns as he looks over my shoulder. "Do you think Miles is okay?"

Following his gaze, I see Miles pressed up against one of the mirror-tiled walls, where a girl in a tight shiny dress has him cornered. He's smiling, and laughing at her jokes; she is handing him a drink she has just bought him. There used to be a time when being a nerd was kryptonite when it came to attracting girls, but these days it's positively an aphrodisiac. He does look objectively hot standing there, laughing and flirting like the attractive, well-adjusted, and solvent good catch he is.

"I think he is doing just fine," I say to Rory, ignoring the familiar sharp pang of wistfulness I often feel in the middle of my chest.

"It's just that she looks like she wants to sniff his butt, and you told me that was not a good thing in humans."

"He's a big boy," I say with a determined shrug. "And this is my birthday party! Come on, Rory, uncover both your ears and let's dance!"

It takes precisely as long as I do to say that sentence for Rory to start leaping around like that time he found a live frog in the garden, only more happily. A few seconds more and he's nodding his head to the beat and flinging his arms around.

"This is BRILLIANT!" he calls to me. "I never got the point of music before!"

"Must be a human thing," I say, glancing over at Miles, whose face is getting closer and closer to Shiny Dress Girl. Then he looks up at me, and I *think* I see him jerk his head as if he wants me to go over. But the lights are flashing different colors and I'm not sure if it's wishful thinking, so I just stare hard at him. If he's totally okay with this girl's interest in him I will look really weird, but that's not new for me. Then he does it again, when she's turned to pick up her glass. He beckons me over and mouths, *Help*.

Well, it's either *help* or *why are you staring at me when I'm flirting with a girl, you nutjob?* I'm no lip-reader, but I go with the former just in case.

"Hi," I say, arriving at their side just as a fully loaded kiss is incoming. The music changes abruptly, just like magic, to the song of the summer that Miles and I first became friends, "Beautiful Monster" by Ne-Yo. Excellent timing, DJ, luck on my side for once.

The dance beat kicks in; Miles's and my eyes lock, our shoulders moving in sync with the rhythm, as he steps around the girl, and we pull some 2010 club moves like two fully grown adults who don't care what the cool kids think.

The girl, halted mid-move, looks at me, affronted. Grabbing Miles's hand she regains his attention, rather forcefully. My hackles rise in a way that Matilda would be proud of. Nobody shoves Miles in the corner and then tries to kiss him.

"Er, we're a bit busy, love," she says, waving me away as she all but pins him up against the wall.

"Yeah, but . . ." I look at Miles, and think of about three innocuous but not fun things I could say and go with the nuclear option. ". . . with *my* husband."

The look on Miles's face, a mixture of relief and disbelief, tells me he knew I would go rogue. Sort of resigned, and kind of amused but also a bit tired. Maybe I am too much. Apart from the times when I am not being enough, that is.

"You let me buy you a drink when your *wife* was on the dance floor?" The girl turns back to Miles with flashing eyes.

"I didn't let you," Miles says. "You just did it."

"And then you didn't think about mentioning your wife after that?"

"Typical Miles," I tell her. "I love him, but he just can't help being a woman magnet."

"I mean, he's all right but . . ." Shiny Dress Girl looks him up and down. Miles widens his eyes at me. "Why are you still with this prick?"

"The heart wants what the heart wants," I shout at her earnestly, pressing the back of my hand to my forehead. "Oh, Miles, why am I never enough for you?"

"Oh, you are more than enough," Miles says, repressing a smile as he turns to Shiny Dress Girl. "Look, the truth is this is Genie my friend, not my wife. I should have just made it clear earlier I'm not in the market for anything right now. I tried but you weren't really listening."

"Listening?" she asks, incredulous. "What am I, your shrink? I haven't got time for your issues, mate. I'm going home in the morning, I'm on a deadline!"

She leaves, making a beeline for another guy across the room.

"Sorry," I say once we are alone. "I was trying to be funny."

"You don't have to try," Miles tells me, with a small smile.

"I'd have come over sooner, but it looked like you were into her for a while there," I explain.

"I told you, I'm waiting for a certain someone."

"Oh, Miles," I say teasingly, cupping my palm to his cheek. "You should have invited Claudia-from-work, if you are that keen. We wouldn't have minded!"

"Genie." Miles sighs, gently removing my hand. "I've lived next door to you for half my life, more or less. And yet still, you do not get me at all, do you?"

"I do, I do," I promise him, warming to the subject, which means I can avoid feeling feelings. "Is it that you don't know how to ask her out on a date because you like her, and if it all goes wrong, it will be awkward because you work together?"

For a moment I am locked into his eyes. The colored lights cast a rainbow of colors across his skin. That ache I felt when I saw him talking to that girl seems to intensify, and the edge of the thought I'm trying so hard to have comes into focus. But, that's just crazy, right?

"Yeah," Miles says, his shoulders falling. "That's basically the problem. We geologists are rarely known for our dating game."

"You'll never get anywhere if you don't tell her how you feel," I tell him, running as fast as I can from those confusing almost-thoughts. "Like, sure, everything might go tits up and be a terrible disaster and ruin your life forever, but you have to try. Apparently. That's what everyone says."

"It's the ruining my life forever bit that makes me a tad uncertain," he confesses.

Miles looks like he's about to say something when Rory crashes in between us.

"Stop talking!" he says, leaping up and down like a human pogo stick. "Talking is boring, do the dancing instead. The dancing is tremendous!"

"Shall we, Milesington?" I offer Miles my hand. He hesitates for a fraction of a second before breaking into a huge smile. Suddenly everything feels better.

"We shall, Eugenie," he says. That funny little thought wafts away and out of my mind and is replaced by the all-consuming joy that is unplanned choreography.

Funnily enough, if someone had ever asked me if going to a club with my dog would be fun, I would definitely have said, No, are you mad? What a terrible idea. But Rory's got moves. And he's properly smiling for the first time since he transformed. That's the best birthday present I could hope for.

Kelly goes to hand him a beer and I swoop in and snatch it from her, giving her a stern warning look. Because I can take a lot of things, as it turns out, but not a drunk former dog. A girl has to draw the line somewhere.

WE FALL IN THE FRONT DOOR at about a quarter to four in the morning, and somehow Miles comes in behind us. Maybe he forgot which house he lives in. Fortunately, the hallway wall catches me and I lean against it hard as Rory dances past me.

"I don't see why it has to close," Rory says. "Why do things close?"

"Honestly, I have never thought about it," I say as Miles goes through to the kitchen and puts on the kettle. "I suppose people have to sleep sometimes?"

"What was your favorite part of the evening, Rory?" Miles asks him, popping four slices of toast in the toaster.

"When we went for a kebab," Rory tells him, adding proudly, "and I chose my own kebab without any lettuce. But anyway, you are in the wrong house. If I went to the bathroom for a drink, and then came out and saw you, I might forget you are a friend and accidentally tear you limb from limb."

"Not my chief concern, I'll admit," Miles tells him.

"Genie needs a protector," Rory goes on, warming to his subject. "There are so many dangers out there. What about postpeople, right? Sure, in the morning they are shoving death threats through the inexplicable door hole, but where do they go to at night? Have you ever thought about that?" He peers out of a gap in the curtain. "I think they live in the trees . . ."

"Are you sure Kelly didn't give him anything?" Miles asks.

"No, I think it's a mixture of excitement and the additives in kebab shop chili sauce," I say, fishing his toy out from under the sofa. "Come on, Rory, here is Diego. Why don't you sit down and watch telly? I'll put David Attenborough on—I know he's your favorite."

"He has a kind voice," Rory says as he sinks onto the sofa hugging Diego to his chest.

"So, I know you've had a few things on but did you like the gift I got you?" Miles asks, buttering the toast and cutting it into triangles just how I like. He hands me the plate.

"Oh, what with one thing and another I haven't opened it yet!" I say, shoving one triangle of toast into my mouth. "Let's open it now!"

"Oh, while I'm watching?" Miles looks alarmed.

"Yes, while you're watching." I laugh. "Why, what is it? Does it require batteries or something?"

"What? Oh god, no. No. I just . . . what if you don't like it?"

"Come on, stay and watch me open my gift and eat toast with me?" I entreat.

"Matilda will be worrying about me," Miles says.

"Only that you might have dropped dead outside the home and she won't be able to eat your corpse," I reply.

His mouth twitches in a smile.

"Go on, then."

We leave Rory falling asleep on the sofa and, fetching the small gift, we go out into my little garden, lit only by the slice of light that comes through the curtain and the glow of Scarborough. I put the toast down on my outside table and sit on one of my two chairs.

"I keep meaning to get some pretty outside lights," I say. "For all the imaginary garden parties that I will never have. But it is nice to sit out here, and look up at where the stars should be if it wasn't for light pollution."

"You can still see the North Star." Miles points. "And that— that's Mars."

"Shut up, no, it is not!" I squint at the distant light.

"It is too!" Miles laughs. "See how it's kind of orange? Mars."

"That's crazy," I say, and we fall into several moments of silence as Miles contemplates the vastness of the universe and I wonder how to eat toast without crunching too loudly. This is why I prefer to eat alone.

"Right, let's get this open." Pushing the plate away I pick up the gift. Miles squirms. He's wrapped it with so much tape that it takes me several minutes, some swearing, and finally a trip to fetch a pair of nail scissors to get into it.

"Have you never heard of a gift bag?" I ask him with a smile.

"My mum used to say that a badly wrapped gift is a badly wrapped thought. And I thought about what to get you a lot. So, I wrapped it . . . a lot."

"You sure did," I say. Finally, I slide out what is a small rectangular brass box, about the size of the flat of my hand.

"If you press down on the lid, the sides slide out," Miles says, watching me turn it over as I examine it. Glancing up at him, I slide the sides out until I hear them click. And then what I see pleases me enormously.

The two little sliding doors reveal on one side a set of six watercolor paint tablets, and on the other a ceramic palette. In a groove that runs the length of the box are a pencil and paintbrush. And in the middle a small pad of watercolor paper, no more than five-by-five inches square. And last but not least, a very small glass bottle with a cork stopper, just the right size to add water to. It's a tiny, portable painting set, and I love it.

"Oh. Miles." For reasons I don't really understand, but it's probably got to do with the hour, the alcohol, and the magic dog thing, my eyes fill up with tears. "It's so perfect."

"Really?" Miles asks softly. "It's just, I would really like to see you painting and designing again, Genie. You were always so—"

"Oh god, I can never use it!" I say, looking up at him wide-eyed.

"What? Why on earth not?" Miles is confused. "If it's because you don't think you're talented enough . . ."

"No, I mean, *yes*. I never really had what it takes, but that's not what I mean," I say, close it, and then open it again, just to relive the thrill of delight. "Look at it, Miles. It's perfect. It's absolutely perfect. I don't want to ruin something so beautiful with my non-sense."

"Back in the day, when you were at fashion school, and painting everything, all you ever did was make the world more beautiful," Miles tells me. "You could never ruin anything, Genie."

"Oh, really?" I put the box down on the tabletop. "Have you met Rory?"

"Rory isn't ruined," Miles says. "He's just a little bit different. And it's temporary."

"I hope it's temporary," I confess. "I just have the horrible feeling that Eugenie Wilson's unerring ability to make the wrong choices at exactly the wrong moment has struck again."

Miles falls quiet. Have I hurt his feelings? His gift is perfect, and I do love it very much. But it's a gift for the girl I used to be. Not the woman I am now.

That girl believed herself to be extraordinary. This woman knows she only just about meets the criteria for average.

"So, what's next in your quest to fix Rory?" Miles asks, eventually.

"Don't call it a quest. I am not a quest sort of person," I tell him. "What's next is that I need to find Nanna Maria. So, I'm going to go to Whitby first thing. I can't wait for her to be in a sex lull. I don't have that kind of time. Kelly said she'd come, but she'd have to bring the kids and there's no way you are getting those two through Whitby without spending a week's wages on ice cream and fudge."

"Want me to come?" Miles asks, sort of casual like he's not bothered either way. I do my best to be the same when it comes to my response.

"Do you want to?"

"Might as well, I've got nothing else on," he says.

"Yeah, might as well, then," I say. "God knows I need all the help I can get."

"That reminds me, on the way back," Miles says. "When you and Kelly were doing ABBA's greatest hits, I remembered something."

"Was it your taste in music?" I ask.

"Heavy metal forever," Miles says. "Before I came to Scarborough, when Mum was already sick?"

I nod.

"I had no idea how bad things were; she protected me as much as she could, but secretly she was getting me ready for after she'd gone."

"Ready?" I ask gently. Miles was half my age when he lost his mum, and I know I couldn't cope without mine now. I can't imagine how he made it this far, and is still so . . . complete.

"She said it was for sixth-form college, but I realize now, it was for after she'd died. For coming up here to live with Gran. She made me a list of all the things I needed to navigate a new school, new friends." Miles smiles as he looks up at the North Star. "My mum was so cool, Genie. You would have liked her a lot, and she would have loved you."

The thought makes me smile.

"Mum was the sort of person that just commands every room she was in. She could hang with anyone, make friends with anyone. Change people's minds about anything, if she wanted to. But me? I was in chess club and I read books when I wasn't playing at being a Jedi. I had my little gang of mates and we were solid, but she must have thought I might struggle, in a new town, being the new kid and all that. She didn't know I'd meet you on the first day, and you'd look out for me."

"Someone had to," I say. "But it wasn't all altruistic. Hanging out with a kid from Hackney got me some serious cred back then. I was *well, gangsta, innit*."

He shakes his head at my attempt at a North London accent.

"Mum made me a list to fall back on. Do's and don'ts of getting on in life on your own. Real basic stuff, you know? After she died it was a sort of whirlwind of sadness and change. I forgot about the list until I was going to uni. Then I found it when I was packing up to go and it was a little bit like having her with me again. Stand up straight, never settle for second best, eat your veg, Miles. That list really helped me out when I was far away from home and you. It gave me the confidence to get through the door and just start a conversation with strangers. After a while I found I didn't need it anymore." He smiles, and I smile because he does. "I thought maybe Rory could use that list now. Or a version of it, at least. A sort of 'how to be a human' list."

"Miles, that's a wonderful idea!" Before I know it, I've covered his hand with mine, as I lean toward him. It stays there for a moment and I slowly withdraw it, glad that the dark is covering the blush that is creeping up my neck as I slowly sit back in my chair. "We should write it out new, though; the original must be precious to you."

"It is," Miles says. "Have you got a pen and some paper? I can remember it by heart, and I'll edit it for Rory as I go."

A few moments later I am sitting opposite Miles holding my phone torch over the paper while he writes. His head is bent in concentration, his dark lashes looking so much fuller and thicker than they have any right to be on a boy. I like to watch him write, the way he lightly holds the pen, the movement of his hand across the paper. It's somehow intimate. As he works that familiar feeling bubbles up in my chest again, one I've known on and off for a long time now.

Maybe once, a long time ago, there could have been a me and Miles. If I'd made different choices, and the things that had happened hadn't. But if there was ever that moment, it's long gone now and even though that version of reality never existed, sometimes I still miss it. And I'll just have to keep on dealing with that because when it comes to love, Miles deserves someone really wonderful. Someone who's good enough for him, and when she does finally realize that he likes her, then I'll just have to deal with missing something I never had, just like I always have, in secret.

There's a soft plop and a quiet padding of paws, and before I know it Matilda is sitting at my feet looking up at me, her tail swishing slowly back and forth.

"Oh god, she's hunted me down at last," I say.

"Hello, Matty," Miles coos at her. "Wow, I thought she'd never come into your garden. Not these days anyway; she's not as nimble as she used to be."

As if to prove him wrong Matilda jumps up into my lap, turns around once and then settles down.

"What's happening?" I ask. "Am I going to die right now?"

"You are the chosen one this evening," Miles tells me, his face alight with pleasure. "Matilda wants you to scratch her just behind the ears."

After another second or two I comply. Matilda is warm and soft; her breathing becomes slow and steady and after a few minutes she even starts to purr.

"I have to live in this chair now," I tell Miles, smiling down at the elderly cat. "It's like, it's like being visited by royalty. Or a goddess. Wait, is she doing this just to get me into trouble with Rory?"

"Maybe," Miles says. "But more likely she was lonely, and wanted to see what had happened to her midnight snack."

"Am I her midnight snack?" I ask.

"No, a bowl of tuna is," he says. "Here."

He pushes the piece of paper across the table to me and I shine my phone light on it, careful not to disturb Matilda.

1. Don't panic! Change is hard, and it's scary. Sometimes it feels like too much and you will want to run away and hide, but standing your ground and discovering more about the world will give you so much more. Remember you are loved, you are strong, you are kind, and you are brave. You've got this.

2. Listen. If you want to know the secret to good conversation and making friends, then learn how to really listen. Plenty of people are good at talking, but they don't pay attention. It's when you really hear what a person is telling you that you learn how to truly communicate.

3. Practice. At first everything is scary, from catching a bus to making an appointment. It's okay to rehearse what you are going to do and say, to write it down and put a list in your pocket. Pretty soon you won't need it anymore.

4. Embrace the unexpected. Sometimes things happen that you didn't plan for, and sometimes those things are hard to bear.

Don't stand still and let circumstance direct your life for you.
You can make the change that changes everything for the
better.

5. *Most people are kind, even if they don't know how to show it.*
   Treat everyone you meet on this basis, give them a chance. If
   they don't take it, let them go.

6. *Do not, under any circumstances, sniff another person's or dog's*
   behind in public unless you have their written consent.

There are tears in my eyes by the time I've finished the list. I turn my face from the light, brushing them away with the heel of my hand.

"This is a good list," I say, reaching for his hand before I think about it. "You must miss your mum a lot."

"I do." The evening is warm and peaceful. The dark soothes and surrounds us, hiding all our faults and frailties. Miles's hand rests in mine and for this one perfect moment all the endless rushing thoughts that run around and around in my head are silenced. When I turn my head to look at him, I find him looking at me.

For five whole seconds I wonder what it would be like to lean forward and kiss him.

"Well, it's getting late," is what comes out of my stupid mouth instead.

"It is," Miles says. He yawns and stretches, so that his muscles flex against the material of his T-shirt. "I've got to go to bed, Genie. I never usually stay up this late unless there's a *Star Wars* marathon at the Rex."

Carefully he lifts Matilda out of my lap and puts her back on the fence.

"You'd better go that way, Matty," he tells her. "Don't think Rory could stand the shock of seeing you in his house."

Matilda leaps down into his garden and a moment later we hear her enter through the cat flap.

"I'm knackered too." I smile. "This was actually a pretty great night, all things considered."

"I'm glad." He tilts his head to one side as he looks at me for one moment more. "See you in a few hours, Genie."

"Hope your cat doesn't kill you in your sleep!" Rory calls out sleepily as I let Miles out the front door. Just as he's about to leave he turns on his heel and engulfs me in a hug. It's brief, but tight enough to make me a little giddy when he lets me go.

"Birthday hug," Miles says with a shrug. "Annual event."

I haven't managed to think of a snappy reply by the time he has closed his front door behind him.

WHEN I GO BACK into the living room Rory is stretched the full length of the sofa with Diego clutched to his chest, fast asleep. I pull the throw over him, my heart full of complicated feelings.

There isn't time to feel wistful about Miles. There isn't time for might-have-beens. If there is one thing I have taught myself over the last ten years it's that you can never go back, no matter how much you might want to. I have to focus on now. I have to focus on Rory.

I love Rory so much, you see. He is my best and goodest boy. And although I am freaked the flip out by the turn of events, the fact that he has grown into a great hulking dude hasn't changed all those maternal, soppy feelings. He is still the same Rory: sweet, loyal, loving, and flatulent. So I have to do what's best for him, what he wants. Because none of this whole improbable mess is his fault. That's what parents do, isn't it? They love and protect, no matter what. That's why I *have* to get it right.

I suppose that at least now he can tell me exactly how he's feeling.

"Is there any more toast?" Rory mutters, hugging Diego closer. Mostly hungry, it seems. At least some things never change.

Chapter Ten

IT'S BEEN A WHILE since I really had a hangover.

I don't normally drink that much anymore, except for birthdays and impossible dog-to-human transformations. Not since I was a kid myself and could shrug off a hangover like it was nothing. She wasn't around long, that wild, carefree version of me who didn't mind being noticed. I think about her sometimes. As if she still exists in a parallel universe somewhere, living my best life.

But I woke up thinking about Miles's list and how I have always done pretty much the opposite of everything on it. It's almost like I know how to be happy and just decide not to be. Something about everything that's happened in the last couple of days has got me wondering, Why? Why in a universe where dogs sometimes turn into men have I just given up hoping for a happy ending?

Back then I needed to protect myself from hurt and love, and so I did. Except when it comes to dogs. But is it possible that maybe, just maybe, that time is over? It's too scary to think about. Besides, I have a huge man-dog who doesn't understand the concept of dwelling and wants his breakfast.

"Rory, it's Sunday," I groan at him, opening my bedroom door, which he has been knocking on quietly but consistently for the last fifteen minutes. "We don't have to get up this early on a Sunday."

"Well, you say that, Genie, but I am pretty hungry and I think if you don't feed me soon there is a pretty good chance I could die," he tells me sincerely. "Also, my head hurts and I did an orange poop and I think that could be a sign I need bacon."

"But I showed you how to use the toaster," I grumble.

"Yes, you did," he says. "We've run out of toast."

"Right, if I make you bacon and eggs, will you let me go back to bed for a couple of hours?"

Rory ventures into the room and peers at me, his face very close to mine. He looks confused.

"But the sun is out, Genie. I bet the sea looks like Princess Dolly Daydream's collar, all sparkly and pretty, and I think the tide is out right now so the sand will be all firm and a bit wet and perfect for racing on."

"Hmm, well," I mutter, hauling myself out of bed and shuffling into the kitchen. "Maybe later. Right now I need sleep."

"But what if you die when you are asleep and never get to race on the firm wet sand under a blue sky and next to the sparkling sea again?" Rory asks as he follows me. "It could happen. Jeff from the park went to sleep one day and never woke up."

"Jeff was a bulldog and he was fourteen," I say. "He was like, old—really old."

"But you're really old," Rory points out.

"I'm willing to risk it."

I do feel a bit bad when I slink back into bed, leaving Rory sitting on the sofa looking out the front window into our narrow little street, where the nearest thing to action is a lost blackbird stopping by to get its bearings. On the other hand I need to be in full possession of my brain to face today's activity. So I take paracetamol, set the alarm clock for eleven, and pull my duvet over my head.

Approximately twelve minutes later I am up, dressed, and ready to go to Whitby. It seems human Rory is much better at making his feelings known than dog Rory. By singing. Outside my door. Over and over again. In imaginary Korean.

"Are you ready, Miles?" Rory calls through Miles's letter box when Miles neglects to open his door five seconds after I ring the bell. "Are you ready? Shut the cat in a box and hurry up!"

"Rory," I say, "calm down."

"I feel all wriggly and full of energy," he says. "When I was a dog you would have taken me out for a walk ages ago, but just because I am human now you neglect me. I would call the RSPCA if it wouldn't be so awkward."

"We aren't quite there yet," I assure him. "And yes, any other Sunday I would have taken you down to the park ages ago, but today I just wasn't quite up to it. "

"And I'm not even going for a walk now," Rory complains. "Instead it's more cars, more talking, more unresolved sexual tension."

"What?" I guffaw in his face. "What did I miss in the club?"

"Nothing! I mean you and Miles!" Rory says, as if he is declaring the most obvious thing to happen in the history of creation.

"You are way off on this one, mate," I tell him. "Miles and I are friends, that's it. That's how it has always been, and how it will always be."

"That is because you only think with your mind," Rory says, pityingly. "I think with my nose, and I know when I smell attraction. It is in the air. It's been in the air so long, it's going a bit stale, to be honest."

"Shut up," I tell him firmly just as Miles opens the door. "You think anything smells great—literally anything. Don't forget you once rolled in a dead hedgehog."

"May he rest in peace." Rory nods. "And?"

"Sorry for the delay," Miles says. "I had to unhook Matilda from my arm."

"Ow," I say, looking at the scratches on his arm, "What did you do to piss her off?"

"I attempted to pet her when she did not wish to be petted," Miles says. "My mistake. I think you are her favorite now."

"What?" Rory asks.

"Nothing," I say.

"Matilda came over the fence last night while you were napping," Miles said, "and Genie petted her."

"What?" Rory squeaks with horror, his eyes wide. "I feel so betrayed."

"I just scratched behind her ears a bit." I stare hard at Miles and his unremitting loyalty to the truth. "It meant nothing to me."

"Not to you, maybe." Rory turns his back on me.

"Are you sure you are okay?" I ask Miles. "You don't need to stay in and placate her? Maybe feed her the souls of innocents or something? I don't want you to neglect your pet, running around trying to save mine, who has already threatened to call the RSPCA and it's not even nine a.m."

Rory sobs as Matilda makes an appearance, winding in and out of my legs in a figure eight.

"Now you are just taunting him," I tell Matilda. "Rory, I was just being nice. You know I could never care for Matilda the way I care for you. Would a packet of crisps help?" I offer him a packet out of my bag.

"No," Rory says, taking the crisps. "I'll wait for you in the car."

"Why?" I ask Miles.

"Because things are way less complicated when you are just honest," Miles says.

"Less complicated," I say, glancing at Rory, who has tipped his head back and seems to be wearing the crisp packet like a nose bag.

"Sorry," Miles says. "I'm just practicing being open and honest about everything. Like you told me to, remember?"

"So, you can ask the girl from work out?" I ask him.

"Claudia," Miles reminds me.

"Dude, just tell the girl you like her and get it over with."

"Easier said than done," Miles mutters, ushering Matilda back in before closing his front door and getting in the car with us.

"You can't spend your whole life like a virtual monk!" I tell him. "You're in your prime, you should make the most of it, mate."

"It's not a lifestyle choice," Miles says. "Also, have you met yourself?"

"That's different, I was cool at school. I peaked early and now my life is all downhill. You were the loser nerd and are about to reach your peak potential and show all the ex–cool kids at the school reunion what we are not going to have. Have you never seen an eighties high school rom-com?"

"I've seen them all, thanks to you," Miles said. "I just don't consider them a guide for life."

"More fool you. But seriously, do you like this Claudia-from-work?"

"I think she's nice," Miles says. "But I have other priorities."

"What other priorities?" I ask. "Don't say organizing quartz."

"Well, helping you with Rory seems more pressing right now. And finding ways to get you to use the painting set I gave you."

"I'm not your project, Miles," I tell him.

"I never said you were, it's just that . . ." He sees my hands ball into my waist. "Whatever. You are impossible, Genie. The worst friend ever. It's like trying to talk to a brick wall."

"What is? Anyway, come on," I say, climbing into the car. "I thought that we could stop at a clothes shop and buy Rory some stuff on the way. I feel like he should have some clothes that fit him before we take him to see Nanna Maria."

"Question," Rory says from the back seat. "Is a clothes shop in any way like a vet?"

"Well, no one has ever tried to take my temperature via my behind in a clothes shop," I say.

"Well, that's something," Rory says, as I hand him the list.

"Can you read?" I ask him.

"Obviously," he says. "I'm not an idiot."

"This whole dog-to-man deal is so lacking in consistency, it does my head in. But anyway, Miles wrote you a list of helpful advice about being human. Here."

Rory takes the list and scans it.

"Like literally no butt sniffing whatsoever?" he asks.

Seems like we have a ways to go.

THERE'S NOT A MASSIVE CHOICE LOCALLY. It's either the generic sports store that seems to clothe most of Scarborough's, and indeed the nation's, teen boys in their uniform of hoodies and joggers, or TK Maxx, neither of which really seemed like Rory—which I admit is weird given that Rory only started seriously to wear clothes yesterday.

We wind up in a surf shop, where I spend my time going around reading the price tags and whistling through my teeth. Who knew it cost so much to look like a dropout?

Rory is uncertain about the whole thing at first.

"Go have a look round," I say. "See what takes your eye. Maybe check the sales rack!"

Rory frowns at me over his shoulder as he hesitantly makes his way in among the railings. He sniffs a wet suit and wrinkles up his nose, and sticks his tongue on T-shirts.

"This is not going well," I mutter to Miles.

"Never fear," Miles says. "I've got this."

Miles goes over to Rory, putting his hand on his shoulder.

"So, you decide what sorts of things you like," Miles says. "I like a white shirt and dark jeans, for example, but you might like this fun T-shirt or—"

"I like this." Rory picks up a brightly colored Hawaiian shirt.

"Excellent," Miles says, squinting at the noisy pattern. "And I would say that you would want to pair that with some nice shorts. Perhaps these?" He picks up a pair of light khaki denim cargo shorts. Miles has a surprisingly good eye for a man who dresses like a geologist. "Let's do the shirt in extra large, I think, at least across the shoulders. Let me take you to the changing room and you can see how you feel."

"I feel smooth," Rory tells him. "And sometimes squidgy and sometimes hard . . ."

"That not exactly what I meant," Rory says as he ushers him into the changing room.

I DON'T KNOW what takes them so long to get Rory into one shirt and one pair of shorts, and I don't want to know, but when he finally emerges I have to admit that despite the shirt being the ugliest thing I have ever seen Rory looks great.

"Wow, it suits you!" The young shop assistant suddenly perks up. "Not many men could carry that off, but you can."

"Oh, great, she says we can carry it off," Rory says, heading for the door.

"Hold on, we need to pay for them with money," I tell him, taking the trouble to show him getting my card out of my purse. "And you will need another set, so one more pair of shorts and this shirt?"

Miles fetches another pair of shorts and Rory chooses another shirt and I pick up a couple of T-shirts and some swim shorts that will do as underwear-slash-pajamas and pile them up at the till.

I won't say how much they come to but basically he's blown his annual Bonio budget in less than an hour.

"Rory, come here. Life skills." I beckon him to my side.

"So, when you need to pay for something you take your debit card and sometimes you can tap it here to pay, but when it's this much you have to put in a PIN number, which stands for a personal something number . . . number. A PIN—you put in a PIN. See?" I hand him my card and he frowns at it with the same kind of precise concentration he gives a ham sandwich when he attempts to psychically levitate it from the table and into his mouth.

"I don't get it," he says.

"Don't worry," Miles says as he comes over to join us. "We'll keep practicing until you do, like it says on the list."

"Hey, cool hat," I say, looking up at Miles to see he is wearing a straw fedora, which normally I would abhor, except it suits the heck out of him. "You should buy it!"

"Oh no." Miles snatches the hat off his head and returns it to the hook. "No, couldn't possibly. Hats, they're for losers."

"Yeah, but you're a loser already and you look good in it," I say with a grin.

"Do I?" He looks at me suspiciously, like I might be about to pull the rug out from under my compliment.

"Oh, you do," the shop assistant says, winking at Miles with a flirtatious smile. "You'd stand out in a bin bag."

Miles looks at her. "Um, thanks."

"Of course you would," I say. "Anyway, you shouldn't worry about what other people think. If you like a hat, wear a hat."

"I know, but I do," Miles says. "And presumably so do you, which is why you always wear black."

Suddenly I stop in my tracks.

"You know what, Miles? I do worry. Every single day. I worry about what my family thinks of me, my friends, the people in the shop. I worry about it all the time even though I pretend that I don't care. It's bollocks to just tell people to be themselves and live for the moment and dance like no one is watching, because people *are* watching, Miles. They are watching. Put the hat back."

"That is not the takeaway I was expecting from this moment," Miles says.

"People are watching because you are an excellent dancer," Rory says, producing exactly the same fedora from a bag and dropping it onto Miles's head. "And in your case, Miles, because you are very handsome. So, you dance and you wear the hat."

He returns my card to me.

"I did the tappy thing," he says.

This is like the time he learned to open the dog-proof bin with his nose all over again.

Chapter Eleven

WHEN WE ARRIVE Kelly is leaning up against the wall of the inn that, when I phoned her earlier today, Mum told me is where Nanna Maria is staying.

"What are you doing here?" I say, giving her a hug. "I thought you didn't want to bring the kids over?"

"Well, Dave was about to slope off, and I thought, You know what, no," Kelly says, giving Rory a big hug, before kissing Miles on the cheek. "My best friend is having a crisis and he's off to see his fancy woman? I'm not having it. So, I told him, Dave, I said, Genie needs me, you've got the kids. And I grabbed the car keys and walked out."

"Well, I'm glad you are here anyway," I say. "Nanna Maria always liked you."

"I've always believed in her," Kelly says, "plus, I've always wanted to see what the inside of this place looks like. Just like old times, isn't it, Miles?"

"Old times were never quite like this." Miles smiles.

"EXCUSE ME," the receptionist says when we start to creep up the dark-oak stairs of the sixteenth-century inn. "Upstairs is for guests only."

"And ghosts," Rory says, looking at the landing anxiously. I don't think I'm going to ask him if he sees dead people, because there is one corner in my front room that he will never sit in and sometimes at night he stares at it and whimpers. Ignorance is bliss in my book.

"Don't you take a tone with me, sunshine," Kelly tells him. "I've got Tripadvisor, and I know how to use it."

"My grandmother is staying here," I tell the young man, gesturing to Kelly to stand down. "A Mrs. . . . Miss Maria Martinelli?"

The receptionist checks the register.

"We have no one staying here with that name," he tells me curtly, as if I am a legit commoner attempting to get an audience with the king, which is a bit much if you ask me. This is only a three-star B and B in Whitby, not the flipping Ritz. I sigh, glancing at Miles, who shrugs.

How is it that my nan is always finding new ways to embarrass me, even when she's not trying? Shouldn't she be at the knitting-and-handing-out-toffees stage of life by now? Not the sexual-adventuring stage. I positively long for the day when people don't ask me if I'm married or a mother or how my career is going. I'm counting down the days until people don't judge me for staying in all the time. But, oh no, not my nanna Maria. Her milkshake, as she would proudly say without a hint of irony, is still bringing all the boys to the yard. Oh well, there's no way out of this. I'm just going to have to go there. I look at Kelly, who nods in encouragement.

"A Miss B. Bardot?" I ask, nonchalantly scratching the back of my neck and lowering my voice a notch.

"Nope," the receptionist says.

"Marilyn," Kelly whispers.

"Miss M. Monroe?" I ask quietly, leaning in over the desk.

"'Fraid not," he says primly, ushering me back from the desk with a wave of the hand.

"I've run out of bombshells," I tell Kelly.

"What's going on?" Miles asks.

"Nanna Maria likes to go undercover," Kelly tells him. "She has a list of iconic sex symbols that she rotates regularly. The other day she booked in to get her roots done at my aunt's salon as Gigi Hadid."

"There's loads yet." Kelly turns to me, ticking names off on her fingers. "Jean Harlow, Rita Hayworth, Jayne Mansfield, Jane Russell—"

"That's it, Jane Russell, ballsy, brunette, bosomy. It has to be . . ." I mutter to myself.

"Miss J. Russell?" I say.

"Ah yes, we have a Miss J. Russell and a Mr. B. Lancaster in room twelve, the honeymoon suite," the receptionist tells me. "Lovely to see a couple so in love at their time of life. It was a pleasure to upgrade them."

"The honeymoon suite?" I say, rolling my eyes. "She's only just met him!"

We begin to head up the stairs but the receptionist calls us back.

"I'm sorry," he says with far too much pleasure. "Those stairs are only for guests. Can I relay a message?"

"Yes," I say with a careful smile. "Please make sure you take it down very carefully." I wait until the receptionist has got a piece of paper and his pen is poised over the pad.

"'Oi, Nan, I thought you were supposed to be psychic, question mark, how come you don't know that I am in reception in your hotel right now having a total mare, question mark. Lots of love, Genie. Kiss kiss.'"

"Darlings!" I swear, five seconds later Nanna Maria arrives on the landing wearing a long scarlet silk dressing gown, her perpetually dark hair tumbling over one shoulder and, yes, in red lipstick. "Come up, come up at once, my love! Bring your entourage and tell me what has been happening in the five minutes since I left you to your own devices."

I take a certain amount of pleasure in the slack-jawed look of amazement on the receptionist's face as I swan up the stairs with the team in tow. A couple of days ago I would have put this down to coincidence and Nanna Maria's uncanny ability to always pick exactly the right moment to make the most impactful entrance. Today, though, I am not so sure.

"OH DEAR," Nanna Maria says, once she has shut her bedroom door behind her and got a good look at Rory. "Oh dear, oh dear, oh dear. What were you thinking, Eugenie?"

"That the wish thing was a pretend, made-up thing." I shrug, sitting down on her messed-up four-poster bed for precisely one nanosecond before realizing I don't want to think about that either, so I go and look out the window instead. The street below is packed full of Goths. You have never seen so much black and purple velour in your life. There must be some kind of Dracula festival going on. Just in case you didn't know, parts of *Dracula* are set in Whitby so there is always some kind of Dracula festival going on, or just rando vampire wannabes trailing around under black umbrellas.

"It's rubbish, Nanna," Rory says, sitting at the table where there are the remains of two full English breakfasts. "Can I eat this?"

"Of course you can, darling," Nanna Maria says, ruffling Rory's blond shaggy hair. "Hello, Miles, how nice to see you. Kelly, my love. Still worrying about Dave?"

"Nice to see you too, Genie's nan," Miles says, which is what he has always called her because he never could quite bring himself to call her Maria.

"I am worrying about him," Kelly says. "I keep thinking about coming to you for a reading, and then I think, I don't want to know. I want to know, but I don't want to know, you know?"

"I know, dear," Nanna Maria tells her. "I can't see anything clear, I'm afraid, around Dave. But for what it's worth it doesn't feel like an affair."

"Really?" Kelly half sobs. "And to think Genie never believed you were magic, Nanna Maria."

"To think," Nanna says, narrowing her eyes at me. "How's work at the museum?"

"It's great," Miles says. "But I do think we all need to focus on Genie and Rory right now."

"You're right, of course," Nanna says.

"Do you *still* think the wish is a pretend, made-up thing?" she asks me, one eyebrow raised.

"Well." I gesture at Rory, who gives a little cheer when he comes across a whole sausage under a piece of fried bread. "Not so much, no. I need your help, Nanna Maria, please."

"I'll do my best," she says, looking Rory over sadly. I refuse to believe that things are as bad as Nanna's face says they are.

"Anyway, where's your 'husband' gone, Jayne?" I ask. "I don't want a strange bloke coming in while we are in the middle of some naked rune casting or whatever we have to do to reverse the spell."

"I'd rather rune cast with clothes on," Miles says.

"Rupert has gone home," Nanna says. "I think I wore him out a bit. But I'm not leaving until checkout time. I like to get my money's worth, you know?"

She goes over to Rory and puts her hand on his head, closing her eyes for a moment, and then envelops him in a red satin embrace. Rory tolerates it for a moment then wriggles out to lick the butter off cold toast.

"You are coping amazingly well, Rory," Nanna tells him fondly. "You really are. And so clever too, to be able to have your soul transformed into a male human body without your consent and not go completely Cujo on Genie's backside. No one would have blamed you."

"Don't give him ideas," I say. "Anyway, Rory's not like that. He wouldn't hurt a fly. He would hurt a squirrel, in theory, but he can't catch one."

"I could if I wanted to," Rory says. "Thanks, Nanna Maria, I'm okay. Luckily I have Diego and toast. And Genie. She has helped me not be scared of most things since I went to live with her, and I trust her. I know she will get me back to my dog self in no time, won't you, Genie?"

"I'll really try, boy," I say, looking from Rory to my nan. "Right, Nanna Maria?"

"Don't get your hopes up. You may recall that the rules of the wish clearly state that once it is made there is no turning back."

"I don't want to be human, though," Rory tells Nan. "Genie used to make me have a bath up to two times a year, and I don't know why because it's humans who stink—of stress and secrets and lying about things. You people think about thinking all day long, and it's rubbish. I don't want to think about thinking. I don't want a job. I just want to be me. On the sofa with Diego. And a biscuit." He pauses for a moment, downcast. "I already told you how unhappy I was before Genie came and took me home. What I didn't say was that I know she feels like I did before I found her lots of the time. She tries to hide it but she can't."

"You got that from me?" I ask Rory gently.

"Sorry," he says, not able to look me in the eye.

"Before all this happened," he says, gesturing at his human body, "being a dog meant that I could do something about it. That I could make your heart beat slower, make you smile and forget everything. Now I am just making everything worse for you and that sucks."

"Oh, baby," Kelly tells him, putting her arms around his shoulders. "You could never do that, babe. You got Genie out of her shell again, and that's no mean feat, let me tell you."

"I wasn't in a shell," I say.

"You were a bit," Miles says.

"You're at least half out now," Kelly adds. "Like a snail."

"Anyway," I say, returning my focus to Rory with a shake of my head. "You are still helping me, honestly. If you hadn't been so good at handling this mess I would probably have exploded with anxiety. And besides, it's my job to look after you, Rory, not the other way around."

"That's not how it works, Genie," he says. "Things that love look after one another."

I know that he is right, and it hits me that all this time I have felt alone, I never have been. Not since the day Rory took up residence on my sofa.

"See?" I say to Nanna. "You need to turn him back. He's not into it. I am not into it. We need things to go back to the way they were on Friday before you gave me the wish. Normal, predictable, boring."

"Darling," Nanna says, throwing her hands up in despair, "if you had paid attention, you would know that there is no way to reverse the wish! I made that perfectly clear. I told you several times. You ignored me. Just like you are ignoring your own magical potential."

"She did tell you," Kelly says. "I wasn't even there and I knew the rules by heart."

"I know, I know I messed up," I admit. "It's just that I didn't think that the wish would actually come true . . . I mean, would you?" I look to Miles for backup.

"Honestly, no, I don't think many people would," Miles says apologetically.

"I believe," Kelly adds, glancing at me and then at my nan adoringly.

"I wouldn't have expected you or Kelly to believe," Nanna Maria tells Miles. "But Eugenie here should have realized. She would have, if she just had a little faith in me, in the family, and in herself."

"Yeah but . . . looking at a cloudy sky and predicting rain doesn't seem that magical," I say desperately. "Or telling a woman crying her eyes out that she's had her heart broken? Even choosing an under-twenty-five-pound winning scratch card almost every time isn't really definitive, is it? Like, you could have turned Dave into stone before my very eyes and that would have been conclusive, but you didn't and what I am really trying to say is that none of this is my fault."

"Could you turn Dave into stone?" Kelly asks thoughtfully. "How much would that be, out of interest?"

"Not in my remit, I'm afraid, Kelly dear," Nanna says. "Genie, I know that's what you are trying to say." She purses her lips. "But as a woman of thirty, don't you think it is time to take responsibility for your actions?"

"Nanna!" I wail. "Please just do your witchy stuff, whatever it is, I beg of you!" I clasp my hands together. "If not for me, for the poor innocent golden retriever?"

"I can't, my love," Nanna Maria says, cupping my cheek in her hand. "The wish is irreversible."

"You can't be serious?" I ask. "Can't you go and look in the big book of family lore or something like that? There must have been someone in the whole history of the ancestors who made a mistake that needed correcting. I can't be the only one since records began."

"You'd think," Nanna Maria says, following it with a heavy, sighing "hmmm."

"What does 'hmmm' mean?" I ask her.

"Do you remember my nickname for you when you were little?" she asks me.

"Your sunshine girl," I mutter, glancing at Miles.

"You were the most optimistic, the most hopeful, the most delightful child. Rainbow colors poured off you wherever you went. And then . . . then you let the rain get in. And now . . . Now you are on mute."

I did not expect those words to sting so much, but they do. They whip right through me and leave a hole on the way out. When did I stop being the girl that always saw the bright side? Of course I can count back to the exact hour, but that doesn't help.

"That's not nice, Nanna Maria," Kelly says, taking my hand. "And it's not true either. Please don't take away my boobs."

"Genie is very loud—you take that back," Rory says, standing up. "Last night she sang 'Bohemian Rhapsody' so loudly it set off the neighbor's car alarm. And Genie is clever and kind and funny. It was Genie who came and got me when I was really scared and hurt in the shelter. And Genie who made me feel safe and gave me Diego the squeaky pigeon to protect me. Genie can do anything she wants. You are the one who needs to have more faith, Nanna Maria. In Genie."

Rory takes my other hand.

"I have to say I agree with Rory here," Miles says. "Any other human being on the planet would have checked themselves into a mental-health facility by now. But not Genie. She is determined to make things right again. She is taking responsibility and maybe she doesn't do things your way, but she does them. And she might seem on mute to you, but to us she's turned up to eleven."

"Guys," I say, looking at them each in turn. "Thank you."

Nanna Maria thinks for a moment.

"You're all right, of course," she says unhappily. "I *am* being unfair. I just want so much for you, Genie, and I know that everything you deserve can be yours if you will only find the courage to take what's within your reach."

"So, will you at least try and find out?" I ask her.

"I'll try," Nanna agrees. "I'll speak to my cousin in Valetta and ask her if there is anywhere to look that I might not know."

"Like through your mind powers?" I ask her.

"No, darling, on Zoom," she says.

"Thank you, Nanna," I say, hugging her tightly.

"Thank you, Nanna," Rory says, joining in.

"Thanks, Nanna Maria, you're the best," Kelly says, basically curtseying.

"Thanks, Genie's nan," Miles says, offering her his hand. "I'm sorry if I got a bit heated back then."

"Don't apologize," Nanna tells my friends with a smile as she takes Miles's hand. "You care about Genie, and that's a beautiful thing." And then the worst happens. A shadow crosses Nanna's face, tears spring into her eyes. Miles removes his hand from hers, but it's too late.

"Miles, your mum wants you to know," she tells him with a gentle, sad smile, "that she is so proud of you, and now is the time to make the change that will change everything."

The color drains from Miles's face and he walks out of the room, leaving the door open behind him.

"What just happened?" Rory asks, bewildered.

"Did you just talk to his mum in spirit?" Kelly asks, agog.

"Nan!" I cover my face with my hands.

"I'm so sorry," Nanna says. "His mum was insistent. I had to say something."

"No, no, you didn't," I say. "Not everyone wants your advice or unsolicited spirit texts, Nanna! God, poor Miles. I hope he's okay."

"He has you as his friends," Nanna says. "So he will be. I truly am sorry, Genie. Will you tell him that? Will you tell him he is loved. More than he knows? Tell Miles he is loved."

"If we can find him," I say, glancing out the window at the crowded narrow streets. It's just a hunch but I'm pretty sure a busy seaside town in mid-vampiric mode is not really Miles's cup of tea.

"Bye, Genie's Nan!" Kelly gives her a big hug.

"This conversation is not over," I tell Nanna. "Love you, bye!"

We hurry down into the lobby. No sign of Miles anywhere.

"You're friend left." The receptionist gives us a haughty look, as if he is hoping we will follow suit.

"We'll find him," Kelly says as we hurry out onto the street. "And then you'll make him feel better, Genie."

"Me?" I say. "You're Mrs. Bosomy Hug."

"And you are one of the only people that makes him really laugh, like a proper belly laugh. Or haven't you noticed that?" Kelly asks.

"It's true," Rory says. "Although I don't know why. Your jokes are terrible."

Chapter Twelve

KELLY AND I FOLLOW RORY out into the street and we are immediately caught up in the flow of people heading up toward the ruins of the abbey, which stand hard against the sky on top of the headland.

"Here," I say to Rory, guiding us all into the shelter of a doorway. "Now, which way would Miles have gone, do you think?"

A parade of vampire fans files slowly past, making its way through the tightly packed streets, taking enormous delight in swooshing their capes and wearing more top hats than is sensible—I don't care how undead you are.

Belatedly I realize that Rory is holding my hand and tugging on it.

"Sorry, bud, is this all too much for you?" I ask him. Dog Rory never got fazed by crowds. He was just delighted by the number of people who wanted to admire him. Judging by the side-eye a lot of these Goth girls have been giving my blond Adonis, not much has changed there. But maybe he's not that into it now.

"No, I just found Miles," he says.

"Really? Where?" Kelly asks, peering into the crowd.

Human Rory is a good foot taller than us and half a foot taller than most people, so as we stand on the stoop of a jewelry shop, he can see over most of the crowd.

"I can't see him, but I can smell him," he says, his eyes scanning the crowd. "I can follow his scent. He went that way, for starters, with all the weird, scary people." He nods up the hill, where the flow of the crowds is processing toward the abbey.

"That's brilliant," I say, giving him a hug, which makes him smile, pleased with himself.

"He's like a superhero," Kel says. "Mind you, you always were, hey, Rory?"

She reaches up to ruffle his shaggy blond hair and he beams.

"It's weird that even as a human you have dog super scent," I say as we follow him into the slow-moving crowd. "I wonder what the rules are. You can talk, you can read, you seem to understand a lot of the world around you, like a human. But you can still smell like a dog. It's weird."

"Not really, if you think about it," Rory calls over his shoulder, his pace picking up as he weaves in and out of the Draculas—Draculae—whatever. Kelly does CrossFit, and strides along like it's a stroll in the park, but I have to break into a trot to keep up with them. "If you think about it, back in the day when humans and wolves first got together, humans used all their six senses all the time—they had to just survive. I think you lot have just got out of the habit, a bit like we dogs have got out of the habit of hunting for food. Maybe I am like an early human, still half wild."

"Rory, you were never any wild," I tell him. "But good theory."

"And you talk to me a lot, Genie. I don't think I understood the words before, but they must have gone in somewhere, because now I remember most of them, and a lot of the things you told me when I was a dog."

"Not all the things, I hope," I say, thinking about my goofy dog who would roll on his back with his tongue hanging out in a bid to get a belly rub while I told him my innermost thoughts and feelings. "Have you always known that? Like, is that knowledge built into your dog instincts?"

"No, I got it off *David Attenborough*," he says.

"You know they won't let you take part unless you are in costume?" a girl with jet-black hair, wearing a dark-ruby number that looks alarmingly like something Nanna Maria might wear on your average Wednesday, tells me.

"Take part in what?" I ask her with a laugh. "In this?"

"Yes—biggest-ever gathering of vampires in one place! It's a Guinness World Record attempt." She smiles excitedly, showing her stick-on fangs, which she has applied at something of a jaunty angle.

"You all look amazing," Kelly tells her.

"Shouldn't that technically be the biggest gathering of people dressed up as pretend vampires?" I ask, her smile faltering.

"OK, well, bye," she says, and in a moment I have lost her in the crowd.

"Genie," Kelly admonishes me like she would one of her kids. "You don't always have to be the Christmas Grinch, especially not in August."

"You should let people have their things," Rory tells me sternly, slowing down to talk to me. I've never known Rory to be stern before so I am a little bit taken aback. It's not that he's angry, but more disappointed, if you know what I mean. It's like Year 7 PE all over again.

"What do you mean?" I ask him.

"Well, when it comes to me, Genie, you are always kind. You let me have my things, like Diego. And you never make me feel bad about how much I love Diego or David Attenborough."

"Oh god, you're right," I say.

"I'm just saying you should try being as nice to people as you are to your dog. Let people have their things that give them comfort, even if it's not a squeaky pigeon with one leg. The list says most people are kind, and I know you are. But you hide it a lot, for some reason."

"Oh," I say, feeling chastened. I hadn't meant to mock that girl, but she had obviously felt mocked. I suppose I had been needlessly pedantic. "I am a cow. I don't know when it happened, but I am."

"You're not a cow," Kelly says. "Sandra Michaels from the One Stop is a cow. You are defensive. You're always worried someone is gonna hurt you, so you strike first. Luckily for you, your mates worked this out years ago."

"Humans are far more complicated than they need to be," Rory says, with a sigh. "Maybe you should take some pointers from David Attenborough. He seems to be very good at it."

THE INCLINE GETS HARD-GOING, not that you would know it by the way Rory bounds effortlessly on ahead, and Kelly skips on after him, giving a thumbs-up and a compliment to every Goth she passes. Soon we are on the packed steps up to the abbey, with Rory hopping up two at a time, weaving deftly in and out of the throng. Meanwhile, I need to stop to catch my breath and hold the stitch in my side every four steps. Kelly must already be at the top by now, but whenever Rory thinks he's got too far ahead he turns around to find me in the crowd and comes back again. And then we begin the whole process over, me two steps forward, him ten steps back. Before all this madness happened I was the one who took Rory for all his walks every day. So why aren't I fit as a fiddle like him? Then it hits me—apart from walking him, or sometimes even driving him down to the beach, I just stand still and watch. Usually with a scarf wrapped around my head, and my hands thrust deep into my pockets if it's cold. Sometimes even with a takeaway hot chocolate and a freshly fried doughnut, even though that always results in me getting wool fluff in my mouth or doughnut sugar in my mittens. Totally worth it, either way.

If I do move it's to lob a tennis ball into the surf for Rory to run after, dancing and vaulting over the waves and doing all the cardiovascular exercise that his healthy little heart desires.

It never occurred to me that I should do at least some of the running.

And less of the doughnut eating.

Two life-changing revelations in one day. If human Rory keeps on dropping epiphanies at this rate then I will have evolved into a higher species by Friday.

After a full 199 steps we are finally at St. Mary's Church, sitting low against the constantly buffeting wind and surrounded by gravestones, many of which have been worn away entirely by the elements.

Kelly is nowhere to be seen. My phone vibrates and I read a text from her.

Gone to Abbey giftshop to spend
Dave's money on fudge. Get me when
you're done. Be gentle with Miles.

"This way," Rory says, beckoning me into the graveyard.

The noise just drops away the moment we step in among the tombstones, and I take in a deep breath of relief, leaning into the muffling whispers of the wind, and the ripples in the long grass that grows between the graves. Rory leads me along the narrow pathways in an arrow-straight beeline to the ocean-facing cliff edge. Sure enough, there is Miles sitting on a bench, looking out to sea, earpods in. It touches me to see him there, occupying the very center of the bench to dissuade strangers joining him because that is exactly what I always do. Do I look as lost and lonely to everyone else as Miles looks to me now? I have never thought about it, but right at this moment I know how Miles is feeling.

"Good job, Rory." I reach up to ruffle his hair and think better of it, at the last minute giving him a pat on the arm instead, and a fizzy lemon candy I have in my jeans pocket. I stop him before he races over to Miles.

"You wait here a sec, yeah?"

"Okay." He nods and sits down on the grass in the middle of the path as he begins to unwrap the sweet. Taking a wide approach, I go sideways a few feet so that Miles can see me coming. He looks up, and for a second he appears exactly like he did on his first day at our school, vulnerable and wary. I perch on the very end of the bench, which, if I'm honest, is not built for a behind like mine, as he takes his earpods out.

"Hiya," I say. "I'm so sorry about what Nan said. She means well, but her mouth gets going before her brain engages sometimes. She told me to apologize on her behalf, and she never says sorry. She is famous for it. And she said to tell you that you are . . . a great person, Miles, and that she is an absolute dick."

"She did not say that." Miles eyes me sideways.

"Okay, she didn't say it in those exact words, but she did feel it," I confess.

"It's not so much what she said," Miles says. "It's more that I really miss Mum, Genie. And the way your Nan spoke it was . . ."

"Weirdly intrusive?"

"It sounded just like Mum." Miles gazes out to the far horizon of the sea. "I thought I had gotten used to not having family around. Had to. Mum died when I was fifteen, Gran when I was twenty-four. Dad . . . don't even know if he is alive or dead. I've always had you guys, and your families and Matilda, and I feel pretty lucky about that. But when your nan spoke to me the way she did . . . turns out I still really miss my mum."

"Of course you do," I say, edging closer to him. "You never stop missing the people you've lost. Missing them becomes a part of who you are. A good part, I think. A part that knows what it's like to really care."

"Yeah." He smiles at me. "I guess you are right."

"For what it's worth, you've got me. And Nanna said . . ." I take a deep breath. "She said to tell you that you are loved. And you are, Miles. You are loved."

"Am I?" He turns to look at me. I swallow.

"Yeah, me and Kel, we love you. Rory loves you. Matilda thinks of you as her preferred food dispenser. And . . . and what about all those rock nerds, they think you are the Harry Styles of geology. And rocks, rocks love you too."

Miles laughs, throwing his head back and guffawing.

"The most stable relationship in my life," he says. "You always know where you are with a rock."

"That's because they don't have legs." He laughs again and I wonder if he really is the only person in the whole world who finds me as funny as I do.

"But also . . ." I pause for a moment. "You know what I think? I think your mum and Gran's love is still going strong. I don't think love stops just because people do."

"That's an uncharacteristically woo thing for you to say. Bordering on magical." Miles's smile is so impossibly gentle. I'd fight the whole world to protect it. "I like it, though."

"Me too," I say.

"Mum wants me to be brave, but there are some things that scare me shitless," he confesses as his smile fades.

"Like what?" I ask gently. "You know you can say anything to me, right?"

Miles looks at me for a long moment.

"Not everything," he says. I must admit it stings a bit, to have him put that wall up.

"That's cool too," I say, doing my best to shrug it off. "I'm not a talker either."

Miles raises an eyebrow, and we both laugh.

"Not when it comes to, you know, real stuff. But it is about Claudia-from-work, right?"

"The thing about Claudia-from-work is—"

There's a sort of strangulated cry from behind us, and we turn around to see Rory come racing our way, his mouth wide open and flapping his arms as if he's about to take off.

"*Gahhhhp*," he sort of says as he drops the half-eaten candy right out of his mouth at my feet, staring at me wide-eyed.

"What the heck is that?" he demands. "Why did you not warn me it would taste sweet, sweet, sweet, EVIL, EVIL, EVIL?"

"Oh, I should have warned you about the lemon," I say.

Rory's face screws up into a ball of distaste.

"I need some grass—yes, that's what I need. Grass and a good vomit."

"Or . . ." Miles offers him a bottle of water he must have had in his rucksack. "You could have this instead."

"*Gahhhp*," Rory says, taking the water and gulping it all down in one go. "Must run really fast! Get away from the taste! Escape the taste!"

Miles and I watch as Rory races at speed down the grassy lanes between the ancient gravestones, yelling at the top of his voice, taking sharp turns here and there, and at full pelt. I've seen Rory do zoomies a hundred times, but nothing prepares you for the human version. Vampires stop and stare as a garishly dressed man races around, his arms flailing.

"Should we try and catch him?" Miles asks.

"I'm not sure we can," I say as Rory vaults over a headstone. "Do you have any food in your backpack?"

Miles hands me his bag, and, peering in, I see an eighties Sony Walkman, Miles's mum's Walkman, from when she was a kid. He showed it to me once. I never knew he carried it with him. I also see something in bright green shiny satin, covered with leopard print. Is that something that belongs to Claudia-from-work? He is carrying her stuff around?

I find a Mars bar and take it out, and wonder about asking him about the shiny material. Probably best not.

"May I?" I show him the Mars bar.

Miles seems a little sad about his chocolate, but he nods.

"Go for it."

"Rory!" I yell at the blur of Hawaiian-clad Rory that races past. "Want some chocolate?"

"Oh yes, please," Rory says, stopping at once and strolling back to us. "I think I've escaped the lemon now. Shall we go and look at all the vampires?"

"Yes," Miles says, standing up decisively. "Let's find Kel, and take a look at this world record attempt. I can't miss out on a vampire rally."

"Are you sure?" I ask him. "That is a lot of nerds."

"About to be joined by four more," he says, flashing a smile at me. When Miles smiles hearts skip beats. Well, mine does, anyway.

"Told you," Rory says, trotting along at my side. I scowl at him. He smiles at me.

"Well, anyway," I say, changing the subject. "Nan is not hopeful about an anti-wish, so I think our best bet is Miles's list and trying to teach you how to be human, Rory. How hard can it possibly be?"

"Squirrel!" Rory yells and runs right into a tree.

Chapter Thirteen

"DO YOU WANT to come in for dinner?" I ask Miles as we get to the front door. I surprise myself with the invitation. We hang out a lot, usually on the doorstep or over the fence. Today I find that I don't want to say goodbye to him just yet.

Before he can even think about it, though, a gray elderly ghost appears at the window of his front room, her yellow eyes boring into us with unremitting fury. Very slowly Rory crouches down behind me so that he is not in her line of sight at all.

"I don't know why, but I get the feeling that I should probably pay attention to Matilda," Miles says, pressing his forefinger to the windowpane, which she softly bumps with her head, "but thank you for the invitation. I'd like to, another time?" He pauses as he puts his key in the door. "I was thinking—there's the house-warming for the new people over the road . . ."

He nods at number 27, one of the two dozen identical little terraced cottages that our two are part of.

"I wasn't going to go because . . ."

"Couldn't think of anything worse," I finish for him.

"Exactly, but for Rory it would be a good chance to practice his small-talk skills. So why don't we go together? All of us, together."

"Like a date," Rory says, his head popping up over my shoulder.

"Hardly!" I say with a laugh.

"Like neighbors," Miles adds, his eye widening at the very thought.

"Just two neighbors and a man-dog . . ."

"Walking across the road together," Miles finishes.

"Okay," Rory says. "It's just that they said on *This Morning* that when two people finish each other's sentences they are. . ."

"Very hungry and probably would like some steak," I finish for him, opening my door before he can offer any more sage advice.

"That does appeal," Rory says as he bolts in.

"So, I'll see you tomorrow evening, six-thirty." I nod.

"Yes," Miles agrees. As he opens his door Matilda rushes out, wrapping herself around his ankles and purring. I get a glimpse of him picking her up and burying his face in her soft belly fur as he closes the door. I suppose there is a small chance that cat people are people too. Or even—and I would never say this to Rory—that cats aren't totally horrible either. Small, but definitely a chance.

RORY IS NOT HARD TO FEED. He is delighted by almost every taste sensation I put in front of him, lemon candy notwithstanding. The problem is that he is impossible to make full. I don't know why it bothers me more than it did when he was a dog. Maybe because when he had four paws I could look him in the eye and say, "No more cheese for you, sir. The vet says we have to watch your weight. Don't give me those eyes—it's for your own good." But now that he is human, and doing his best to keep his cool in a strange body and a world that he has never experienced this way before, it is much harder.

Also, because since we finished our steaks I have hoovered

down an entire tub of posh ice cream in one sitting. You see, some-time in the past I discovered that really going to town on a ton of carbohydrate or sugar or ideally both is a surefire way to calm and sometimes even quiet the constantly chattering thoughts that tear around and around my brain on a mad loop. Kelly tells me that this is me self-medicating; I say that it's self-soothing and that's a totally different, probably quite healthy thing.

Anyway, scoffing down Häagen-Dazs while limiting Rory's food makes me feel like a bit of a hypocrite.

The thing is, I'd planned for me and Rory to be together, just us two, until one of us popped our clogs. And, yes, I'd assumed, that it would most likely be him that bought the farm first.

Now I'm confronted with the real possibility that we have fifty years left together, and at the same time as I love that thought it also terrifies me. What if I have condemned Rory to a long life wishing he could just go back to when he was happy and carefree? And he has to spend every day with the person who's to blame?

Or what if . . . what if Rory ends up left all alone with no one to look after him? Alone and confused in a world that wasn't made for him.

This calls for another tub of ice cream. This time I get two spoons.

"WHAT SHALL WE DO NOW?" Rory asks a little later, jumping up and down like he's on an invisible pogo stick.

"Well, it's nearly midnight and I am about to slip into a carbs coma, so I was thinking bedtime?" It occurs to me that if Nanna Maria is right and there is no way back, then I will probably have to buy Rory a human bed and clear out the box room of all the things that I can't bring myself to throw away but also don't want to look at. It's a good job we are out of ice cream.

"Yeah, but I'm not tired," Rory says enthusiastically. "I know—let's put on the music and do that dancing, or, or, or go out to the dancing place and do that dancing and get a kebab on the way home as a snack, or just get a kebab?"

"I know what the problem is," I say, hitting my forehead with the heel of my hand.

"What, what is the problem?" Rory asks me, looking around him like a problem might be something cat-shaped. "And how did it get in?"

"You haven't had a proper walk since all this started."

"Yeah!" Rory says. "Let's go down to the beach—the tide is out and it will be awesome!"

"How do you know the tide will be out?" I ask him, checking on my phone, which confirms he is right.

"I don't know—I just know," he says. "There's sort of a pattern that doesn't repeat but it goes in a . . ." He makes a looping motion with his hand. "So, if you keep that in your head you can sort of see where it is, and anyway, can we go? Can we go? Can we go?"

"Okay," I say, marveling at his hidden talents, which it seems are more than just howling to the theme tune from *EastEnders*. "Let's go out."

Who needs the blissful oblivion of a carb coma anyway?

THE TIDE IS FAR OUT ON NORTH BAY, leaving long stretches of wet sand shimmering invitingly, gilded by the light of the full moon. It's quieter here than it would be even at this hour on South Bay, where the music will still be pumping, the chips will still be frying, and young love will be blossoming up against the outside wall of the King Richard III pub.

On North Bay everything is closed. All you can hear is the rush and receding of waves. All you can see is the ruin of the castle perched high on the headland overlooking us all, and the faint lights of a cargo ship far out at sea that seems to hover like an alien craft above the lost horizon.

Rory kicks off his shoes at once and rushes toward the water, whooping and yelping for joy.

"Did you bring the ball?" he asks me when I eventually catch up with him as he dances and skips in and out of the waves.

"Er, no . . ." I say.

"Why not?" He is instantly sad. "How can I chase a ball if you haven't brought it?"

"Because . . . humans don't tend to do a lot of chasing balls."

"Er, football, tennis, rugby, cricket, rounders . . ."

"I mean, people don't chase balls just for the sake of it."

"Er, football . . ."

"Fine, you win," I say. "But I forgot the ball. Just run around, pretend there's a ball. Pretend the moon is a ball!"

"Are you having a breakdown?" Rory asks, bemused, as the water foams around his ankles. "The moon is a great big lump of rock in the sky. Anyway, you should play ball with me next time. It's great—you see the ball go, you get the thrill of running really fast and getting to it before all the other dogs, and then it is yours and you are the winner and you get to do it all again!"

"When you put it like that . . ." I say. "I'm sorry, Rory. I didn't think."

"Oh well, we'll just have to play in the water, then," he says, wading in deeper until the water is at the bottom of his shorts. "Come on, Genie!"

"I'll watch you from here," I say.

"No." Rory shakes his head. "Nope."

"What do you mean, no?" I ask him, taken aback. I am not sure that Rory has ever really refused anything before unless you count his worming tablet.

"I mean that before when you stood on your own throwing the ball, or on the edge of the sea, watching me play, you never seemed to understand when I was asking you to play with me, no matter how hard I tried. But now I have words and I can say it out loud and I want you to play. And it's your fault that I have these words. So just come and play with me, Genie. Just come. Please?"

It's the last word, so determined and hopeful, that gets to me. Before I know it I have kicked off my trainers and am wading into the water. The North Sea is always bloody freezing, even in the height of summer and especially at night. At first it takes my breath away, and I want nothing so much as to turn around and go back. Rory keeps calling me forward, though, his arms outstretched, a delighted smile on his face.

Eventually the water is around our waists and he ducks right under, emerging a second later, making a huge splash of freezing moonlit drops that cascade over me.

"Jesus effing Christ!" I squeal, and laugh at the same time.

Let the splash wars begin.

I DON'T KNOW when we stop splashing and just start to wallow, but I do know that I haven't laughed so much for such a long time. Now, as we float in the palm of the sea while it gently rocks us, I can see why Rory was so determined to give me this. I feel calm and connected to everything, from the gleaming white tops of the lapping waves to each star that sparkles overhead. For a few seconds it seems perfectly logical that magic is real, and that nothing is impossible. Not even happiness. Not even love.

"See how much more fun life is when you play?" Rory asks.

"I do," I say. "I see all the beauty in the world."

"I think happiness is a thing that you can catch in your teeth, if you are always on the lookout for it and ready to jump," Rory says.

Is it possible that my dog is the wisest human being that I have ever met?

Chapter Fourteen

FEEL SORRY FOR MONDAYS, I do. Imagine being the most universally hated day of the week. Even if you work weird hours like me, and sometimes have a Monday off, it still comes weighted down with that whole, oh-god-not-this-crap-again feeling. Look, I'm not a philosopher or an academic, but it is always on a Monday that I most wonder what the point is: of Life, the Universe, and Everything. Maybe someone should look into that and see if there's a correlation or something. Between Mondays and existential crisis.

(Sidenote: it turns out this state of being is highly exacerbated by the knowledge that you accidentally turned your dog into a human being.)

Rory, however, does not have this problem. While my fleetingly smug feeling of oneness with the universe that came from our midnight dip has evaporated with the dawn, my darling dog still thinks the world is a constant delight, even on a Monday.

"I'm ready!" he declares cheerfully as I shamble into the living room to find him already dressed in a fresh set of shorts and a bright shirt and some shades he's found somewhere that are adorned with rhinestones on each batwing corner. They suit him.

There's a plate with the remains of some sort of concoction that I don't want to think about on the counter.

"I had toast," Rory confirms when he sees me looking at it. "But then I was still hungry, but I am a bit scared of the fire thing that makes sausages brown."

"Hob," I remind him. Weird how he knows some words and is basically fluent in English—erudite, even—while others are a total mystery to him. One day I would like to speak to the manager of transmutation and have a word with him about the vagaries of the ground rules.

"So, then I had the butter . . ." He shows me the thoroughly licked out tub.

"Just the butter on its own?" I ask him, noticing that there is no bread left.

"No!" he says. "That would be gross. I had it with the rest of the cheese. And four packets of cheeseballs. Which are like eating cheesy dust. And then some of your emergency chocolate, because I can now. I'm ready to face the day!"

Maybe I'll just have a coffee, then.

"I LOVE COMING TO WORK!" Rory says happily as we arrive at the shop. I unlock the door, and he positively bounds inside, intent on cantering around the table in the middle of the room. The ancient lighting system, designed by Nan sometime in the eighties, flickers then begins to boot up. Red and purple bulbs start to glow behind clamshell-shaped wall lights. A disco ball, for some reason, begins to slowly spin in the center of the room, setting off a swirl of spinning, glittering lights that Rory finds endlessly delightful.

"Like inside stars," he tells me as he follows the repeating pattern.

You'd think there would be some kind of backup lighting. Like for when the shop is closed and you need to mop the floor. There is not. Everything here is done within the weird disco twilight world of my nanna Maria's 1990s imagination.

"Ooh, brilliant, new biscuits," Rory says, after sniffing the air, immediately going out to the back room to investigate the snacks. He sticks his head in the cupboard while I put the kettle on. Nan isn't here yet and we are already late opening. It's not unlike her to be late—she will sweep in at some point and tell us she was delayed by spirits, or an angel with a message for her.

I peer out the shop window down the front toward the castle. It's going to be a warm day—kids with families are already out and about. Fat little toddlers trail about after dads with no tops on, and girls who wear their long hair on top of their heads in big looped buns parade up and down like they are in Cannes looking for the next movie star to whisk them away on a yacht. Beyond, the stretches of golden South Bay shimmer and gleam like they're made of gold dust. The sea is a startling blue.

We are going to be busy. The warmer the weather, the more people want their fortunes told or to chat to someone dead.

"Where are you, Nan?" I mutter as I turn around the *Open* sign on the door and hope that she arrives before the first customer does.

"I wonder who we'll meet today?" Rory says, sitting in Nanna Maria's red velvet chair and putting on the silk turban she sometimes wears if she's feeling extra theatrical. I'll say this for Rory, he certainly is making full use of his new motor skills. Except that he's put it on upside down, and the long, pink plume attached to it is face down, covering his nose. "I hope we meet nice people. Most people are nice, though, aren't they? The only people I've ever met who aren't nice are vets and people with beards. Why are people with beards weird? You'd think the more hair a person has the more doglike they would be, but it's the opposite . . ."

Before I can even begin to think of an answer the bell on the door rings and a woman walks in. Even though it's already scorching outside she is wearing a pale blue raincoat buttoned all the way up to the top. She sees Rory sitting at the table and hesitates. I'm about to tell her to come back in ten when I see her straighten her shoulders with resolve and take a seat at the table. Nan is still nowhere to be seen.

"I need a sitting, please," she says. "I've got contactless—is that okay?"

"Fortune?" I ask. "Madam Martinelli will be with us any—"

"No, I need to speak to my husband." She sits down and looks at Rory, who puffs the feather away from his nose and smiles at her.

"Hello," he says warmly.

"Hello, I need to speak to my husband," she says. Oh god. It has taken me several seconds too long to work out what is happening.

"No, excuse me, sorry, this isn't . . ." I begin, but the woman is dead set. She's worked up her courage and nothing is going to delay her now.

"Can you help me speak to him, please?" the woman says. She leans forward in her seat, her narrow face pinched and pale. I watch in horror as Rory reaches across the table and takes her hand in his.

"Have you thought about phoning him?" he asks.

"He's gone to the other side," she says.

"Of where?" Rory asks.

I'm rooted to the spot with a kind of immobilized panic, somehow unable to intervene. This is going to be a train wreck.

"Of life," she says.

"Oh!" Rory exclaims, puffing the feather out of the way again. "You mean he's gone over the rainbow bridge. Don't worry, a lot of my friends are there."

"It's been a year, but I don't feel any better, you see," she says unhappily. "I just want to cry all the time, and tomorrow it's the anniversary. I thought, I thought, if I could just speak to him one more time . . . it might help."

"And what do you want to say to him?" Rory asks, gently and soft.

"I'd say, What were you playing at, you stupid git? Not telling anyone you had chest pains?" she says, with a sort of cross sob.

"And what else?" Rory asks.

"I'd say that the last year has been nothing but gray and cold since he left. Don't matter if the sun is out or if it's snowing. Every day is the same, miserable and lonely. I try, for the kids and the grandkids, I try to keep my chin up, you know? But all I can think of is the conversations that we are not having, and all I can feel is the empty space where he used to be, and I miss him so much. I don't know how to keep going."

It feels to me like this is getting out of hand. This poor woman is expecting a professional not a puppy, but still, she is gripping on to Rory's hand, and he is gazing into her eyes. And what I see there stops me from intervening. He is listening to her, really listening. As if he is feeling every word.

"And what would he say to you?" Rory asks.

"He'd tell me not to carry on so," she says with a faint, remembering smile. "He'd say, I was always getting under your feet anyway." Her eyes brighten just a little. "And then he'd say, Do you know I love you, Dolly? Just as much as I did the day I married you? And that won't ever change, girl."

Dolly bows her head, tears sliding down her face onto the back of Rory's hand. He doesn't try to withdraw it.

"But how do I keep going, Jack?" she asks Rory as if he is her husband. "How do I keep going without you hanging around, getting in the way? Bringing me home a bar of Cadbury's milk chocolate on a Friday night?"

"You just keep going," Rory says. "And one day the cold and dark hours will start to have little sunny warm minutes happening. And the minutes will turn into hours and then even whole days and weeks. The dark cold days will still be there, and the sadness. But Jack isn't the only person who loves you. Your kids and your grandkids do too. And all your friends, I bet, and that dog you left tied up outside though you could have brought her in, because we have a well-behaved-dogs-welcome policy. She loves you very much, that dog."

"And I love her," Dolly sniffs. "Saved my life, she has."

"You might feel alone," Rory says, "and sad and scared, but people love you and there are a lot of really good ones who care about you. And when one day you go over the rainbow bridge you will see Jack. He will come running down the big green hill full of long, good-smelling grass, and he'll leap into your arms and you will roll about in the flowers and it will be epic."

"Epic," Dolly echoes with a faint smile. "Jack's favorite word. He picked it up off the grandkids and kept using it, even when they told him it wasn't cool anymore. Oh, thank you, thank you. Thank you so much."

Then something really weird happens. I hear a voice, a local accent and male. Conversational and calm, just like there's someone standing next to me. Only there is not.

"Um, also just to add," I say as the voice repeats itself. "The gold cuff links that Jack wanted to give to your grandson are in his lockbox under the wonky floorboard in the spare room and he loves you."

"That's where they are? I've looked everywhere!" Dolly exclaims, bursting into happy tears. "Oh, Jack, you are still looking out for me, aren't you?"

Always, Dolly, love.

"He says always. Would you like a tissue?" I offer a box of three-ply enclosed in a plastic gold box while I consider if swimming in the North Sea at night can lead to delusions. Or tinnitus. It's probably tinnitus.

"Thanks, love. Thank you so much." Dolly hugs me tightly. "How much will that be, please?"

"No charge," I say.

"But—" She looks from me to Rory. "You've made my day, my year!"

"You're our millionth seeker of the light," I say, using one of Nanna Maria's phrases. "So no charge. You have a nice day, now."

"You wait till I tell my Alison what her dad said," she says as she leaves the shop.

"You are a very kind human," I say, sitting down and looking at Rory. "But we probably shouldn't do that again. We were lucky that she took what you said and turned it into a message from beyond."

"It wasn't me that got a message from Jack," Rory tells me. "All

I did was ask her what her human would say to her, and she knew. He did talk, through her memory and her love for him. She just needed someone to listen so that she could hear it too."

For a moment I just sit there looking into Rory's mismatched eyes, and wonder at how, after only forty-eight hours, he is so much better at this than me with thirty years under my elasticated waistband.

"It was you who got a message from a dead person," he says.

"That's not what happened," I insist. "It was auditory pareidolia. I've just got a bit of seawater in my ears."

"Oh yes, that's definitely what happened," Rory says, glancing at a spot over my shoulder and giving a thumbs-up. "Really lucky it made sense to Dolly, right?"

"Right," I say, resisting the urge to look where he is looking.

"Anyway, good job, Genie," he says. "You deserve a treat!"

"You know, you are a really nice person, Rory," I tell him again.

"So are you, Genie," he says. "You are the best person I know."

When he says it I want to believe him, and I've almost decided to, when the bell on the door rings and Nanna Maria walks in in a hot-pink wrap dress and a huge pair of fake Gucci shades.

"Brace yourself, my darlings," she announces. "For I have tidings from the motherland."

Chapter Fifteen

EATH," I SAY. "Are you serious?"

"I'm afraid so, darling," Nanna Maria says. She pauses, looking around as if she can detect some unseen residue in the air.

"Have you already had a client in this morning? Why didn't she wait for me?"

"Turns out that Rory has a knack for this," I say. "Death? You are telling me that the only way for the wish I made to be reversed and for Rory to be turned back into a dog is death? What does that mean? Do we have to find someone and kill them, because I can think of a few candidates . . ."

"No, Genie." Nanna Maria sighs. "No, if you had wished for something for yourself and changed your mind then it would be your death that would reverse the wish."

"I'd call that less of a reversal and more of a termination," I say.

"But as it is, the only way for Rory to become a dog again is for . . . well, for him to die."

"Not doing that," Rory says. "That is a big no from me. What's the alternative?"

"There is an alternative, right?" I ask Nanna, circling the table toward her.

"What part about 'the only way' do you not understand, dear?"

Nanna Maria asks. Rory and I look at each other. Rory sits down on the floor and then rolls backward, where he lies prone, staring at the disco ball. Rory can't accept that there is "no alternative" and neither can I. This can't really be happening, right?

"Only me. Only I could be granted an actual once-in-a-lifetime magical wish and fuck it up this badly," I say, tangling my fingers in my hair. "Yep, that's some grade-A Eugenie Wilson for you. The Unluckiest Girl in the World—"

"Stop that right now," Nanna Maria says. "For goodness' sake, girl, you are not in the least bit unlucky. Or at least not more than the next person."

"Er!" I exclaim, gesturing with some emphasis toward my dog-human, who is lying prone on the floor while the processing chip of his brain reads *Error 404*.

"That is not bad luck," Nanna Maria says. "That is bad judgment, and now you must consider how to make the best of the situation."

"I hate it when you are right," I say unhappily.

Nanna Maria smiles, turning on her high heels to head for the kitchen.

"There is one alternative," she says in an offhand way.

"What?" Rory sits up.

"What?" I demand.

"Well, it's not so much dead cert, pardon the pun, as a possibility . . ."

Rory and I wait till Nanna Maria boils the kettle and makes a cup of tea. We both know there is no point in trying to hurry her up, that she will tell us when she is ready and not a moment before, because Nanna Maria is infuriating like that.

"What?" we repeat in unison as she appears from the kitchen carrying a *Best Psychic Ever* mug.

"I didn't mention it before because, well, Genie, you have never really embraced the notion of . . ."

"What?" I ask her.

"Self-reflection and improvement," Nan says. "But specifically, your own magic."

"A, I am not magic. And B, how is this suddenly about me?" I ask.

Rory looks at me. Fair enough.

"So according to my cousin, *if* the conditions are right you might be able to . . . cancel out the wish," Nanna says. "But the conditions have to be right. You have to commit. And there is no replacement wish. It would just be as if the original wish never happened."

"Fine," I say at once. "Let's do it."

"Well, obviously it's not as easy as that," Nanna Maria says. "Like I said, conditions have to be right."

"Obviously!" I will admit I am now slightly fraught.

"Mariella said that she had heard of a family legend from long, long ago. When a distant relative wished to marry the richest man in the village."

"Right," I say. "And how did that work out for her?"

"Well, she regretted it because she was really in love with a goatherd called Sebastian."

"Like how long ago was this, and did it actually happen?" I ask her.

"Hundreds of years, and it's in the family lore so I'd say there is a fifty-fifty chance of it being true," Nanna says. "Maybe sixty-forty."

"We're doomed," I tell Rory. "Go on."

"Well, the girl knew she had made an awful mistake. But it was too late. She was married. She thought the trappings of wealth and power would replace what she really longed for, which was to live with purpose, kindness, and love. But money never did buy happiness."

"I do kind of beg to differ on that one," I say. "I mean, for starters I'd be willing to give it a good go."

"So she began to live as if she had nothing. To give away her clothes and jewels and to see the beauty and rarity in every normal, mundane thing. She saw that her existence was the most precious thing she had, and that to squander even one second of it was a terrible waste. The power of her realization was so great that she canceled out her misguided wish with the power of her fulfillment in discovering her life's true purpose and her inner priestess." Nanna Maria smiles at me. "So, you know, you could try that?"

"This sounds suspiciously like a hackneyed attempt to get me to go on dating apps while I get used to having a human Rory," I tell her, narrowing my eyes.

"Which is why I didn't tell you," Nanna Maria says. "I knew you'd think something cynical like that. But the point is that becoming the person you are meant to be isn't about meeting boys or falling in love. It's about appreciating your own existence as a unique miracle that will never be repeated again in the entire history of the universe. And the family magic."

"We're doomed," I tell Rory.

"We're doomed," Rory agrees.

"Oh well," I say. "Better crack on with Operation Pinocchio."

"That's not a good name," Rory says. "Pinocchio wanted to be a human boy and he lied! I wanted to be a *dog* dog and I never lie."

"You think of a name, then," I say.

"Genie." Nanna makes me sit at the table with an expression that is gentle and loving but also quite scary.

"Why are you so willing to dismiss the possibility that there might be a better way of living your life?" she asks. "A way that can help Rory get back to his natural form and help you see how beautiful life can be. It's very small, I know. But it's a possibility. And where there is the smallest possibility there is hope. Hope for Rory and for you. Would it be so wrong to try and find your way back to the girl you used to be, and to be the woman you *should* be? The one who was so full of ideas, imagination, and color? The girl who always had hope?"

When I look into her eyes I see the grief there. It's hard when you realize someone is grieving for the person that you used to be. Nanna Maria must have missed me for a long time.

"I'm so sorry, Nanna," I tell her, "but that girl is long gone. I can't bring her back. I don't want to. It would be wrong even to try."

"Why do you think that, Genie?" Nanna grabs my hand. "Why would you even think that?"

"Because how can I go on like nothing happened? How could I do that to . . . how could I do that?"

Nanna's gaze drops. One tear falls onto the tabletop.

"You, you are different to me," I tell her, bringing her hand to my cheek. "Somehow you, Mum, and Dad have managed to keep your shiny coating of weird endemic joy, and I love that about all of you. But mine is chipped and cracked and rubbed away. I used to see magic, now I just see the truth. This is my normal." I gesture at myself. "It's just who I am, and you know, I like what I have. It's good enough. It's more than I deserve."

"Darling, it's not," Nanna says. "And I truly believe that if you would only try you could—"

"I can't try any harder," I tell her, caught off guard by the catch in my voice. "I try every single day, and this is me at maximum capacity. I am trying, Nanna. Right now. This is it."

"Genie . . ." Nan trails off. Rory comes over to the table and puts his arms around my shoulders, resting his cheek on the top of my head.

"Don't be sad—it's fine," I tell her. "I've still got Rory to look after me, see?"

"I see," Nanna says.

"Now I'm taking Rory home to get ready for the housewarming party tonight. There's going to have to be prep."

"Going home?" Nanna Maria exclaims. "But you only just got here!"

"No, you only just got here—and you are the one who granted me a wish without doing the proper health and safety checks on my mental acuity, so I think the least you can do is give me an afternoon off."

"Go on, then," Nanna says. "And try not to worry, Genie. Things usually have a habit of working out for the best if you only let them."

Whatever, Nan.

Anyway, it's official. Operation Man-Dog is a go.

Maybe that name still needs some work.

Chapter Sixteen

RIGHT, SO WHAT do we need to remember?" Miles asks. He's wearing a white shirt with one button open at the neck, which for some reason is maddeningly alluring to look at. I'm wearing a dress! It's a black dress and it reaches my ankles, so it's basically a habit, but it does have a sort of swishy cowl neckline that isn't not flattering when it comes to cleavage. I feel sort of attractive, which is weird, because I don't care, but also, I do want Miles to notice a bit.

"Look interested, nod a lot, don't say your inside thoughts out loud, and be prepared to stay for a minimum of one hour."

"Excellent, Genie." Miles looks over to the front door, where Rory has been waiting eagerly since we got home from work. "And what about you, Rory?"

"New friends? New snacks? I was born ready!" Rory assures me.

"Right," I say, nodding, and Miles offers me a firm handshake, which I take with grim determination. "Let's get this over with."

SUSAN AND AMANDA GREET US with warm smiles and a plate of sausage rolls. Inevitably Rory takes the entire plate from them with a big grin and a thank-you before charging into the room firing off a succession of cheery hellos and one "Your head is so shiny—how do you get it that shiny? Is it from stroking? Can I stroke it?"

Miles and I stand by the door.

"How does he do that without people wanting to punch him?" I ask Miles.

"He's naturally charming," Miles says. "Charming people find this sort of thing effortless."

"Aren't psychopaths charming?" I ask, squinting at Rory as he bows his head for Mo from number twelve to admire his lustrous locks.

"I think some of them are," Miles said. "But I think you can be charming without being a serial killer. Anyway, Rory was a dog for most of his life, and he was used to nearly everyone being very pleased to see him. He doesn't have—"

"Hang-ups," I say.

"Or social anxiety," Miles says.

"He doesn't care what people think of him," I add.

"Because he assumes that everyone thinks he's great."

"Because he is great," I say. Miles and I look at each other.

"Maybe we should have got Rory to write a list for us," I say.

"We don't need a different list—the same list will do," Miles says.

We stand for a moment observing the gaggle of effortlessly mingling humans.

"You look very nice, by the way," Miles says, looking in precisely the opposite direction to my face.

"You have very nice manners," I tell him. "Your mum would be proud."

"She would, and I do, but I mean it," Miles says, studying the dusty lampshade. "Anyway, come on, let's go and talk genially to virtual strangers and pretend we are fascinated."

There's a second's delay before I follow him. A second in which I try to imagine myself telling him how nice his neck looks, and then all the resultant weirdness that would surely follow. Best avoided.

"Genie!" Rory grabs my wrist and pulls me over toward the lady who was just patting his head. "Come and say hi to Mo. Did you know that her family has lived on this road since the houses were built, like five thousand years ago?"

"More like a hundred and fifty, lad." Mo chuckles.

"Yeah, but what's that in dog years?" Rory asks her.

"Really?" I ask. "In the same house?"

"Oh yeah, my great-great-great-granddad lived there first off. He worked on the railway. After the First World War we were able to buy the house. We handed it down. One day it will be my grandson's. I was born in the upstairs bedroom." Mo smiles. "That place is part of the family."

"Isn't that amazing?" Rory says. "To have all that history going all that way back? Like you can know that wherever you go in the world there is always somewhere you really belong."

"That is nice," I say. "Do you feel that when you go home, Mo?"

"Oh yes, I say hello to my nan every morning," Mo says. "And all the others."

"Can you see them?" Rory says. "I can see ghosts, but I don't tell Genie. She's funny like that."

"I did think I saw my dad on the stairs once," Mo says thoughtfully.

"I don't even know where my mum is now," Rory says, "or who

my dad is. I had about nine brothers and sisters but they could be anywhere. I just hope they got a better home than me—before Genie, that is. Genie is the best. Complicated, but good at heart, you know?"

"Oh, you poor love!" Mo hugs him spontaneously. "Genie here's a good girl. Not one to stop and chat, but she always puts her recycling out. You make a lovely couple."

"Ew, gross," Rory says. "It is not like that AT ALL. We are just best friends."

"I thought I was your best friend?" Kelly arrives from somewhere, slinging her arm around my shoulder.

"I don't judge," Mo says. "I heard on the radio about you young people giving up sex."

"I never really think about that stuff," Rory says with visible distaste. "I do think about cheese a lot."

"I'd rather have a nice cup of tea," Mo confesses. "Do you know, I saw some cheese and pineapple on sticks in the kitchen. And a kettle."

"That sounds wrong, but I'm prepared to give it a try," Rory says as Mo hooks her arm through his and leads him away.

"I need to talk to you right now," Kelly says. "Come outside, yeah?"

"Yeah, 'course," I say, scanning the room for Miles. He is frowning very earnestly as the two guys from number 40 explain to him why Scarborough Athletic is the best football team in the world.

"So how's Rory doing, then?" Kelly asks once we're outside, flopping against the wall as if she's about to faint. "I went to the parlor but your nan said you bobbed off early."

"He's trying to be upbeat," I say. "But looks like he's going to be stuck as a human unless I find my life's purpose, and honestly I sort of thought it was sitting down and eating crisps. I'm not sure it's really sunk in yet. For either of us."

"Shit," Kelly says. "Well, you could give it a go, the life's purpose thing? For Rory. Even if it does sound like a ploy to get you on dating apps."

"That's what I said!" I exclaim. "And anyway, who's to say this is not my true life's purpose. Me now. Just as I am. With crisps."

"Yeah, but it's not, though, is it?" Kelly says.

"What?" I ask, aghast.

"You forget that I've known you all your life. You used to be leader of the pack. You were voted most likely to be famous for being a fashion designer in Year eleven. You had a glow of confidence about you. And an imagination that could conjure up these drawings and designs out of thin air that took our breath away. Remember when you made your own dress for your Christmas dance, in your first term at college? Crazy green beautiful gown. And you wanted that wanker Aiden to dress to match you, and he refused, so you designed an outfit for Miles, and it was crazy but together you looked amazing. We all came to wave you off, and that dress was rad."

To be honest I try not to think about that night. I'm afraid that if I think about it too hard, I'll see the exact moment I made a wrong turn and never found the way back.

"None of us could believe how clever you were. You were going places. And then Aiden fucked it all up. Don't get me wrong. He was a grade A wanker. The way he treated you and . . . what you went through, darling, that was so hard. But you are the one that let it stop you in your tracks. And you never got moving again. So no, love. This isn't how you are meant to be. It's how you want to be and it's a waste."

"Shit," I say. "Tell me what you really think."

"I did, for a long time, but it never did any good. Maybe now. Maybe because it's for Rory, you might just listen."

"That girl everyone keeps talking about, she wasn't real. Back then I thought life would be like it was on the telly. I didn't know better until I did. Life isn't always about massive achievements, fame, and success, you know. Sometimes it's about just getting through."

"Fuck off, no, it isn't," Kelly says. "We all have our different purposes in life. Some people are astronauts, some people are beauticians, some people are nuns and that. If you find what's right for you, you're happy, right? Genie, you were special. You have a talent that no one else does. I still think of all those drawings and designs that must be stuck in your head, and how great it would be to see you creating that stuff again. It made you happy. And you happy is like a comet streaking through the sky, lighting up the dark."

"Really?" I ask her.

"Yeah, really." She smiles. "So, don't totally discount the life's purpose thing, okay? At least think about it, yeah?"

"I'll try," I say. Kelly drops her chin, and sighs forlornly.

"Now could you help me with my life's purpose? Or at least the love of my life."

"What's up, Kels?" I ask

She searches her pockets for a pack of cigarettes.

"Dave is what's up," she says. "He's been cheating on me, Genie. I know he has. He came in tonight and it was the same as it's been for weeks. Barely even looks at me, he's so ashamed. And he stinks of some bloody cheap body spray. So I asked him, I said,

Are you seeing another woman, Dave? And he said to mind my own business, Genie. I told him, Our marriage *is* my business, Dave. And he said, I'm going to the pub, and walked out. Can you believe the front of him?"

"So, he didn't actually admit to cheating?" I ask.

"It was written all over his face!" Kelly says. "I don't know what to do about it, Genie. I love him, the bloody git. I thought we were so tight. And now . . . he's like a stranger."

"It is a bit iffy," I say. "But you know it might not be another woman. Maybe he's got a gambling addiction or . . . was abducted by aliens."

"What are you talking about?" Kelly asks me. "This is Dave we are talking about. Not Dr. bloody Who."

"No, fair. Have you thought about talking to his mates?"

"No," Kelly says. "But I've decided. We're following him. Tomorrow. After he finishes work."

"We?" My eyes widen.

"I need you to come with me to make it seem like I am not some crazy bitch who is completely off her rocker."

"Kelly! You drive a hot-pink Nissan Micra with *Kel's Mobile Beauty* emblazoned in hologram glitter lettering on the side. I'm pretty sure he's going to know it's you."

"That's why we're going in your car," Kelly says. "I bought us wigs."

"My car that Dave did the MOT on?" I ask. "Last week?"

"Look, I don't know what else to do," Kelly wails. "I have to know, Genie. I have to! I can't bear this uncertainty. It's not fair to me or the kids."

"Okay, fine. Tomorrow after work. I'll pick you up from your place and we'll go and follow Dave, but when he sees us, which he will, you will just have to try and talk to him about it, okay? Like adults."

"I did try, but okay," Kelly says, rifling in her handbag. She brings out two wigs that for some reason she has brought to the party. "Do you want to be blond or ginger?"

Kelly pushes two bunches of nylon hair at me.

"Are you kidding? Blond all day long," I say, taking the wig. "Everyone knows they have more fun."

Chapter Seventeen

NO WAY," Rory is saying in utter fascination as he talks to Kath Simpson from number 33. He sees me, wig in hand, and calls me over. "Hey, Genie, did you know that Kath goes swimming in the sea every day for at least ten minutes whatever the weather? Just like we do!"

I shove the wig in my handbag.

"I didn't know you were a cold swimmer, Genie," Kath says. "I'm in a club—only ladies allowed, I'm afraid, Rory, but you'd be welcome to join us any time, Genie."

"Oh, well, I . . . er . . . um . . . thank you," I say. "It's more Rory's thing, really—I've only actually got in once."

"Yeah, but that was before," Rory says. "Now that I, a human, live with Genie, she is going to get in the sea with me every day. Why don't you allow men, Kath?"

"It's just more relaxing without them," Kath says. "Most of them are awful, but I think we might make an exception for you, Rory."

"That is brilliant! Really?" Rory claps his hands. "I'd love that, Kath. Me and Genie are definitely up for that. What time do you meet?"

"Normally about five a.m.," Kath says.

"Oh yeah, no, that's way too early for us." Rory shakes his head. "We don't get out of bed until eight-thirty a.m. even on a workday. I would, but Genie says morning people are bastards."

"That's not exactly the word I used," I say, glancing over at Miles where he is listening very intently to how much Neil Parsons loves his 1978 Ford Capri. He must feel me watching him, because he looks up and smiles. I feel better knowing he's in the room.

"Yeah, it is," Rory says. "Remember when that delivery guy knocked at the door really early one Sunday? You said he was a stone-cold bastard and you hoped he burned in hell."

"But I definitely am not a morning person." I smile at Kath, who stifles a giggle. Miles comes to join us, just as Rory spots another instant friend.

"Hi, Steven!" is how Rory greets the guy from number 45. "How's your toy poodle, still evil?"

"So evil," Steven says, completely unoffended, and as if he has known Rory all his life. "I'm at my wits' end, to be honest. Yesterday she bit me on the nose and wouldn't let go for three minutes. I mean, I know she's only tiny, but three minutes is a long time to have a bitter poodle hanging off your nose."

"I told you dogs are more violent than cats," Miles says softly in my ear.

"Poodles are the exception that proves the rule," I whisper back. "Them and Chihuahuas. Like someone put cat energy in a dog body just to mess with us."

Miles chuckles, the top of his arm brushing against me with a friendly nudge.

"Have you thought about toothache?" Rory tells him. "Hetty's always complaining about toothache. No one likes going to the vet, am I right?" Rory looks around the room for affirmation. "But if you pop a bit of lavender oil on her collar and get someone to check out her gnashers I am pretty sure she would chill right out. I mean, obviously she'd still want to prove her supremacy in battle over all other creatures, but in a more chill way, know what I'm saying?"

"Not entirely," Steven says, "but you know I haven't even thought about her teeth. That's a really good idea, Rory."

"You're welcome."

"I didn't realize you were a specialist in dog psychology," Steven says. "Study their body language, do you?"

"Not exactly," Rory says. "But I do know what dogs are thinking a lot of the time."

"Like a dog whisperer?" Steven asks.

"Mostly just like in a normal voice," Rory says.

"Thank you so much for coming," Susan says, catching Miles just before he gets to me and Rory. "And you, Genie. It's so nice to move into such a welcoming community."

"Oh, pleasure," I say, reaching the end of my small-talk capacity at alarming speed.

"Delighted," Miles says, arriving at the end of his just after me.

"More sandwiches?" Rory says, perusing Susan's selection with naked delight.

"So, what's the inside scoop on the neighbors?" Amanda asks. "Who's fun and who should we avoid?"

"We'll, you're clearly wonderful." Susan nods at Rory.

"Yeah, I am," Rory says.

"Yes, Rory here is my . . . lodger," I say. That's a concept that is taking quite some getting used to.

"Don't you mind that, Miles?" Amanda asks.

"Mind what?" Miles asks.

"Your girlfriend having such a hunk of a lodger." Amanda laughs, just as she catches Susan's eye and realizes she's made a faux pas.

"Oh, Genie and I are just friends," Miles says with quite some emphasis. "Just old, old, old, old, old, old friends."

"I think that was about five 'olds' too many," I mutter.

"Oh," Amanda says. "I'm sorry, I should be the last person to make assumptions, but it's just that you came together and Rory is so vocal about you not being his girlfriend, Genie, and I"— Amanda catches Susan's eye—"will just shut up now. Would you like a mini quiche?"

"No thanks," Miles says. "It's getting late so . . ."

"It's eight-thirty," I say.

"Still," Miles says. "I think I'll probably . . ."

"You're tired," I say, but before Miles can leave there is suddenly a burst of enthusiastic cheers from my neighbors, who are almost all gathered around Rory.

"Genie! Miles!" Rory calls to us. "We're going to go in the yard and howl at the moon to get in touch with our inner wolves! Wanna come?"

I look at Miles.

"Rude not to," he says.

"I THINK I'LL GO HOME," I say after the people from the street that backs onto ours call the police, fearing some kind of drug-fueled zombie attack. "Do you want to stay, Rory? I think the party is going to keep going, if a lot more quietly and lot less ferally than it was."

"Without you?" Rory asks, looking suddenly worried.

"Yes, it's allowed," I tell him. "You are technically a grown-up, and it looks like you're having a great time. You really are a people person."

"I am," he says. "Most dogs are. Still, I think I'll come home with you, Genie. It's nearly time for our TV series. And you did really well tonight. You probably need a sit-down and several uninterrupted hours of silence."

"You get me," I say, putting my hand on his arm, almost weepy with gratitude.

I hang around for another ten minutes while Rory says goodbye to all his friends. It's almost ten as we head over the road.

"Our boy's a natural," I say to Miles as we pause outside our front doors.

"We make pretty great parents." Miles chuckles.

I can feel the heat blooming in my cheeks, and a tug of sadness too.

"I didn't mean like a . . . couple or anything," Miles says hurriedly.

"Duh, obviously not," I say, making a theatrical gagging noise.

"Just a good team."

"Such a great team." I nod, offering him a fist to bump.

"'Night then, Eugenie," he says.

I hear the click of his front door shutting, and it's only then that I close my front door. Lean my forehead against it. It's crazy to think that the me and Miles that might have been, back when we were kids, would still be together now. Fifteen years later and we would definitely have grown apart; that's the accepted wisdom on childhood sweethearts, right? And anyway, I'm not even certain if we would have been might-have-beens, if you get me. There was chemistry and flirting. If you call some kid bringing you pretty rocks flirting, which I do. And there was one moment. One moment when our lives might have taken a different path.

I'd been going out with Aiden for three months when I asked him to come with me to my college Christmas dance. Everything had been so perfect up until then that when he laughed in my face over the dress designs I showed him, and said that pretentious bollocks like the dance wasn't his scene, I brushed it off. I thought he was just a bit shy, not the kind of guy to step outside his comfort zone. That I was wrong to even ask him. So, I asked Miles instead, because even though he wasn't the kind of guy to step out of his comfort zone either, I knew he would, for me—he was that kind of friend. I was too young to see that meant that Aiden wasn't the right guy for me. Too stupid to realize who was.

I was standing right here on the night of the Christmas dance, waiting for Miles, and I felt so good. If I concentrate really hard, I can just about remember that sense of confidence and certainty. To experience even a fraction of that again is all kinds of wonderful. I knew my designs were good, I knew I looked great, I felt *fantastic*.

Mum and Dad are standing on the stairs with a camera when Miles knocks at the door.

The flash goes off as he gives me flowers, pink roses tied with a pink bow and, threaded onto the ribbon, a pink quartz bead; Mile's love language, I know that now. At the sight of him I feel the familiar bubble of happiness that his smile always set off in my chest. The simple joy of knowing that he is part of my life, and that he always will be.

His mouth falls open when he sees me, his eyes wide with wonder. There's hardly any space in our little hallways, so he leads me out onto the street and twirls and twirls me until my skirts flare out; our laughter echoes off the rows of houses and I'm so dizzy that for a moment it feels like I'm floating.

In that moment anything was possible. Now, all these years later it feels like hardly anything is.

When Miles said we made good parents, I caught a glimpse of a different future for a different me. Nothing concrete, nothing certain, but a sharp sense of possibility. And in that different future from the one I've been so certain of for so long, all the things that my friends and family have kept telling me about myself for so long were true. And right at the heart of that was something else that is certain, that is constant, no matter what version of my life I'm living.

I am so in love with Miles. I always have been.

"Hey," I call to Rory as I walk into the living room. "Do we have any more ice cream?"

Then I catch a glimpse of myself in the mirror and lean in for a closer look. It looks like . . . no, it can't be, it's August. Yet, it looks like there are a handful of *snowflakes* melting in my hair.

Chapter Eighteen

"WHAT'S GOT YOUR GOAT?" Nanna Maria asks me as I lay out a new tablecloth, ready for her first client of the day. "You've got a face like thunder and your aura is all muddy and sickly looking."

"Oh, let me see," I say, tipping up the battery-powered tea lights so they begin to flicker and glow. "Could it be because my beloved grandmother neglected to tell me that the wish she granted me on my birthday would actually ruin my life?"

Obviously I plan to blame her for all the feelings that caught up with me yesterday. At least for a little while.

"Ruin *my* life, you mean," mutters Rory, who is in as bad a mood as me. I don't know what happened. He was in high spirits after the party and talked about his new friends nonstop. I was starting to think that maybe he would be okay with the change in his circumstances and that, somehow, we would all just muddle through. I had visions of my dog moving out, getting his own place, developing an amazing career as an animal psychologist and eventually getting his own TV show. I thought, yep, my actual dog having a more fulfilling existence than me would accurately reflect my life. And then on the way to work this morning, it was like someone just switched a light off in him. The bounce went from his step, the glint went out of his eye. Normally I'd have put it down to worms, but in this instance I doubt it. All he's been doing since we arrived at the shop is leaning on the door and gazing moodily out the window. I have yet to get to the bottom of what's upsetting him, mostly because I am too busy wallowing in my own self-inflicted misery. Or I would be if Rory wasn't so keen on being super-specific about it.

"Are you really still trying to blame me for that?" Nan asks, with a huff.

"It's not your fault, Nanna," Rory tells her. "Genie is in a mood because she finally realized she is in love with Miles and has decided to be all complicated about it."

"That is . . . fairly accurate," I admit.

"Ah." Nanna Maria comes to scrutinize me under the mirror ball, taking hold of my chin and twisting my face this way and that, as if she can see my existential crisis imprinted on my face. Who knows, maybe she can.

"Well, this is a good sign," she says with a nod. "Rory, can you turn the *Open* sign to *Closed*, please?"

"Wait." I motion to Rory to stop. "What do you mean, this is a good sign? How can years of nameless yearning and unrequited love be a good sign?"

"Depends how you look at it, darling," Nanna Maria says. "You could look at it that way, or you could decide it's better to feel *anything* rather than nothing."

"Not this again." I sigh. "Rory, open the shop."

"Wait," Nanna Maria instructs Rory.

"You have hidden yourself away from hope and love and—"

"Misery," I add.

"For far too long. It's time to start living again, my darling girl.

Even if that means you are rejected and your heart is broken. It's a start, a step to discovering your true purpose."

"Whoa, whoa, whoa there." Crossing to the door I flip the sign to *Open*. Rory flips it back again, crosses his arms, and gives me a just-try-it look. I narrow my eyes at him, but he is resolute. "Me acknowledging a feeling for a moment, before I repress it right back to where it belongs, does not mean that I am going on your stupid quest to 'find myself' or whatever it is. I have found myself, I am right here, being just below average. I am not the girl who goes on journeys of discoveries. I am the girl who watches other people do it on TV. I'm just a dumb, stupid, nothing special human."

"Tell me about it," Rory mutters.

"I see," Nanna Maria says, giving me that look of hers that says she knows something I don't. "Why don't you just ask him how he feels now?"

"Ask who what now?" I ask as my phone rings and I see Miles's name appear on my phone screen. Nanna preens. Narrowing my eyes, I turn my back on her and answer the phone.

"Milesington," I say.

"Eugenie," he replies.

"I had an idea about how to help Rory," he says. "I thought we could talk about it."

"Oh?"

"I thought in person might be better," Miles tells me.

"In case the phone is being tapped?" I ask. I'm not sure what it's going to be like being near to him, now that I definitely know I want to be near to him all the time. But I suppose I can't avoid him for the rest of my life either.

"You never know," he says, so deadpan that for a moment I think he's being serious. And then he chuckles, a deep warm throaty laugh that makes me think about what it would be like to kiss his neck and, anyway, shut up.

"Then come and meet us on our lunch break, about noon? Eleven-thirty if Rory gets his way. We'll be over the road with chips. Code word: 'seagull.'"

"Excellent. Goodbye, Eugenie."

"Goodbye Milesington," I say. I do my best not to smile with the pleasure I feel after our exchange as I turn back to Nanna and Rory, but it takes effort, and like everything that takes effort with me, I fail miserably.

"I see," Nanna repeats herself, arching an eyebrow.

"They've had special feelings for each other for years," Rory adds with a grin. "And don't think I've been too busy with my security duties to notice all the long lingering looks and pregnant pauses whenever you see Miles."

"My pauses are not pregnant," I protest. "My pauses are positively virginal. And don't forget Claudia-from-work. Miles has told me to my literal face that he really likes her."

"I really like dried pig's ears, what's your point?" Rory says.

"Not really the same thing . . ."

"What I don't get is why all this is so hard just because you are human. I never fancied anyone in that way, but I've seen other dogs who wish to mate, and so they do mate. It's usually quite weird, and it makes small talk awkward, you know, when they are there getting it on, and you're just passing, but anyway, they do it and then it is done, and the dog's sperm travels up the girl dog's—"

"Enough with the *David Attenborough*!" I say. "Being a human is much more complicated than being a dog."

"Tell me about it," Rory says. "I can see that, but I don't see why. You like someone, so tell them. If they like you, yay! If they don't, oh well, you tried. Everything out in the open, no secrets, no games, no nonsense. Done."

"Because that is not how society works," I say. "Civilization is built on secrets, lies, and mistrust. Miles and me . . . maybe once, but not now. Now we are just friends and that is it. And it's best we stay friends. I like him, he's a good neighbor. Don't want to ruin that and I don't want to interfere in this Claudia-from-work thing. Miles deserves a nice geologist girl who is not weird and tangentially magical-adjacent."

"Today you are friends and neighbors," Nanna says. "Who knows about tomorrow?"

"Who knows?" Rory echoes.

"I'm telling you right now," I say, pointing at both of them in turn, "that this double act is not happening. You are not bullying me into a quest. I am not the sort of person who goes on quests. So knock it off."

"Very well," Nanna concedes. "Besides, it doesn't matter if your feelings are fleeting—at least you have them. Like I said, a good sign."

"Ugh, I hate feelings!" I proclaim as a gaggle of giggling hens tumbles in through the door.

"Can you tell our Steph if her marriage is gonna last?" one of the girls asks Nanna. "We've got a sweepstake."

"Of course." Nanna waves regally at the table. "Take a seat, ladies, and let me reveal the secrets of your love lives to you."

"YOU CAN'T BLAME NANNA for all this," Rory says at lunchtime as we lean against the railings that separate the sidewalk from the beach, eating chips and looking at the sea like two French lieuten-

ants' women, but with chips. The beach heaves with holidaymakers, and it's impossible not to smile at the kids galloping through
the surf, at the old ladies in deck chairs eating ice creams in their
shades, looking like a couple of mafiosi matriarchs.

"Can't I?" I say. "You watch me."

"She did tell you to be careful," Rory says. "She gave you rules!"

"Details! Anyway, what about you?" I ask him.

"What about me?" he says.

"You are down, and you being down is really unusual, even in
these circumstances. Why are you down?"

"We didn't go through the park today," Rory says.

"We were a bit late, and I thought we didn't have to because . . ."
Suddenly I get why Rory is sad.

"Now that I'm human it doesn't matter if I see my friends for
our morning play," he finishes for me. "I thought I'd be okay about
it. I thought after the party that maybe being human could be
okay. But then we walked past the park this morning and I realized that we never have to go to the park again. I miss my friends.
And now that I am one of you, that's all over. It's over and I didn't
get to say goodbye."

"Oh, Rory, I'm so sorry." I put my hand on his shoulder, and he
tilts his head to rest on it.

"And you don't cuddle me anymore," he goes on. "I get it. I
get why. You're worried what people will think. But I miss your
cuddles, Genie. They made me feel safe."

"Oh, Rory." Dropping my chips into a bin, I put my arms
around Rory's waist and hug him tight. After a moment he hugs
me back. I don't even know why I was worried about hugging him
at all. What does it matter what people think or the assumptions
they might make? Rory and I know what we are to each other, and

that's all that matters. Our hug is warm and comforting and it makes me feel safe too.

"This is awkward," Miles says, appearing at our side.

"Miles, buddy," Rory says, offering him an arm. "Join us!"

"I'll pass," Miles says. Rory and I break apart.

"Rory was feeling sad, and we realized that since Rory turned human, we don't really hug anymore, and I couldn't think of a good reason not to, so . . ." I explain with a shrug.

"Genie is the best hugger," Rory says. "You should try it."

"I've hugged Genie," Miles says. "Not for a few years now, but back in the day, sure. She is a good hugger."

"Then hug now! It doesn't have to mean you want to have sex or be in love . . ."

"Blaughshgigff," I splutter.

"Or anything." Rory gives me the side-eye. "Anyway, why did you stop hugging? Genie hugs me and we are just good friends, also."

"Oh." Miles looks at me. "I don't know . . . maybe because . . ."

"You know what, I just had the best idea," I say, before my dog goes any further with his pseudo Dr. Phil skills. "It's Tuesday!"

"So?" Miles shrugs.

"It's the Tuesday pup meetup at the park. Let's go and see some of your friends right now!"

"Really?" Rory says, his eyes lighting up.

"Yes," I say. "I'll text Nanna to say we are taking a long lunch. She won't mind. Let's go!"

"Good idea," Miles says.

"I mean, I hang out with dogs much more than I hang out with and talk to people. There's no reason you can't still see your friends anymore, Rory! No reason at all!"

Of course there was a reason, as I was just about to find out.

Chapter Nineteen

BECAUSE RORY STILL UNDERSTANDS DOG. Not a huge problem in itself—it just sort of attracts a lot of attention when a big blond bloke in a Hawaiian shirt starts making small talk with a dachshund.

"How were you to know?" Rory says. "I mean, anyone would think that if it's okay to eat a biscuit on the sofa it's okay to take it into bed? Bed and sofa are the same thing. What did you do?"

The little dog rolls on to her back, waving all her legs in the air.

"Classic," Rory says. "Works every time."

"I really don't get any of this," I say to Miles as we watch him. "He looks like a man, he has the digestive system of a human, he is really quite thoughtful and intelligent, but also he can still smell like a dog and apparently understand Bark. I mean . . . who makes up the rules?"

"Maybe there are no rules," Miles says with a frown. "Which is kind of scary."

"Anyway, what idea did you want to talk about?" I turn to him. It's a bright day and he's wearing a pair of classic (presumably prescription) Ray-Bans and a navy T-shirt. Has he deliberately decided to get more stylish for Claudia-at-work? As he watches Rory a tiny smile tugs at his mouth, revealing a comma-shaped dimple.

Probably best to stop looking at him in this new light. No good can come from it.

"Ah, well, so I was reading a book and I suddenly had a thought and . . ."

"And?" I prompt him after a long moment of silence.

"Genie, can I be honest?"

"I don't know," I say, frowning.

"I don't have a plan. I just realized I would really like to see you."

"Oh." I look straight ahead. It's safest.

"Both, both of you." Miles coughs. "Is that okay?"

"Yeah, 'course, no problemo," I say. *Problemo?*

"Back when we were kids, we used to hang out all the time and we never needed a reason. It was like a given. But these days, I don't *really* get to see you, not like I have these past four days. I realized I really miss just . . . being with you."

"Miles . . ."

"Genie . . . You know, Claudia . . ."

"From work. I doooooo."

"She asked me out. On a date."

"Oh?" I try to process this information. I mean, I knew it was coming, I just didn't see Claudia-from-work taking the initiative. "So that's good, is it?"

"What do you think?" he asks.

"Well, what did you say?"

"I said I'd think about it," I said.

"Miles!" I turn to him. "The girl put herself on the line for you and you left her hanging!"

"Well . . . it was just that." Miles takes a breath. "I wanted to ask you . . ."

"Why, I'm not your mum!" His face falls, and I feel terrible.

"Oh god, Miles, I'm such a klutz. What I meant to say is that the chick is clearly into you, dude!" Apparently, I've turned into a surfer bro from the 1990s, so I punch him in the arm for good measure. He winces. I wince too, but on the inside.

"She is clearly into me," Miles agrees. "It's refreshingly obvious, in fact."

"There you go, then," I say, desperate for this conversation to be over.

"There you go," Miles repeats. "Thanks for the clarification."

"Who's that hot dish?" It's a relief when Sally, the blond, pigtailed, young local dog walker comes to join us, pointing at Rory as he sits right on the daisy-studded grass surrounded by a circle of excited, barking, sniffy dogs.

"I know!" I hear Rory say. "I was pretty shocked too, and let me tell you, you know that big white drinking bowl in the bathroom? That's not for drinking out of . . ."

"My lodger," I tell Sally. "He's Australian."

"Oh," she says as if that explains everything. "He really loves dogs, doesn't he? It's a very attractive trait in a man. Hello, I'm Sally." She waves at Miles; he bows slightly back.

"I'm Miles," he tells her.

"Well, Genie, you've brought all the talent to the meetup today." Sally giggles, nudging me in the ribs. "You dark horse, you."

Rory rolls onto all fours, and is engaged in an enthusiastic game of tug-of-war with an old English sheepdog called Dusty, thankfully not using his teeth.

"He's so cute with them," Sally says, gazing at Rory. "It's like all the dogs are really listening to him."

"He knows a lot about dog psychology," I say.

"Dog psychology, huh?" Sally says. "I'd lie on his couch any day of the week."

"He's not into girls," I tell her, without even thinking about it.

"Just my luck," Sally says.

"Meh, men, who needs them?" I say, just as I glance at Miles and his so kissable almost-smile.

"Me," Sally says, "but then, I am in my twenties, and it's all about sex at my age."

"I'm only just thirty!" I protest. "I like sex too!"

"Do you?" Sally looks very surprised.

"Yes," I insist, looking at Miles, who has taken a deep interest in a cloud. "I have sex. I have fine, fine sex."

What I mean is two years ago I had a one-night stand, and when I say it was fine I mean a howling void of misery and despair, but still.

"How about you, Miles?" Sally asks. "Are you on the market?"

"I'm not," Miles says firmly, which, when I think about it, is probably the right way to go about handling Sally's questions.

"Shame," Sally says as Rory suddenly takes off, followed by six or seven dogs, just running for the sake of it. "I don't really want a boyfriend. I just want some really hot sex. But I suppose that's what the apps are for."

"Yeah, totally," I say.

"The initial flirtation, the buildup, the naughty sexting, the skin on skin, the orgasms, the afterglow. You know, that really satisfying feeling of have a stubble burn in all the right places?"

I'm still reflecting on "orgasms," plural. My brain seems to have shut down, and all I can do is stand here, my mouth flapping up and down like an out-of-sorts goldfish. Miles has wandered away several feet and seems to be closely examining a tree. Before long he will be having orgasms with Claudia. I could have said, Don't do it, Miles. Claudia-from-work isn't the girl for you, I am! But I didn't. And that's why I don't do quests because quests are for people with hope and who can stand to fail. I don't have either of those qualities.

"Stubble burn . . ." I mutter to cover my misery.

"Sorry," Sally says. "Mum's always telling me I'm a bit much."

"*Pffft*," I say with a devil-may-care wave of the hand that secretly agrees with her mum.

"Well, he's certainly a tonic." Aida, at least a comforting twenty years older than me, arrives and nods at Rory as he leads the excited yapping pack round and round the park in one great crazy chase.

Aida lets her collie, Pip, off the lead, who races toward where Rory and a half dozen other dogs are rolling and wrestling, chasing each other. It's good to see Rory laughing and smiling as he plays with his friends. For the first time since this whole thing happened he looks truly relaxed and like his doggy self again. More or less.

"Listen, mate, they left the bin open. What else were you going to do?" I hear him say as he jogs past, before throwing a ball which everyone chases after, including him.

"He's a dog psychiatrist," Sally says. "Not into girls."

"How does he feel about women?" Aida says.

"Oh god, what's all this show?" Pete Strange, the big-I-am dog-trainer in town, joins our group, hands on hips as he surveys the chaotic scene of romping man and dogs. His two beautiful German shepherds sit perfectly still, one on either side of him, waiting to be given permission to leave his side.

"My new lodger," I say.

"Dog psychologist," Sally says.

"Fancies fellers," Aida adds.

"You know what, I could have worked all that out without any of you saying a word," Pete says, squaring his shoulders. "That's the trouble with the so-called dog owners of today. They forget that dogs aren't pets."

"Um, they sort of are?" I query, but Pete ignores me.

"They are wolves, descended from wolves. Apex predators with a killer instinct that could emerge at any moment. They need to be dominated, controlled, trained to obey every command. Psychology? It's all about letting them know who's the alpha." Pete puffs out his chest. "Treating your dog like a 'fur baby'—" He grimaces with disgust at the hated phrase. "It's like having a deadly weapon and calling it Fluffy."

"The only thing deadly about my Pip is his farts." Aida chuckles.

"You laugh," Pete says, "but if push came to shove any one of those dogs would eat your rotting corpse."

Somehow Pete makes Miles feel safe to wander over toward us again.

"I hope not," Sally says. "Rusty's a vegan."

"Hey, guys." Rory trots up to us, his face flushed and beaming with pleasure. "Come and say hi to the guys! They've got a lot they want to say to you. Oh, hi, Sheba, Darth—it's me!"

Sheba gives a high-pitched yelp.

"I know, it *is* mental," Rory says.

"Hi to the guys?" Pete shakes his head in disgust. "These are animals, my friend. You don't say hi to them. You command them."

"Talking of animals," Aida says, "where's your lovely boy today, Genie? I've just realized he's not in the scrum. Odd to see you here without your dog."

"I'm at the vet's," Rory says quickly. "By which I mean the dog is at the vet's. I took him. Though I am not there myself. Right now. Phew."

"Can you let Sheba and Darth off so they can come and play, please?" Rory asks Pete, who has already jerked Sheba back into heel.

"I'll let them off when I'm ready," Pete says. "The dogs follow me, not the other way round. Now, you run along, sunshine—go and do your soppy, touchy-feely, woke nonsense."

I swear I just saw Sheba roll her eyes.

"Hey, Sheba," Rory says, wiggling all five digits at the dog, "watch this!"

Within a matter of seconds Rory has unhooked both dogs from their leads and is racing away, calling for them to follow. Sheba looks up at Pete for permission.

"You stay right there," Pete warns her.

"Oh, sod this," I say. "Come on, Sheba, down with the patriarchy."

As I race into the thick of the dog park Sheba is at my heels, and not far behind Darth follows, pouncing and bounding in the grass more like a lamb than an attack dog. Miles runs beside him, cheering Darth on. I know this is terrible behavior but right now I could not love him more. As we race toward the horizon Pete stands next to Aida and Sally, shouting in fury.

Aida is pissing herself.

Picking up a tennis ball that I spot shining in the long grass, I hurl it as far as I can. Then, like everyone else in the pack, I race after it. For a few brief seconds I feel like I am flying down the hill, my hair whipping behind me, the sea air blasting into my face. It's exhilarating, it's hilarious, it's ridiculous and *wonderful*.

Before I know it Sally has joined us, and is diving on the ball before Lucy the labradoodle can, whooping with joy as she throws it in another direction. Off we all go again, half feral, half mad, and 100 percent happy. Aida claps and shouts encouragement from the sidelines, while Pete eventually subsides into silence, his hands on his hips as a couple of kids with a football get in the middle, and suddenly this is a game of two halves and two balls.

Then my body remembers that usually the most exercise it does is standing; my knees buckle and I fall into the soft grass, entirely out of puff, as I roll onto my back and assume the snow-angel position.

"I'm tapping out!" I gasp to anyone who will listen. "I don't think I've run about so much since Year five PE!"

Miles sits down next to me, a bead of sweat tracking down his neck.

"You make me laugh, Genie," he says, very solemn.

"I do, don't I?" I say.

"All the time," Miles says with that small smile.

He lies back on the grass beside me, and just for a moment there is nothing but the blue sky overhead and heat coming off Miles's body, which is inches from mine. It would be so easy just to roll over and plant a kiss on his beautiful mouth. But even though terrible choices are my specialty, for once I hold back. He's going to say yes to Claudia.

"I'm out too," Sally says, puffing, flopping down next to me, wiping away the glimmer of perspiration from her forehead. "I think we can all learn a lot from your lodger. What's his name, by the way?"

"Rory," I say.

"Like your dog?" She laughs.

"Yeah, but with an . . . *i*."

"Well, I think we can learn a lot from Rory with an *i*. I never really thought about joining in with the playing instead of just watching . . . It was . . . magical."

"Did you have fun, Genie?" Rory crashes down, grinning from ear to ear, as one by one the other dogs come and join him, including Sheba and Darth, sitting around us, panting. Stiffly Pete approaches with a collapsible dog bowl and fills it with water. All the dogs partake.

"You know what? I did," I say. "How about you?"

"Yeah, this is good," Rory says. "I realized not everything has to change. Sometimes I can even be mostly dog again."

"I am worried about Darth and Sheba," Sally says under her breath. "Pete was pretty cross when you freed them."

"You aren't really mad, are you?" I ask Pete.

"What you just did was highly irresponsible," Pete tells me. "Dogs racing around in a pack. Anything could have happened."

"I know, I'm sorry," I say. "But it was my fault. You won't take it out on Darth and Sheba, will you?"

"I'm not a monster, Genie," Pete says. "A dog is only ever as good as its owner. Or its owner's casual and questionable acquaintance. Now, Darth, Sheba, come here. You look like you both need a dip in the pool to cool down."

Pete waits as the dogs trot over and then ruffles each behind their ears, kissing them on the tops of their heads in turn.

"Well, that was fun, wasn't it?" I hear him say as they walk away. "Genie's as mad as a box of frogs, though."

If he only knew.

"Oh yeah, don't worry," Rory says. "Darth says Pete's all bark and no bite. When he gets home and gets on his fluffy slippers, he's sweetness and light."

"You got all that from body language?" Sally laughs. "Are you sure you're not a dog psychic?"

"A what?" Rory asks.

"I was telling Sally that you understand dog psychology really well."

"Oh yeah," Rory says. "No, I'm not psychic or anything, I just listen to what they tell me. Dogs, humans. Most of the time they just want to be heard."

"That's so wise, sweet, and sensitive," Sally says, tilting her head. "Of course you only like boys."

"Oh, I like girls too," Rory says. "I like everyone. Except men with beards."

"Anyway," I say before this goes any further, "lunch break is over. We'd better get back to—"

But before I can finish my sentence Rory and the dogs take off once more, haring toward the treeline.

"Squirrel!" Rory shouts over his shoulder as he joins the chase.

"Off I go again!" Sally yells as she scrambles up.

"Shall we . . . not?" I say to Miles, flopping back onto the grass. He does the same. Very slowly I turn to look at him to find that he is looking at me. There is something in his eyes, something that makes me start to think something half formed and hopeful. But before I can get it straight in my head Rory crashes back down next to me, and he is very upset.

"We've got to go, Genie," he says. "We've got to go now."

"What?" I sit up, looking around. The dogs are all still playing over on the other side of the park, and a little way off there's a man with a small Lab mix on a lead, jerking her to heel every few seconds even though she's not pulling.

"It's him," Rory says, keeping his face down and his eyes averted. "It's the man that had me before. I can't let him see me, Genie." I put an arm around Rory's shoulders and feel him trembling in fear. "Don't let him take me away again, Genie."

"He's got another dog?" I mutter, watching the man yank the poor animal on after she dared to stop and sniff for a second. I see that her tummy is swollen, she is expecting puppies, poor, poor girl. "Rory, are you sure it's him?"

Rory just nods, trying to make himself smaller and smaller, cowering behind me.

"It's okay, Rory," Miles tells him. "He won't recognize you now, and even if he did, he couldn't hurt you. He is a weaselly little bully and you are a huge great muscle-bound giant. If anything, you'd scare him."

Rory doesn't seem to agree; his shoulders are hunched, his eyes are fixed on the ground. I'm reminded of when I first brought him home from the shelter. Even after weeks of care and therapy he was still so scared when I took him home. For the first few hours he wouldn't even sit down; he'd just stand in the corner looking at me, panting with anxiety. That night we had both camped out in the living room, me on the sofa, him exhausted and as far away from me as he could get on the other side of the room. That horrible little man over there had frightened my Rory so much that it had taken months for him to trust me, months more for him to finally feel safe. And now he has another dog?

"I'm having a word with him," I say, starting to climb to my feet.

"No, no, Genie, no." Rory drags me back down. "Please. Please, can we just go away from him? Now?"

"I think Rory needs a safe space," Miles says.

I look from Rory, who's curled himself up into as small a shape as he can, his knees tucked under his chin, to the dog who trots alongside the man, her head and tail down. Miles is right.

"Come on, then," I say reluctantly as I see the little dog vanish among the trees. "Time to go home."

I make a promise to that little dog. As soon as I've got Rory sorted out, I'm going to find her and get her to a safe place too.

Chapter Twenty

*S*OME THINGS HAVE GOT TO CHANGE," I tell Rory as I let us into the house before we head off to take Kelly on her stakeout. "You can't just go around chasing squirrels now that you are a six-foot-something man. You'll get arrested by the RSPCA or something."

"You don't understand, Genie," Rory tells me earnestly. "Squirrels might look cute, with their fluffy tails and chubby cheeks, but they are evil. And it is every dog's sacred duty to protect mankind from the scourge of squirrels. We practically take an oath."

He's been much more like his old self, minus the tail and floppy ears, since we got away from the park. Like the minute he couldn't see that horrible man, he forgot he existed. I hated seeing him like that, just as I hate that there are people in the world who seem to exist to make other humans or creatures feel afraid. I really hate the thought that Rory could turn the corner one day and be right back there in that same, terrified space again. I really wish I could change that for him, forever.

"Rory, are you fibbing about that oath?" I ask.

"I said 'practically'!" he adds, offended.

"Well, I wish you felt the same about spiders."

"I don't like spiders—they've got way more legs than is reasonable," Rory says. "The thing is, when I see a squirrel I feel the same way that you do when someone jumps a queue in the store. It's like a red mist comes down and all I want to do is violence."

"That was one time," I say, reflecting on my lifetime ban from the grocery store for aggravated assault with a home-baked baguette. "Anyway, you never even come close to catching one."

"It's like David Attenborough says about global warming," Rory says. "It might seem impossible, but you can never give up."

"Not a hundred percent sure about that analogy," I tell him, "but either way, the next time you see a squirrel you've just got to let it go, Rory, okay? Take a deep breath and let it go . . ."

I'm secretly trying this policy in my bid to stop wanting to snog my neighbor and good friend who is about to have an office romance with a colleague. Because when has that plan ever gone wrong?

Miles went back to work after the walk, and we went back to the parlor. We didn't talk about Claudia anymore. Probably just as well.

"But their horrible little hands, and their nasty fangs, and they could have rabies . . ." Rory is still going on about squirrels.

"Rory, let it go," I tell him firmly as he goes into the kitchen in search of predinner snacks. "Let. It. Go."

I will take my own advice. I *will* take my own advice. I will.

Something in the garden catches my eye and I look out the back window. The golden light of a perfect summer evening makes everything beautiful. Miles is standing on a ladder fiddling about with something in his cherry tree.

"What's all this, then?" I call as I head out, leaving Rory with a packet of digestives. Miles's head and shoulders appear over the fence.

"When I was on the way home I saw these Christmas lights on sale," he tells me, showing me a length of those old-fashioned lights with the big colored bulbs. "We used to have lights just like this when I was a kid. Mum would hang them across the balcony of our flat, and on the way home from school I could see them twinkling on the twenty-third floor. I know it's not Christmas, but I was thinking about what you said, how you'd like some garden lighting, and I thought, Well, this can work for both of us . . . Do you mind?"

"No, I love them!" I drag my garden chair over and stand on it to get a better look. "It will be so pretty."

He nods with satisfaction as he weaves the lights in and out of the branches.

"I miss Mum a lot right now," he says, as he studies his handiwork.

"Any reason," I ask, "why you are missing your mum so much right now?"

He looks at me across the top of the fence.

"I'd really like to ask her advice on a few things," he says, lowering his gaze. "I tie myself up in knots trying to figure stuff out, sometimes. Mum had a way of making it all clear for me. I miss that. And her smile. And her cooking." He laughs a little. "Not her singing, though."

"Don't they look lovely?" A pretty blond girl, around twenty-five, comes out of the back door carrying two glasses of Coke. "Oh, hello, you must be Genie, I've heard all about you!"

"And you must be Claudia-from-work," I say brightly. "I've heard all about you too."

"Claudia offered to help me get the lights up," Miles says.

"Isn't it a lovely idea?" Claudia says, flicking her long hair off her creamy shoulders. "Christmas lights in August? It's crazy, I love it!"

"Well." Miles hops off his chair. "Just a bit of fun, nothing more, really."

"Well, it's lovely to meet you," I tell Claudia with my most genuine fake smile. "And Miles, I think you are doing just fine. Your mum would be proud of you. But I've got to get going. I'm doing a stakeout with Kelly to help her sort out her marital problems."

"Wait a moment while I switch these on," Miles asks. "Then you can give me your final verdict."

A few seconds later the trees' leaves glow with colored light that scatters across the grass and fence, making everything in their path a kaleidoscope.

"It looks like disco fireflies have moved in," I say as Miles's head appears over the fence again. "I love them, Miles. I love them a lot."

We smile at one another for a long, sweet second.

"They are perfect!" Claudia laughs, handing Miles his drink.

"Anyway," I say, "I've got to go and pick up Kelly for the aforementioned undercover operation . . ." And I don't know why I suggest it, but I do: "I don't suppose you feel like joining? You might be able to give us the typical male perspective on the situation."

Miles purses his lips.

"Tempting as the offer sounds . . ." he says. "I generally think you and Kelly work best as a pair, don't want to turn your double act into a throuple."

"Well, I'll see you . . . sometime. If I'm not in prison for stalking or something."

Matilda emerges from the shadows and leaps up to the top of

the stepladder, where she rubs her head under his palm. Absently Miles scoops her up into his arms and holds her tenderly to his chest. Damn that cat.

"You can call me if you need bailing out," he offers. "Oh, and what's next for Rory's person training?" He looks at Claudia. "His work experience, I mean."

"Well, tomorrow is normally our day to volunteer at the care home," I say. "Rory's visits are really popular with the older folk down there. But I'm not sure if we should still go."

"Go!" Miles says. "You saw Rory at the party—he's an old lady's dream date. Take him down and he'll charm the pants off them. Tell you what, I'll come too. I'm supposed to be collecting oral histories and memories as a wider part of my project anyway."

"Really?" I ask him, with a surge of pleasure at the suggestion. "Sure you shouldn't be dusting some dinosaur bones or something?"

"That's a paleontologist," Claudia says with a smile.

"Genie knows that," Miles says, shaking his head.

"Then come, yeah—that'd be nice," I say. "Well, better get my wig on."

Somehow determined to make an idiot of myself, I jam the stupid thing on my head. Miles smiles, Claudia laughs.

"Blond suits you," she says with a flick of her own golden locks.

"You look better when you look like you," Miles says. Of course I do—that is really just stating the obvious—but it feels like he has just given me the greatest compliment since Romeo told Juliet she was a bit of all right. (Look, I've never actually read any Shakespeare—I'm paraphrasing.)

"Genie," Miles calls to me just as I'm about to head back inside.

"Yeah?" I turn to him.

"Be careful on your stakeout," he says. "I'd hate to lose a good neighbor to jail."

"Thanks," I say. "You're not bad yourself."

By which I mean that I am desperately in love with his stupid, gorgeous face.

Chapter Twenty-One

WHAT ARE WE DOING AGAIN?" Rory asks as he sits in the back seat. I am trying to discreetly parallel park, which, when it comes to my spatial-awareness issues, is something of an oxymoron.

"We are spying on my Dave," Kelly says. "The kids are at my mum's, so this might be my only chance." She's in a shiny ginger bob wig and a pair of shades. "He never comes home straight after work anymore. So we are seeing what he is up to, the dirty bastard."

"Maybe he just likes rolling in mud. It's very cooling, you know, and good for fleas."

"I don't mean literally dirty, Rory," Kelly says. "I'd actually go for that. He'll be out in a minute." Behind her dark glasses, Kelly is intent on the closed doors of Dave's workshop and garage, which is all locked up for the night. Only a dim light, just visible in the back where his office is, tells us that he hasn't left yet. The next few minutes pass in near silence except for Rory eating his way through a box of doughnuts.

"I've seen TV," he'd told us when he demanded we stop at the bakery on the way. "Everyone knows you need doughnuts if you're going to do a steakout. And by the way, when is the steak part?"

It had seemed safest just to get him the doughnuts and break the news about the "steak" later.

Suddenly there is movement from the garage. Dave steps out of the door.

"Shhhhhhh!" Kelly hisses for some reason, as if Dave might be able to hear Rory's munches as he locks the door behind him. Sliding down in her seat, she peers at his every move over the dashboard.

"There he is!" Rory points.

"Don't point, we are in disguise!" Kelly says. I find myself sinking down in my seat too, more out of shame than a need to be discreet. Dave pauses outside the garage and checks his phone, then he looks up at the still-light sky and sighs. It's such a heavy sigh that I can almost feel it in my chest. I can almost feel the sorrow and wistfulness that runs through his frame. And then he walks right past his van and into town.

"What?" Kelly says, open-mouthed. "Where's he going, the shady git? We need to follow him!"

"We can't follow him, not in this car or on foot. He'll see us right away," I tell her firmly. "Look, Kelly, for what it's worth, he doesn't look like a man in the throes of a passionate affair to me. He looks kind of tired and deflated."

"Yeah, from all the sex," Kelly insists.

"We don't have to follow him," Rory says. "At least not right away. If you have something on you that smells of him, give me a whiff of it, then I can track him like I did Miles."

"Oh yeah!" Kelly exclaims. "Good one, Roar. I forgot you can smell like, seven million times better than humans.

"Well, I could," Rory says, his face falling. "Every day my dogness seems to fade a little bit, and I'm not as good at things as

I was the day before." He dips his head for a second, but then straightens his shoulders and grins. "I think I still have enough scent to follow Dave, though, so don't worry, Kelly."

"Thanks, babe." Kelly reaches into her jeans pocket and produces a sock. "That'll stink of him."

"I'm not going to ask why you have one of Dave's dirty socks in your pocket," I say. "But why do you?"

"I picked it up off the bathroom floor to put in the washing machine and keep forgetting it's there until I get a whiff."

"Mmm, pungent," Rory says as he inhales the sock.

"Never ever think you have lived through the oddest moment of your life," I reflect. "Because you never have."

We wait until Dave is completely out of sight, then get out of the car. I ditch my wig in the boot.

"We might still need that," Kelly says. "If we need to go incognito."

"I think I'm safe, and anyway I prefer it when I look like me," I say primly.

"Yeah, he's got a very distinctive smell," Rory says, holding the sock to his nose with the authority of an expert.

"Paco Rabanne?" Kelly asks.

"Grease and smoke," Rory replies.

"I love that bloody smell," Kelly says with a sob, turning into my shoulder to hide her tears. "What if I never get to smell that smell again, Genie?"

"Come on, Kelly, it's going to be all right," I tell her soothingly. "Whatever it is that's happening, it's best to face it. Once you know what you are dealing with, then you can handle it. And we've got your back. Rory, have you got his scent?"

"Got it." Rory nods. He strides ahead and we follow on.

The walk takes us right through the heart of town, past the faded glory of the Grand Hotel, which stands against the bright blue sea like an ornate birthday cake decorated in gilt.

As Rory leads us over the elegant ironwork of the Spa Bridge, I am suddenly caught off guard by how beautiful my hometown is: the gentle curve of the coastline, the sparkling promise of the sea, the evening song of the birds in the trees that lead down the pretty footpath toward what used to be a Victorian bathing spa. Bright wildflowers nod their heads to the rhythm of the gentle breeze. At this exact moment there is not another more beautiful place in the whole world. How lucky I am to have all this as my home.

"He's gone into that building," Rory says, pointing at the spa complex.

"What's he doing in there?" Kelly asks, hands on hips as she stares at posters for an all-girl Queen tribute act called Yas Kween playing the venue tonight. "He never liked Queen!"

"Well, lots of things happen in there," I say, not mentioning the bar, which is kind of out of the way and pretty perfect for secret liaisons. "Let's go in and have a recce."

Kelly stares up at the spa building, her lip wobbling. She shakes her head.

"I don't think I can," she says unhappily. "Now that we're here I don't know if I can actually stand to see him with someone else, Genie. Maybe I'm better off not knowing. Maybe if I just pretend everything is fine, it will be."

"Take it from me, sticking your head in the sand never works out. You can't go on like this. It's not fair on you or the kids." I think for a moment, glancing back at the building.

"You wait here. Rory and I will go and have a look. We'll find out what he's up to."

Kelly nods and leans against the low wall that looks out over the wilder part of South Bay, turning her face toward the sea.

As we head inside I cross my fingers and pray to the mystic forces that turn dogs into people that everything is going to be all right. Me, I can take all the crap that the universe throws at me. But Kelly and her little family, they need to be okay. Because I am only just realizing they are the reason I sometimes half dare to hope that one day I might have a little family too.

Chapter Twenty-Two

ORY DOESN'T LEAD ME toward the bar, which takes me by surprise. Instead he takes a once-grand central staircase up to the first floor and a landing that is lined with function rooms. He stops outside a door at the top of the stairs. Leaning against the wall outside is a stiff handmade cardboard sign that reads *Fred's Man Club*.

"He's in there," Rory says. "He's in Fred's Man Club."

"In-ter-esting," I say slowly as I look at the door, and then at the sign, wishing Rory had X-ray vision to go with his super smell. "What do we think a man club is?"

"I think it's like a club for men," Rory suggests.

"I think you are probably right," I say. "But men are strange things, Rory. There are many varieties of them. I'm just wondering what kind this lot is."

"Let's go in," Rory says, "and then we will know."

"I am not a man," I remind him.

"Oh yeah," he says. "But what about the patriarchy? Weren't you going to smash it earlier today in the park?"

"What's the worst that can happen?" I shrug and open the door. Inside is a large elegant room that is entirely empty except for a small circle of chairs occupied by eight or so men.

"Hello!" I say, waving lamely. This is a support group. Maybe the secret gambling addiction theory was bang-on after all.

"Hello there, are you lost?" asks a gentleman whom I assume might be Fred.

"Erm, no." I scan the seats, and sure enough there is Dave with his back to me, and I'm desperately reaching for an excuse to explain away this intrusion into the men's group. "I'm here to support my friend Rory. He wants to come in but he's nervous."

"Actually I do not want to come in," Rory says brightly, popping his head around the doorframe. "I don't even want to be a man."

"Ah," Fred says. "Well, all are welcome here. Don't you worry about it, Rory. We get lots of first-time jitters. We've all been there."

"Been where?" Rory mutters, scowling at me.

"Well, what do you say, fellers?" Fred asks the group.

"It's a no from me, Fred," one man says. "You let one woman in, and the next thing you know you're overrun."

"I'm not sure that's entirely reflective of the ethos of the group," Fred says. "Rory needs a friend for a bit of backup, so why don't we let . . . ?" Fred looks at me questioningly.

"I'm Genie," I say, half coughing into my hand. At the sound of my name Dave turns around and looks at me. His face falls down to his feet, and a bloom of color spreads across his cheeks.

"Do we mind if Genie here sits in and gives Rory a bit of moral support just for a couple of minutes?" Fred asks.

Everyone else murmurs their okays while Dave's head drops.

"Come on, then, Rory, no need to be scared," Fred says. "And for the record, what is said in this room stays in this room, okay?"

I nod.

"Go on," I tell Rory, jerking my head inside the room.

"Fine," Rory says. "But only because there are biscuits."

Rory picks up the plate of biscuits and takes an empty chair in the circle. I hover at the back of the room, feeling sick to my stomach. I know I am being a good friend to Kelly, but I am increasingly getting the feeling that I am being a terrible person to Dave. And by the look on his face, so is he.

"Rory, do you want to tell us what's brought you to our man club?" Fred asks him kindly.

"Dave's smell, mostly," Rory says.

Dave sinks down further into his chair.

"Right." Fred chuckles, as if he gets the joke. He's clearly a man determined to put everyone at their ease, no matter who they are. He radiates kindness. "But the men's club is a place for us to be able to talk freely about anything. It's hard sometimes for fellers like us—workingmen, who were raised with a certain idea of what masculinity is—to admit when we're struggling. This is a safe place to do that."

Dave looks at me, and this time it's my turn to bow my head. Poor Dave. Poor, poor Dave. He had a safe space and I blew it.

"Oh, well, I'm okay," Rory says. He pauses. "I mean, I was okay. I thought I had everything mapped out. I knew exactly what my life was going to be like and then one day I woke up and everything had changed. I mean *everything*. I didn't fit in my own skin anymore. And nobody warned me or asked me if it would be okay. And now here I am. Trying to work out how to live with this for the rest of my life."

My heart aches as I listen to him talk. He tries to be brave, he really does. But he doesn't want this life that I've plunged him into. I have ruined everything for the creature that found a way to love and support me, even after everything he went through before I rescued him. I ruined it all, and then I just gave up trying to fix it because it all got a bit hard. What kind of a person am I?

The others in the circle nod and murmur in agreement.

"I felt like that when I realized I was gay and in love with my dentist," one man says. "Seventeen fillings I've had."

"I think we've all felt a bit like that from time to time," Fred says. "I know I have."

"Have you?" Rory asks with genuine disbelief. "What did you use to be before this?"

"A provider," Fred says with a nod. "A Sunday-league footballer, defensive position. A husband and a dad who took care of his family, no questions asked. And then the cancer knocked all that out of me. It kicked me from here to Hull and back. Suddenly I had no choice but to be weak, to need help, and that frightened me more than the thought of dying did." Fred smiles at everyone in the group in turn as they nod along with every word he says. "I've had to rebuild who I am from the ground up, to realize that the people who loved the man I used to be still love me now. Because I am more than just a paycheck or a header into a goal on a Sunday morning. And that's why I started this club. For every other bloke who needs to learn how to talk about what's going on inside."

"Yeah," Rory says. "I think it's a bit of indigestion right now. I ate eleven doughnuts. We had to follow Dave before I could finish them."

"Kelly's got no regard for a man's doughnuts when she's got her mind set on something," Dave says, glancing at me.

"What about you, Dave?" Fred asks. "Last week you said you thought you might be ready to talk today? No pressure, mate, but if you're ready we're here for you."

Dave sighs, shaking his head. His shoulders tremble.

"It's okay, Dave," Rory says. "It's actually all right when you realize you are not the only one who's turned into something they don't recognize."

Dave takes a deep shuddering breath.

"I feel like a fake," he says at last. "Like I shouldn't really be here. I've heard you all talking about what you're dealing with. And there's nothing really wrong with me. The business is doing okay. We're not rich, but we've got all we need. My kids are great, healthy and happy." Dave looks at me and swallows. "I love my wife so much, and I know she loves me. But something bad happened. I don't even know what, really. Something bad happened, and now I'm walking around like an empty shell. Like whatever used to be me, the bloke who enjoyed the taste of food, or paddling in the sea. Or laughing with the kids. Making love to his wife . . ." Dave rubs his hands across his face. "He's gone and I don't know how to get him back."

His whole body shakes with tears as the others in the group gather around him, hands on his shoulders. Soft words of comfort and support are spoken gently. These people need their privacy. I catch Rory's eye and mouth that I'm going to wait outside for him. Very quietly I back out of the door and close it as softly as I can.

Everything is OK, I text Kelly. It's not what you think. Dave will explain. Out soon.

About twenty minutes later I hear a ripple of laughter and the sound of applause. Five minutes after that the doors open and the members of Fred's Man Club file out, chatting and laughing with one another. No sign of Rory and Dave yet, though.

Fred comes out and smiles at me.

"Your lad did grand," he says "Better than grand, actually. He had a few interesting things to say."

"About cheese?"

"He does recommend cheese for most things, yes." Fred chuckles. "He's still in there, actually, talking with Dave. I thought I'd give them a minute, but then I'll need to come and lock up."

"Right. Thanks, Fred." I knock on the door and Rory calls me in.

"So, is this a sting, then?" Dave asks me sheepishly. "I knew Kelly would be on the case sooner or later."

"Kelly's outside," I say. "She thought you were leaving her. She's been in a mess, Dave."

"I know," Dave confesses. "I knew but even though I never wanted her to feel like that I couldn't seem to do anything about it. I've been feeling like I'm stuck in mud. I couldn't even tell her what was going on. I felt . . . ashamed."

"There's no shame in being overwhelmed by life, buddy," Rory says, resting a hand on Dave's shoulder. "It *is* bloody overwhelming."

"But I'm supposed to be the strong one," Dave says.

"You are the bloody strong one," Kelly says as she reaches the top of the staircase.

"Why do you look like Geri Halliwell?" Dave asks her.

"I'm in disguise, obviously," Kelly says. "Oh, Dave, I thought I'd lost you!"

Kelly flings her arms around Dave with such force that her wig half slips off her head and then tumbles to the ground. Dave winds his arms around her and they cling to each other tightly.

"I feel like they don't want us hanging around right now," I say to Rory in a low voice. "Maybe we should be heading off, let them talk it out."

"Hey, Rory, mate." Dave stops us just as we are about to sneak off. "What you said in there, it really helped. I could have done without my missus setting Genie on me, if I'm honest. But what you said made all the difference tonight. I think I can see that what I'm going through now can be over one day. There might be a ways to go, but, like you said, if I am strong enough to ask for help, then I'm strong enough to get better."

"You are strong, Dave," Rory says, flinging his muscular arms around both Dave and Kelly, who both hug him back.

"Bring it in, Genie!" Rory beckons me as Kelly and Dave cling to one another in the shelter of his world-class hug. Normally I abhor this kind of thing, but sometimes there is just not a good enough reason to say no to public displays of affection.

Rory might have helped Dave tonight, but he's helped me too. There's no harm in trying, is there? Sometimes trying is all that we've got.

"Hey, Rory," I say.

"What?" he asks.

"I've thought about it, and, well, it looks like I'm going on a bloody quest."

"Yes!" Rory punches the air.

Chapter Twenty-Three

S O, RE: YOUR LIFE'S PURPOSE, what do you want to do with your life?" Rory asks me after dinner.

We had left Kelly and Dave at the spa, arms entwined around each other. How easy, I'd thought as we left them, for two people who love each other so to somehow become almost strangers, just through forgetting to talk to each other. Or being afraid to, anyway. Lucky for Dave that Kelly has some particular skill sets, and that one of those is never letting it lie. There's a long road ahead for them, I know that. I know that depression can weigh you down, wrap itself around your shoulders and keep out all the light. It isolates you from everyone you love and even the possibility of hope. I know that because that was me once, bricked up inside my own sadness—sometimes it still is for a little while. But then I got a dog.

And then slowly, very slowly, the two of us began to see little chinks of light together. Rory realizing he was safe now, me realizing things weren't so bleak. Slowly, very slowly, we realized we had each other. And every day the dark lifted a little more until the point when I realized I was *almost happy*. Perfect happiness—that is a notion for fairy tales and romantic comedies. But almost happy—that is something real. Something obtainable. Almost happy means that when those rare, fleeting moments of pure joy explode into your life in bursts of Technicolor, then you can recognize them for what they are: perfect, fleeting gifts from the universe to be wondered at and treasured. And almost happy means that when you are nearly completely smothered by that great, dark sadness, you can draw another breath—because you know you have felt, and can feel, better again. Things will always get brighter eventually. That's just the law of averages.

It was on the day I picked Rory up from the rescue home that I began to see the benefits of almost happiness. And then what did I do? I ruined his life by turning him from an uncomplicated, spontaneous, and joyous creature that lived in the moment into an emotionally messy, constantly confused and conflicted dumb animal: a human being.

"When I was a kid, I loved art and drawing and making clothes," I say, picking at the tassels of my favorite cushion. The beautiful little painting set that Miles got me is sitting shinily on the dresser. The ache to open it and start making tiny little paintings is very strong. "I was all set for fashion college; I even did a term and it was amazing until . . . well. That was then. This is now. I can't go to fashion college now, at my age. Maybe I could start wearing hats or something? Take up knitting?"

"It's not too late for you to go to fashion college," Rory says. "All you need to do is to go. To fashion college. Like you go to work, or I go to the park."

"It's not that simple," I say.

"Why isn't it?" Rory asks, grabbing Diego.

"I'm not sure, I just feel like maybe it's not?"

"Well, I know one thing, and that is that hats and knitting are not going to get you back to the way you used to be with me."

"The way I used to be with you?" I ask, confused.

"I know we are okay with hugging now, but you used to tell me you loved me a *lot*," Rory says. "And that used to make me feel happy and safe. But since I turned human, well, you are really kind and funny and you *try* hard. But you never say you love me any-more. Even if I say it first. And I've been really uncertain about if I am a good boy or not for days. And I thought about it, and I think it's because you have a much harder time showing humans that you love them, than dogs. Even human me, and I'm a terrible human. But an excellent dog."

"Oh god, I think you are right," I say, sighing deeply. "Rory, I know I said I'd do the quest, but maybe I'm too far gone. Maybe I am too messed up and not normal to make it."

"Quests are meant to be hard, Genie," Rory says. "And I don't care if you are not normal, because normal is overrated anyway. You are the best person in the world to me. And I know you can do whatever you want to do if you are willing to try, and some-times get it wrong and try again. Like me with not peeing in the sink."

"I love you, Rory," I say. "I love you so much. I'm so sorry that this happened. I can't promise that things won't be difficult, scary, and hard sometimes. But I do promise you that you will never be alone again."

"Even if you get together with Miles?" Rory asks me. "And do the weird face-smooching and rub your butts together?"

"That might be a thing, but it's not a thing I do," I tell him. "And anyway, don't worry. I am not going to get together with Miles. Maybe I can find myself but I can't make a whole relation-ship happen just because I want it to. Love is about choices, and you have to let the person you love decide to choose you."

"Or get Nanna to do a charm thing," Rory says. "Five ninety-nine, or two for ten pounds."

"I'm not saying those charms don't work, considering you and the wish, etcetera," I say. "But I am saying they are not ethical."

"I don't think they work, they smell awful," Rory says. "But what if that's what Miles wants too? And Genie, I'm pretty sure it is. I'm pretty sure you are what he wants."

"Do you really think so?" I ask. "Like, can you confirm it with your spidey senses? Because it seems an awful lot like he's into Claudia."

"I don't have spidey senses," Rory says. "But I have eyes, and he looks at you like I look at cheddar."

"You look at cheddar like it is the most wondrous thing on Earth," I say.

"Exactly."

"But what about Claudia-from-work?"

"I don't think you need to worry about that," Rory says. "Claudia is just a girl from work who asked him out. I bet he doesn't look at her like cheddar. Maybe like those plastic cheese-slice things that will do if there is no cheddar around."

"The last time I was really in a relationship with someone," I say tentatively, "it broke my heart. I lost . . . myself, I suppose. So I'm scared. I'm scared of wanting someone as much as I guess I want Miles. And I'm scared of hurting Miles and letting him down. Most of all I'm scared of losing one of my best friends if things go wrong."

"But imagine," Rory says. "Imagine if things went right?"

I try for a moment to picture that, and immediately shake the thought away. My theory is that as soon as you show the world your vision of happiness it does its best to provide the exact opposite.

Then this image seems to swim into view, at exactly the same time as I am looking at the real world. A blue day, blue sky, blue sea, wet sand turned blue with reflections, and perfect happiness. Suddenly I can feel the sun on my bare shoulders and the soft sand beneath my feet. I can smell the scent of the sea and feel a kind of contentment I have never known. And it's completely real, just as real as Rory and me sitting here in my house. Two realities happening all at once. Desperately, I try to hang on to the seaside feeling for as long as possible, but it fades and almost all trace of it has gone, like a dream just before waking. Except there's a piece of wet seaweed under my foot.

"That's weird," I say.

"What?" Rory cocks his head.

"It was like a daydream, I guess, except normally when I daydream it's me and circa-nineties Keanu Reeves dancing the tango."

"That is too much information," Rory says.

"This one just appeared. Like I could see you, and the room, and also this other time that's not quite yet but already is . . ."

"You know who you sound like," Rory says.

"Nanna! Oh my god, I sound like Nanna, Rory, it's happening!"

"You're growing into the family magic!" Rory says happily. "I thought this for a while. What with the chatting to Dotty's ghost husband, and the snowflakes in your hair—but this is conclusive!"

"I'm going insane!" I reply. "There will be pills for this. I'm sure there will be pills."

"What did the last person do to you?" Rory asks after a moment of silence. "Did they kick you, like the before-man kicked me? And starve you and make you fight bigger dogs?" He looks around, as if he thinks that bad man might be somewhere here, ready to hurt him all over again. "Whatever it was, Genie, it must have been bad. It must have scared you a lot because there aren't many people in real life who get to be a bit magic. That's special. And you want to take a pill to shut it off."

"Because I suppose I find it all a bit hard to believe," I tell him. "I mean, that stuff, it doesn't actually happen."

"Yes, it does!" Rory gestures at himself. "The proof is incontrovertible."

"Well, when you put it like that," I say. "But it's scary."

"Tell me about him," Rory says.

"His name was Aiden. I met him in my first term at college. It was a warm September. So the gang were on the beach and this guy comes over and just starts talking to me. He was a bit older, and so good-looking, with amazing hair. I was smitten. It felt like the start of everything. And he made me feel so . . ." I shiver at the memory. "He made me feel like the most important person in the world. Kelly, Dave, and Miles weren't that into him. They said he was a prick. But I thought he was perfect. I couldn't see anything but how brilliant we were together. The truth is, he wasn't a monster or a genius. He was just an ordinary guy, a couple of years older than me, pretending that he had it all nailed down, when he actually didn't have a clue, just like the rest of us."

That night at the Christmas dance flashes into my mind, and all the things that didn't happen.

"Maybe if I'd listened to my heart then things would have been very different," I tell Rory. "But I thought I knew what I wanted. I was absolutely certain that Aiden was it."

"So then what happened?" Rory asks.

It takes me more courage than I knew I had to talk about this part.

"I got pregnant," I tell him.

"Like with a baby?" Rory asks.

"Yeah, not like that time I had a whole loaf of toast," I say.

"Where is the baby?" Rory says.

"That's the hard part. Aiden freaked out and ran away back to his mum's. He broke my heart, but also, he kind of didn't. Like the second he left I knew he wasn't the right one. I felt like such an idiot. But I knew that I'd get over him one day. What really mattered was my baby. If I was going to look after another human being then I had to start by looking after myself. So I left college—knowing I'd go back one day, and came home to here, and Mum and Dad." I think of Miles, and how he missed his own mum. "I was lucky to have that safety net. Lucky they were the sort of people to always welcome me home. Even I knew I was way too young, but I wanted that baby, Rory. I wanted her so much."

"What happened?" Rory asks, looking around. "Where is she?"

"I can't . . ." I shake my head, feeling the threat of unacknowledged grief bubble and tighten in my chest. "I don't talk about this for a reason. It hurts too much."

"You don't have to talk about it, Genie," Rory says gently. "But has keeping quiet helped you feel better?"

I look into his mismatched eyes, and all I see there is worry and kindness. When Rory has been at my side words have always seemed possible. I told his gorgeous furry head almost all of my secrets when he was a dog. That doesn't have to change. I take a deep breath and tell him about the loss I keep sheltered in my heart.

"My baby didn't make it to term," I tell him. "They said that sometimes these things happen and there is no reason. They said, 'Try not to blame yourself.'"

I hold my hands over my chest, cradling her memory there.

"I'd prepared myself for everything, I thought. How to be a teenage single mum. How to get back to college, with a baby. But not for that. Not to come home from the hospital without her. It knocked me sideways, and nothing seemed to matter anymore. And as for Aiden? He never acknowledged that she ever existed. He never asked me what happened. Mum and Dad did their best. Kelly, she never left my side, and Miles came back from uni for as long as he could. But I couldn't get past the fact that the world would never know how much I loved my little girl, how much she mattered to me. Every decision I made was the wrong one. They said don't blame yourself, but how could I not?

"I wanted time to stop, but it didn't. Dave asked Kelly to marry him. Miles got his degree. Mum and Dad started talking about me getting back out there. After a while I started to work for Nanna Maria just to fill in the time. I always meant to go back to college, but it never felt like the right time. And eventually I realized I was . . . here. Other people lose babies, and they grieve, and they move on. They don't ever forget the love they lost, but they do live again. But not me. I don't know why but I just can't stop thinking . . . thinking it was my fault. That I did something to hurt her." There's a long moment of silence, Miles's lights casting colored shadows through the windows that gently sparkle on the white-painted walls. "Things aren't how I imagined they would be, when I was Nana's sunshine girl, but all in all I'm fine."

"Genie." Rory leans toward me, taking my hand in his. "I don't know how to tell you this, but you are not fine."

Once I start crying, I can't seem to stop.

Chapter Twenty-Four

T O SAY RORY IS A HIT at the care home would be an understatement. When he had four paws he would light up the place with his sweetness and affection. I was pretty sure that he wouldn't be able to equal that as a human, but I was wrong. All morning I have trailed around after him, watching as he sat down with Maura, George, and Violet, listened to their stories, and then made them laugh. Marveled at how easy it was for him to hug them and hold hands without one second of reservation. But it shouldn't have come as a surprise, because that's exactly what he did for me last night. He held my hand while I cried, and then a long time after that, he said, "You know, Genie, I think the hardest part of your quest is already over. I think the vision you had is a sign of that. You are opening like a flower. Or that treat-dispensing toy you bought me once that I had to bash eighty-seven times on the concrete to get the treats out of. Try and embrace it, Genie. I think it will be good for us!"

It's good to hang out with an optimist. It's like their hope kind of rubs off on you. Maybe the weird blue vision, as Rory calls it, was just a one-off. But maybe I am more like Nanna and my mum than I thought, and if I am, then that's something wonderful.

You'd think by now that I'd have got used to how a dog is so much better at being a human than humans ever are, but I am continuously amazed by how very bad we are at using everything we have, from bendy thumbs to capacious hearts and huge brains. We throw so much away on stuff that doesn't matter. But not Rory. Rory knows what matters.

Miles had called for us first thing, with a very angry Matilda in a crate.

"Are you okay?" he asked. "You look like . . ."

"I've been crying." I nod. "Yeah, I've been crying."

"What can I do?" Miles asked.

"Oh, just what you always do," I told him with a smile.

"Why are you bringing the murder cat?" Rory had asked him, nervously edging away.

"Because I thought that as we weren't taking in a dog, per se, then we could take in a cat."

"You realize a lot of the residents are quite frail, don't you?" I asked him. "I'm not sure they could survive a mauling."

Miles gave me a look; I repressed a smile.

"Poor Matilda is very misunderstood when it comes to you two," he chided me. "She's an old lady too, don't forget, and she can be very sweet and affectionate as you know, Genie."

"We don't talk about that," I said, nodding at Rory.

"We don't even think about it," Rory muttered as he climbed into the back seat and put his seat belt on. Miles had kept Matilda in her carrier on his lap in the passenger seat, from where I could feel her glare boring into my skull. She might very well have a cuddly side, but I didn't think it was the side that was facing me right then.

Miles had been right, though. There were plenty of cat people among the residents of the care home, and once the manager had made sure that no one with allergies was in the designated sitting room, Miles had disappeared with Matilda to talk to the cat people, in their satanic cult, or the sunroom, whatever you want to call it.

I peer in through the window for a moment while Rory is doing his rounds. That cat is curled up on the lap of one older gentleman as though butter wouldn't melt. He smiles as he strokes her and tells Miles stories of the long-gone Scarborough of his youth. Maybe he feels me watching—I don't know—but Miles glances up at me and winks when he catches my eye. And I, for reasons that will forever be lost to the annals of stupidity, slowly slide down out of view like a mime artist pretending they are in a lift. No, that's a lie. I do it because Miles's winking is impossibly attractive, and when Miles is attractive I behave like an idiot. It's sort of like the laws of motion: for every cute action there is an equal and opposite stupid reaction.

How am I, the sitting-on-the-floor Genie, ever going to get to a place where I can look him in the face and tell him I am in love with him? Maybe I could write him a letter; no, strike that. I've seen *Romeo and Juliet*.

"Genie?" Miles opens the door, and I almost roll onto his feet. "Want to come in?"

Looking over at Rory, I can see he's doing really well all by himself. Miles offers me his hand, pulls me to my feet. We are standing close together.

"I dropped a . . . button," I tell him.

"Did you get it?" he asks, still holding my hand.

"Yeah, I got it," I say, still holding his hand.

"Where'd it come from?" he asks, looking at my entirely buttonless T-shirt dress over leggings.

"My . . . self," I say. He twitches a smile, and lets go of my hand. I miss it.

Burning with embarrassment, I stroll over to where a lady called Violet had Matilda snuggled on her lap. Apparently the cat is enraptured by her story. Miles and I take a seat next to them.

There's a fresh pot of tea on the table next to us, so I pour three cups. No milk for Miles, two sugars for Violet, and just a spot of milk for me. I pass her a cup and she takes a sip.

"How did you know that's just how I like my tea?" she asks.

"Oh . . ." I think for a moment, realize I don't know how I know. But I know what way Mum always knows. "Family talent, I guess."

"So anyway, then," Violet tells me as if I've been there for the start of the story. "I said to her, I said, 'I love you, Caroline Fisher, and I don't care who knows it.' This was the sixties, mind you. There was a lot of hair spray. Highly flammable. My pal Debbie Rogers set fire to her hairdo with a cig . . ."

"And then what?" Miles asks.

"She had to get a haircut," Violet tells him. "She were the first round here to have a pixie cut. Thought she were the bee's knees, silly cow."

"No, I meant with Caroline Fisher!" Miles chuckles.

"Oh," Violet's face falls. "She said, 'Don't be a daft hap'orth, Dee, I'm married. We can't ever be together. What would people say?' And that were that. She moved away with her husband, and that was the last I heard of her."

"Oh no." Miles holds Violet's hand tight. "I'm so sorry. It's hard to love someone from afar. I hope you found happiness eventually."

"Well, fifty years or more passed," Violet says. "Things happened—a lot of things. Some of them lovely, some of them hard. But I was content, more or less. And then one morning—it was in March, I remember, because all the daffs were out along my path—I opened the door and there was Caroline Fisher. It was like not a second had passed in those last fifty years."

"Just as beautiful as you remembered her?" Miles prompts.

"Even more," Violet says. "And I thought, Oh no, you don't, madam. I haven't spent fifty years getting over you just for you to come back and break my heart all over again, lady."

"So, you sent her packing?" I ask.

"I made her a cup of tea and she sat at my kitchen table and looked around at the life I'd made. It weren't a fancy life—not a lot of money or stuff. But there had been enough of everything. And then she saw my wedding photo.

"'You got married?' she said.

"'People expected it,' I told her. 'He was a good man. A good dad.'

"'I left my husband,' she said.

"I was like, 'Oh?,' pretending I wasn't that bothered, like.

"'It took me fifty years,' she said, 'to be brave enough.'

"'To leave him?' I asked her.

"'To admit to myself that I love you too, Dee.'"

"Then what happened?" Miles asks her, wide-eyed, hanging on every word.

"A lot of talking. A lot of kissing. And then fifteen good years," Violet tells him, tears creeping into her eyes. "Fifteen wonderful years, with my Carrie. If I have one regret it's that there weren't more of them. You mark my words, son: if you love someone, don't you wait or let them go. Maybe you'll get your heart broke, and life will get messy and difficult, but it's a darn sight better than wondering what might have been. You might think that your chance has passed. But you never know, son. You never know until you know."

Miles nods thoughtfully. I snaffle another custard cream.

"Have you got anyone?" Violet asks him. "A handsome young feller like you, you must be fighting them off."

"Nothing serious," Miles says. "There's this girl called Claudia, from work . . ."

"Or just Claudia to her friends," I mutter.

"I hope that . . . well, that's it," Miles says. "I hope."

"Well, hope never got the bread buttered," Violet says rather mysteriously. "You got to find out, son. Do or die. Life's short, young man. You make that hope a reality. There is no try, there is only do."

Did Violet just quote Yoda?

Miles looks at me, and I want to reach out and take his hand and tell him that it's not Claudia-from-work that he's looking for. That it's me, and even though I have been an idiot and let him down, I *am* his person. I will be here for him forever.

Instead, I reach for another custard cream and pour another cup of tea for Mrs. Cundall, who has just woken up from a nap. She likes a lot of milk and no sugar, and no, I have no idea how I know that. But I'm right and it's nice to give her this small gift of having a cup of tea that is exactly right. It gives me a tiny spark of joy. Maybe that's what it's like for Nanna all the time.

"THAT WAS AMAZING," Miles says as Matilda throws her full body weight against the side of her canvas carrier in a bid to break out and kill us all. "I really enjoyed listening to all their memories; it got me thinking that we should have a memory wall at the museum."

"I love that idea. What about the cat, did she enjoy it?" I ask, nodding at Matilda.

"Oh, she loved it!" Miles assures me, as one long claw pokes through a gap in the grille, straining for the nearest jugular. "She's just in a mood because I put her back in the carrier. Usually if we are out and about she likes to ride on my shoulder, but I thought it was safest this way."

The thought of Matilda riding around on Miles's shoulder like a psychotic parrot substitute makes me smile.

"It is interesting," Rory says, "to hear what people who are getting to the end of their lives think is important, isn't it, Genie? Don't you think? Puts everything in perspective, doesn't it? The things you should probably do and say before it's all too late."

"Yeah," I say absently. "S'pose."

"Like how you should always try for what your heart wants, even if you fail. How it is better to have loved and lost than never loved at all, and all that?"

"Have you been reading Dickens?" I ask him.

"There was a film on," he confesses. "But that's the gist of it."

"Did anyone in the care home actually say that, though?" I say, looking at him in the rearview mirror. "Or is this about you not wanting to give up chasing squirrels again?"

"No, it's about *you*." Rory is emphatic. "Not always saying how you feel about things and *people*." He stares hard at the back of Miles's head. "Although I would also like to chase squirrels. They need keeping on their weird, ratty little toes."

"What's this all about?" Miles looks at me, and I avoid looking at him.

"Search me," I say, turning up the radio. "This is all Rory. Five minutes with two legs and he thinks he knows it all."

"I do not think I know it all," Rory shouts over the radio. "I absolutely do not see the point in broccoli."

"Genie, tell me?" Miles asks, turning the radio down again. "I'd really like to know."

I glance at him, trying to get a sense of whether he is looking at me like cheddar, but it's hard when I'm driving.

"It's—" Rory starts.

"No one," I say, panicking. "No one. There isn't anyone. And even if there was, I need to focus on Rory and helping him to adjust to life. So there can be no romance. Or anything of a sexual nature for me." Textbook overexplaining Genie. "And anyway, imagine if I did have a boyfriend coming round all the time, eating all the cheese. Imagine that, Rory?"

"Maybe your perfect man is lactose-intolerant," Rory says, more than a little bit too close to home.

"The thing is, Genie," he says as we turn into our street, "you need to find your life's purpose, like Nanna Maria says, and to do that you just need to say the things that you need to say. Then I will be released from your wish and can go back to being a dog."

"The problem with Nanna Maria's highly questionable oh-find-yourself-and-everything-will-be-fine tactic is that she assumes a person's true self must be all la-de-da and aren't-flowers-lovely? Well, what if your true self is quite cross and largely disappointed? What then?"

"For what it's worth," Miles says, "cross and disappointed isn't who you are at all. You do a good impression of being those things, but really, anyone who really knows you, knows you are the complete opposite."

There's a beat of silence as I park outside our houses. And do you know what? When he looks at me, I think maybe there *is* a cheddarish glint in his eye. This gives a whole new meaning to the *Dirty Dancing* song "Hungry Eyes."

"Thank you, that means a lot," I say. Okay. This is it. There's a dog in the back, but to hell with it. I might look like cheese. The moment is now.

"Miles, what Rory wants me to say is that I—"

Just then there's a sharp rap at the window on Miles's side. Claudia's pretty, heart-shaped face peers in, and she's waving and smiling.

"Claudia?" Miles shoves Matilda in her cat cage at me and gets out of the car. "Claudia! It's Claudia-from-work. Hi! What are you doing here?"

Matilda and I exchange a look.

"Hope you don't mind." Claudia beams as Miles climbs out of the car. "I knew you had a day off, and I had a day off because we were off on the same day." She giggles. "And I thought, Well, what a coincidence! So I was just passing so I thought I'd say hi. But you weren't in, and then suddenly there you were! It must be fate. What with us both having the same day off and everything."

Fate my arse.

"Here I was," Miles says stupidly as he smiles at her. God, he likes her. This is my fault. I encouraged him. I turned his indifference into positive feelings. Why am I such a good friend? Now Claudia-from-work is his cheddar?

Somehow, I clamber out of the car with the carrier containing a homicidal feline doing her best to kill me with one well-placed paw and try to look cheerful and friendly. Matilda is doing a better job.

Rory stares at Claudia with naked curiosity.

"No sniffing," I remind him sternly.

"You've met my neighbor Genie over the fence," Miles says, grinning stupidly. Claudia doesn't take her eyes off him.

"Hi, Genie," she says, like I'm not there.

"And I'm Rory," Rory says, tapping her on the shoulder. When she turns to look at him her eyes widen. "You haven't met me yet."

"Hi, Rory," she says, taking in his golden magnificence. I see she is one of those girls, girls that like boys and dogs that look like boys more than she likes her own kind. And before you say anything, I know it's not cool to judge a book by its cover. And I know it's not cool to be down on another girl because sisterhood, etc. But I am not cool. We've been over that already.

"It's such a lovely afternoon," she says. "I thought you might fancy a walk on Oliver's Mount? I've got my car. And I packed a picnic. Nothing special. Just some crisps, a sandwich selection, a fresh cream Victoria sponge I made last night, and some elder-flower press, but I wouldn't mind sharing it with you."

Just passing, huh?

"I would like to come to that," Rory says enthusiastically. "Let's all go!"

"That sounds nice," Miles says. "I'd like to picnic with you, Claudia-from-work."

"I'm also from lots of other places too." Claudia laughs. "Surrey, originally. I live on Falsgrave Road now. You could just call me plain old Claudia, if you like."

"Well, we must be going now," I say, thrusting the cat carrier at Miles, who fumbles and almost drops it. It doesn't hit the ground, but the catch must have been jiggled because the door springs open and a yowling and furious Matilda bolts out of the cage and straight up Claudia's bare tanned leg. She rakes her claws down Claudia's thigh.

"Owwww!" Claudia does her best to actually scream. "Get off me you little . . . b . . . monkey!"

"I'm so sorry," Miles tells Claudia as he disengages his livid cat, who tries to bat and scratch at Claudia even as Miles encourages her quite firmly into the cat flap, which she kicks at with an angry back paw as she storms inside. "Are you okay, Claudia?"

We all look at the angry pink streaks down her leg, at least one of which is beaded with blood. Remind me to never get on the wrong end of that cat.

"It does sting a bit," Claudia says brightly through gritted teeth.

"Hopefully you won't get rabies," Rory says. "Or septicemia."

"I think a spot of Savlon and you'll be good," I say to counteract my dog's catastrophizing. "I have some inside if you want?"

Claudia looks at Miles with big baby blues.

"Miles, you're the first aid officer at work," she says. "Can you patch me up?"

"Oh yes, definitely," Miles says. "Come in, I'll make you a cup of tea for the shock. I'll pop Matilda in the bedroom where she can't kill anything apart from my pillows."

"Claudia likes jasmine tea," I tell Miles before I know what I'm saying.

"Er, okay?" he says.

"I do, that would be perfect. And I think I'll still be okay, for a picnic, I mean . . ." Claudia says as Miles opens his front door. As she steps inside, he turns around.

"Genie . . ." he begins.

"Miles, the cat's giving me evils," Claudia calls from inside.

"We had a fun morning. Let's catch up tomorrow," I tell him.

He nods and the door shuts on Claudia's giggles and the protest-ing yowls of a very annoyed cat.

Claudia clearly isn't a cat person. I take some small comfort in the fact that Matilda is not a Claudia cat. That, and both of us wishing we could keep Miles to ourselves, while simultaneously not having to admit that we love him, is something we have in common.

Chapter Twenty-Five

Y OU *SHOULD* START PAINTING and designing again," Nanna Maria suggests as she watches me re-chalk the board that hangs outside the parlor. I'll admit, it is probably my favorite part of the job. A nice ten or twenty minutes to be creative and think up as many psychic puns as you can before your boss notices and makes you start again.

"You're an artist, Genie. You can't hide from a talent like yours. When you were a little girl you always had a box of crayons on the go. Felt tips when you were a bit older, though your dad regretted that after you felt-tipped the cream leather seats in his Mondeo . . ." She smiles fondly at the memory. "And then when you were a bit older you'd take your box of watercolors out, sit on the beach and paint. And when you came back after, you'd have this dreamy look in your eyes, like you'd been up among the clouds, flying with the gulls."

"Dive-bombing toddlers for chips and ice cream," I add, as I finish with a flourish my drawing of a luminescent crystal ball. "Anyway, your psychic powers have let you down this time, Nan. I got my sketchbook out last night and started drawing." I nod. "It felt good."

"Genie, I'm so—"

"No, don't make a big deal out of it," I say. "I prefer to think of it as a casual-no-big-deal-type thing."

"Understood," Nanna says. "And you always dressed in bright colors back then too," she adds, looking at my standard ensemble of black T-shirt and jeans. "Making yourself all sorts of clothes, and coloring your hair to match . . ."

"Well, I was a teenager," I say. "That shit's standard-issue."

"I thought it was teenagers who were supposed to always wear black and be surly," Nanna Maria says. "You got it the wrong way round."

"I did sort of stop thinking about clothes altogether," I admit. "Which was weird considering it was all I thought about for most of my life. But not everyone can rock the hot-mafia-matriarch boss-lady vibe like you, Nanna. I can't pull those looks off."

"Well, anyway, I don't agree with you."

"On anything specific or just in general?" I ask, looking at the door a little anxiously. We sent Rory out with Nanna's debit card to pick up some supplies twenty minutes ago, and for the last eighteen of them I've been expecting it to all go horribly wrong. Like that time I went for a haircut, and the stylist asked me if I wanted a French fringe, and I said yes, but I didn't know what a French fringe was, and I ended up looking like I'd hacked at my hair with a pair of nail scissors. Still tipped him a fiver and told him I loved it, mind you.

"You can wear as many colors as you want, and you'd look amazing, because you always knew how to put an outfit together out of any old trash."

"Trash?"

"This isn't about how old you are, it's about getting back your confidence."

Nanna takes a hot-pink scarf from around her neck, and drapes it around mine.

I can't argue with that, and it's annoying, so I change the subject as I get up and go to the mirror. I look at the scarf hanging limply around my neck, and instead tie it in my hair with a big bow at the front like a 1940s factory girl. I meant it as a kind of joke, but actually I like it. If I had a lipstick in that shade . . .

"Here," Nanna hands me a lipstick in that shade. Shrugging, I put it on.

"So, you're saying that if I draw more and put on a pink scarf, Rory will turn back into a dog?" I ask. "In that case, job done."

"No, I'm not saying that it will return Rory to his dog form. Honestly, I don't think there is a way to do that. What I'm saying is that last night you started drawing again, and today you have a spring in your step and a little color. It suits you, sunshine girl."

She's not wrong. After Claudia invited herself into Miles's place, flaunting her Victoria sponge, I had felt pretty low. And then I did something unprecedented, something I never do. I decided not to feel pretty low.

Rory watched as I took out most everything from the understairs cupboard until I found my big sketchbook and an art box full of different-colored pens and pencils. Most of the pens had dried up, but the pencils just needed sharpening, and before long I wasn't thinking about Claudia feeding Miles strawberries at all. I was only thinking about what was on the page, losing myself in the flow of color and form. I was absorbed so intensely that I didn't realize until I took a break how good it felt. How much like *me* I felt. How much I wanted to make the clothes that I had designed on the page and wear them. Top-notch questing even if I do say so myself.

"And, say what you like about this whole Rory debacle, although the situation is not exactly *ideal* . . ."

"Understatement of the year," I say.

"It has been good for you," Nanna goes on. "It's got you out of your comfort zone."

"And taken me on a coach ride to the land of What the Hell NOW?" I add. Still, Nanna Maria is giving me insightful advice, which means I might have to admit that I don't know what I'd do without her. So, I'm relieved that Rory comes stumbling in through the door, stinking like a student's house party, at just the right moment to prevent any more unscheduled personal growth.

"I'm back!" he announces, as if his presence wasn't enough of an indicator. "I went to the crystal shop with the tappy-card thing and I asked them for some incense like you told me to, and Ellie said, 'What kind?,' and I said, 'I don't know, I don't even know what incense is,' so Ellie burnt a whole load of the whiffy sticks and we sniffed a lot of them. I couldn't decide, so Ellie said, 'Why not get a pack of each?,' and she gave me her phone number in case I wanted to know more about crystals."

"I have a feeling that Ellie might have led you astray," I say, narrowing my eyes at him. "Are you high?"

"I think I am quite high, yes," Rory tells me, swaying from side to side a bit. "I am definitely higher than you, and that was weird at first because you were always higher than me and, like huge, sort of like the biggest, most important thing in the world, like massive. And now you are a *teeny-tiny little woman*." He wobbles toward me and boops me on the nose. "Teeny-tiny."

"Okay, point made," I tell him. "Sit down and I'll get you a drink of water."

"Got any biscuits?" Rory asks. "I could murder a packet of bourbons."

"And now my dog's got the munchies," I tell Nanna Maria. "Surely getting your dog stoned must be the low point, and from now on the only way is up."

Of course, the law of the universe dictates that the moment you question whether or not your circumstances could possibly deteriorate any further, they always do. A rookie mistake that I realize about 0.3 seconds later when Miles and Claudia enter the shop. Oh god, did she stay the night with him?

"Oh, this is marvelous!" Claudia says, clapping her hands together and laughing with joy as she turns on her heel, taking in the full splendor of the parlor. "What fun, it's so kitsch! I love it!"

Obviously, I take offense at once. Or at least I would do, if it wasn't for the fact that Claudia's intentions are pure, and she is clearly delighted with everything she sets eyes on, including Nanna Maria. She's thrilled to bits, the bloody perfectly nice woman. And by the way he's smiling—Miles is thrilled to bits with her.

Bloody Claudia in her ditsy floral sundress that makes her look like a heroine from a Hallmark movie being all lovely. Typical of me that my secret archnemesis would be adorable. Wait, maybe I'm the bad guy in this story? Bloody hell.

"Hi, Genie." Miles shoots me an apologetic wave before I can analyze that thought any further. "When Claudia found out your nan was a psychic she *really* wanted to come and have a reading done, made me promise to bring her in on our lunch break, before she went home yesterday."

She did not stay the night, thank god. Of course, lots of things can happen outside the bedtime hours, but somehow it's easier not to think of them if the sun is still out.

"I said, 'Let's wait and book it with Genie. No need to just turn up unannounced,' but . . ."

"I didn't want any special treatment!" Claudia says. "So here we are!"

She bounces over to Nanna, like Tigger but with really good hair.

I look from Miles to Claudia and back at Miles. I don't know what's going on, but Claudia is bringing some serious girlfriend energy.

As Claudia looks around I raise a questioning eyebrow at Miles. He shrugs.

"The thing is," Claudia tells Nanna very seriously, "I've sort of met someone. And I'd like to know if it might go somewhere."

Claudia doesn't look at Miles as she says this, but she doesn't need to. The fact that she's talking about him, and whatever happened between them, is obvious in the coy tilt of her head and the way she twists her hands into her pockets.

"Well, then, let me tell you *for sure* what the future holds for you, my dear." Nanna Maria beams at Claudia. "Come and sit with me, give me your hands." Nanna Maria glances at me and then at Rory, who is about to fall asleep standing up. "Miles, you'd better wait outside with Genie and Rory. A reading requires total privacy. Besides, I think Rory could do with a few lungfuls of fresh air."

"Oh, okay," Miles says. Producing a tennis ball from his pocket, he waves it at Rory. "The tide is out—shall we go for a walk on the beach?"

"Yes!" Rory wakes up with a start and punches the air, making Claudia jump and giggle. "Bally time!"

"Rory just really likes the beach," I tell her as I grab him by the wrist. "He's Australian."

"Take your time," Nanna Maria says as she examines Claudia's palms. "I can see that Claudia and I have a lot of ground to cover."

"Ooh, do I need to cross your palm with silver?" Claudia asks.

"Or I take PayPal, if that's easier," Nanna Maria tells her.

"SO . . . YOU AND CLAUDIA, is that happening?" I half ask Miles as we head to the beach. He lobs the tennis ball, and Rory, who is still a little bit off his head, gallops after it, promptly followed by two springer spaniels and an ambitious Westie, their owners calling them back in vain.

"Not exactly. We are just hanging out," Miles says.

"Even after Claudia's clearly-planned-to-entrap-you picnic?"

"Oh, that . . ." Miles smiles. "Yeah, she's funny."

"So you're not an item yet?" I ask, trying not to sound like I care.

"No, we just talked," Miles tells me. "Claudia is new, and she doesn't know many people. It's hard to find your feet in a new town, as I know. So, we talked about stuff and got to know each other a bit more. It was nice, actually. She's easy to hang out with. Uncomplicated. Nice. I don't want to rush her into anything, if all she needs is a friend. Like I said, she's nice."

"Nice."

"Yeah, like your hair thing, and the lips. Nice. You look nice. Anyway, what were you going to say to me before Claudia turned up yesterday?" he asks, tilting his head. "It felt important."

I look at my darling Miles, just on the verge of being happy with a nice, uncomplicated woman, and I know what to say.

"Did it?" I ask, with a shrug. "Gosh, it's gone right out of my mind."

"Shame," Miles said. "Well, he looks like he's perked up a bit, at least."

He nods at Rory, who is racing through the surf holding the tennis ball aloft, whooping and cheering as the other dogs chase him.

I look into his face, made half golden by the afternoon sun, for as long as I can before I search the horizon for Rory again. About 0.1 seconds by a rough estimate.

We keep walking away from the parlor, up toward the spa beach huts. Running ahead, Rory has made it to the rock pools that are only revealed when the tide is out. I watch him hopping from one rocky outcrop to another, peering into them like Nanna Maria does into her crystal ball.

"It's pretty clear that Claudia is into you, she's not interested in just a friend," I say at length. "You realize that, right? She's into you, dude."

What am I doing and why am I doing it? is what I screech inside my head while grinning like a loon.

"Do you really think so?" Miles asks. "I can never tell when a girl likes me. Sometimes I think I know, and then she goes and says or does something that makes it clear that she can't feel that way about me. It's confusing."

"Really, you're confused by the way Claudia is right now?" I ask him. "She couldn't do much more to make it clear that she likes you. Other than some sort of bat signal in the night sky, I suppose. Or a small plane flying a long banner that reads, 'I think you are dreamy, Miles!'"

"I'm not dreamy." Miles chuckles. "I'm just a quite tall geologist. Nothing special."

"You are special!" I protest, thumping him on the arm. "You are funny and clever and . . . se—stuff. A woman like Claudia would be a hundred percent into you. Any woman would."

"Any woman?" he asks me. And he's not fishing for compliments—he really wants to know.

"Yeah. I'll say."

"Huh," he says. "Could someone tell Zendaya?"

I punch him lightly on the arm again.

There's a lull of quiet between us as we listen to the rush of the waves and cries of the gulls. Rory's stopped splashing and is looking out to sea. I wonder what he's thinking about. Nanna Maria is right about one thing: this whole impossible business with Rory has woken me up from a kind of hibernation. It's made me see how much better life is with more people in it. How perfect it could be with more of Miles in it.

We reach the rock pools in companionable silence, and I can't help thinking how easy it is to be with him. Not just now, but always. That his presence is a salve that always gives me a kind of peace. Maybe I should just . . . tell him? Now before he and Claudia are really a thing.

But then what if I tell him, and he looks at me, dumbfounded, and has no choice but to tell me that although he loves me, it's not like that? Or worse, what if I stop him from being happy with Claudia? And after nothing would be the same, and these little snatches of contentment would be gone forever. That's the problem with pursuing the idea of happiness. There's always a price, and sometimes it's too high. There is no way I'd make Miles pay for something that might not even exist.

Rory has stopped playing. He is just standing there, perfectly still, gazing at the horizon.

"Rory!" I call out. "Ready to come back? Rory?"

Glancing at Miles, I climb out onto the rocks that are normally covered by the sea and begin to make my way over the slippery seaweed and clear pools, followed by Miles. Eventually we get to where Rory is, and when I look at his face I see the very last thing I expected. Rory is crying.

"Rory," I say taking his hand. "What's up, feller?"

"This isn't me," he says, turning to me. "I never really thought about me and what I was before all this. I just thought about the now and cheese. But now suddenly, nothing feels right. Like there's this big jumble of feelings stuff that I am supposed to make fit into this skin, but I can't. There's too many and they are too big and . . . it hurts. Genie, I think I'm forgetting how to be a dog."

"No, no, you aren't!" I tell him, taking his hand. "Only this morning you ate a whole packet of Cheerios off the floor and swore at the postman. You aren't forgetting how to be a dog, Rory. Being a dog is who you are!"

"The real me is fading away, I know it is," he says. "I used to be able to stand here and look at the sea and smell everything brilliant. Chips, seawater, dead crabs, seagulls, seaweed, visiting dogs, friend dogs, cats, little kids and big men. I could take in a deep whiff and I'd get a picture of all of everything, all around me, popping up in sorts of images that told me everything I needed to know. But now when I breathe in"—he takes in a deep breath through his nose—"there's hardly anything there. If I stay like this much longer I won't even remember what it's like to be a dog at all."

"I won't let you forget," I tell him. "I'll remind you every day."

"But you only know what it feels like to be human," he says.

"Being human isn't all bad. Look, Rory, we will figure this out, I promise you."

"I will do my best to help too," Miles says. "And look, maybe there is no way to turn you back into a dog, but on the upside, as a dog you were two-thirds through your life. Now you've got at least another fifty years."

"Fifty years?" Rory looks at me. "Fifty dog years or human years?"

"Human years . . ." I mutter.

"Fifty long, pointless, sad, miserable human years? And I thought this day couldn't get any worse," Rory says.

Please see my earlier note on such comments, and how they tempt the fates.

"OH, GOOD, YOU'RE BACK!" Claudia says as we walk into the shop. "Well, that was very revealing. Genie, it must be brilliant to have a grandma that can tell you what the future holds!"

"It's definitely interesting," I say, with a fixed grin, and suddenly I get another vision, of Miles and Claudia holding hands across a candlelit table, gazing into each other's eyes like they were always meant to be. I know in my heart right now that this is a moment that is happening sometime in the near future. I know this moment will come to pass; more than that, it has to.

Nanna gives me a look, narrowing her eyes, before she turns back to Claudia.

"Such a joy to meet you, Claudia," Nan tells her fondly. "I have no doubt that your love is destined to be reciprocated."

"That's made my day," Claudia tells her, clasping both her hands. I open the door to let them out, but Claudia pauses.

"I don't know if Miles told you, Genie, but I've just moved to Scarborough. And I really want to make some friends. Miles said that when he first moved to Scarborough you were the one that made him feel at home. So I'm wondering: Would it be okay if I invited you and Rory, and Miles, of course, to dinner?" She looks at Miles.

"Oh, um . . ."

"I like dinner," Rory says. "We accept."

"Brilliant." Claudia claps her hands together. "Oh god, I'm not going to get you all into my studio, though. Miles, would it be okay if I hosted at your house? I'll buy everything, cook it, and clean up afterward, I promise. Please?"

"Er, yeah, sure?" Miles says.

"So, you and Rory are invited for dinner tonight at Miles's house. It's going to be great!"

Thanks, fate. Thanks a bunch.

Chapter Twenty-Six

CANNOT TELL YOU how much I don't want to do this," I tell Rory miserably as I stand in front of my bedroom mirror looking at myself in a black dress. When I got in from work, I looked at myself in the pink scarf and lipstick and felt stupid, like a kid playing at dress-up. So, I've gone back to black, and now I look like how an hourglass would look if it featured in an old-school animated Disney movie as a comedy sidekick. "I don't want to go and have dinner in Miles's house with the beautiful but terrifying love of his life. And Claudia."

"Me either," Rory says gloomily, sitting on my bed cross-legged with Diego in his lap. "I am down for dinner, but knowing there is a silent assassin waiting to kill me takes the edge off a bit." He considers the problem. "Why don't we get them to bring it round here? They could post it through the inexplicable hole in the door."

"I have to admit I think Matilda is probably okay for a cat," I say. Rory sits up. It's like I've said the word "bath" or "vet." "Only because she was really soppy when she sat on my lap, and she made the residents' day at the care home. Besides, Miles really loves her. So I'm going to try and stop thinking of her as an agent of Satan, and more like a cantankerous old lady, when all of a person's worst traits become borderline adorable."

"It's like I don't even know you anymore," Rory says, clutching Diego.

"Whatever happens, Miles is my friend and I feel about fifteen years too late, like I should make an effort to like the things he likes."

"So, you are going to be nice to Claudia, then?" Rory asks. Maybe he really is forgetting how to be a dog because he's got his human snark down perfectly. "And not tell Miles that you love him, even though telling Miles you are in love with him might be the key to getting me back to being a dog?"

"Telling a boy I like him is not my life's purpose!" I protest. "My life's purpose is me discovering the best version of myself and how to live the life I'm meant to, or something like that. Telling Miles I love him is at best a quest-adjacent quest. A side quest."

"So, you're just going to let Claudia have him?"

"He's not a prize or an object! And, though I never thought I would say this, I like Claudia-from-work," I say to Rory over the shoulder of my reflection. "She seems sincere, and nice. And it would be good for Miles to have someone. He deserves someone. So, you know, if Claudia is what he wants then that's fine by me. It's not like I haven't had half my life to realize I am in love with him and do something about it and maybe missed my moment right at the last second, right? Maybe the right thing to do, the thing that helps me find my true purpose, is just to let it go. Let him go. Having someone, it's not the be all and end all, right? Purpose comes from what you do, what you put out into the world. That's purpose. And as long as I can find that, then I expect it will be totally fine living next door to the love of my life and his very nice new wife, Claudia-from-work."

"I'm never going to be a dog again," Rory says.

I hold up one silver stud earring against my earlobe and then a gold teardrop. Then I decide against earrings. Don't want to look like I care.

"We're obviously invited to dinner so that she can get to Miles through me, his female friend. And I must be honest, it's a good strategy."

"The way I look at it," Rory says, giving Diego a couple of mournful squeaks, "is that there will be food."

"Okay, you're right, I suppose," I say, as if he has said something wise and insightful, which he kind of has. "Miles has been a good friend to us these last few days. So we are going to be lovely to Claudia. Claudia is here, she is real. We just have to deal with it like adults."

"Yeah," Rory says, when I turn around. "But are you really wearing that?"

YOU HAVE NEVER BEEN STYLED until you've been styled by a dog with an eye for color. When I say an eye for color, I mean a passion for all of the colors all at once.

"Is it a bit much . . . ?" I ask. Nan was right, there was a time when I wore all the colors I could in one go, but now it just feels so . . . loud.

"It's not enough!" Rory says. "When I have dog eyes all the colors are turned right down, but now everything is so bright and noisy and beautiful. Your human eyes are a total trip, so you should make the most of them. Give them something to look at."

"Yes, but . . ." I look at my emerging outfit; the girl who loves this look is still in here, but she's hiding.

The first thing Rory handed me was an electric-blue shirt my mum bought me the Christmas before last. I remember at the time thinking that I would never wear it, and I never have. But now I have it on I see it looks pretty good against my light complexion and dark hair.

"And these . . ."

Rory picks out a pair of pillar-box-red jeans, a present from Nanna Maria the birthday before last—the one when I still thought wishes were pretend and so never came true. I'd asked for vouchers, so I'd been pretty annoyed at Nanna's last not-so-subtle attempt to get me to "take care of myself." As it turns out they are exactly the right cut for my shape, and if I half tuck in the shirt it flatters my curves.

"These . . ." Rory hands me a long string of bright yellow beads given to me by Kelly's kids after I looked after them one weekend. I wind them twice around my neck.

"And finally . . ." Rory hands me a pair of leaf-green heels, only one of which is slightly chewed.

"Sorry about that," he says.

"I look like I present children's television," I say, looking in the mirror. And yet . . . Tipping my head to one side, I examine myself. It's actually not a terrible look—it's even bordering on good. And if I look really hard I can catch a glimpse of that girl I used to be who was so excited to see what the future had to show her. Rory has managed to bring her into focus in my memory. Without really knowing why I take a pencil out of the pot on my desk, twist my hair into an updo and stick the pencil in it to secure it, and, unbuttoning the bottom of the shirt, I tie it into a knot to accentuate my waist, which somehow is still there, despite all the toast.

Then I notice it. An old photo of me that's been stuck in the frame of my dressing-room mirror for so long I've stopped seeing it. Me in my first year at college, pink-lipsticked smile stretching from ear to ear, and wearing all the colors of the rainbow. Together we have brought her—me—back to life.

"Now you look like you," Rory says.

"Now I feel like me," I say. "Which is weird because I thought I felt like me before but . . . you know what? I didn't."

"I don't think there is a before-and-after Genie," Rory says. "I think there is just Genie. Funny, silly, cross, sweary, loving, brave, loyal, colorful Genie. I've known you most of my life, Genie, and the before-man, he was dark and cold. But you, you have always been all the colors, even when my dog eyes couldn't see them. There isn't another long-gone version of you. There is just you."

"Rory," I say, almost overwhelmed with love. "You never showed this much insight when you were a dog."

"I did," Rory said. "I just couldn't put it into words. I've got five years of telling you how much I love you to catch up on!"

"I love you too, Rory," I say. "You were always the best boy, and now you are a very good man."

"I knew it," Rory mutters, with a mini fist pump. He tucks Diego under my duvet, so that his head is resting on my pillow. "So, are you ready to go?"

I look at myself in the mirror.

"One sec." I think for a moment and, picking up Nan's pink scarf, I tie it in my hair again.

"Perfect," Rory says.

"Now I'm ready." As I grab my bag I glance out the window and for a second, I could swear that it's snowing, thick white fat flakes falling softly down. I blink and it's gone, replaced with the summer evening that should be there.

"Huh," I say, peering out the window to zero snow.

"What?" Rory asks.

"I feel like if from now on I am going to see signs and portents, it would be nice if there were some sort of handbook to tell me what it means. I just saw snow, which has something to do with the Christmas dance, so am I just going to randomly see snow to remind me of missed chances now?"

"I like eating snow," Rory offers. "Especially yellow snow."

"I'll make a note of it," I tell him. Snow? Maybe the magic isn't reminding me of the past, maybe it is telling me to go and live at the North Pole.

"Anything you want to tell me not to do or say?" Rory asks me.

"Nothing," I say. "You've got this whole peopleing business down to a tee."

"So does that mean I am allowed to hit Matilda with a stick?"

"Okay, one thing."

Chapter Twenty-Seven

CLAUDIA FLINGS OPEN THE DOOR and greets us as if we're long-lost family, hugging me to her bosom, and then kissing Rory on each cheek. He wipes his face on his sleeve at once, shuddering just like he used to when he was a dog and I gave him too many cuddles.

Miles is standing perfectly still in the middle of his living room like a socially awkward Hannibal Lecter in his prison cell waiting for Clarice. The room is an exact mirror image of mine, except that his was decorated by his gran in 1990 and so everything is in shades of lilac, which apparently was a thing in those days. From the color on the wall to the massive puffy marshmallow sofa and armchair, it's like a symphony of purple pastels. Aside from a few books on the shelf and a laptop on the sideboard, there are no signs that this is Miles's place at all. I bet Matilda had more say in the décor. But there's something so touching about him living alongside all of his nan's stuff. I have my rut, I made it my own. What Miles has are the things the people he loved left behind, chairs, Ikea art, and lampshades, all of which connect him back to the family he no longer has.

He has dressed up for the occasion, wearing a blue button-down shirt and what looks like a new pair of jeans, all shiny and stiff, still with the fold creases showing in the legs. He has shaved, which makes him look younger and somehow more vulnerable. I prefer his stubble, to be honest, but it's not me that's going to kiss him, is it?

"You look beautiful, Genie," Miles says softly.

"What, this old thing?" I lower my eyes. "You look pretty nice too."

"And I had a shower," Rory proclaims. "I didn't even get soap in my eyes this time."

Matilda, who has been lying on the back of the armchair, jumps up at the sound of Rory, arches her back, and hisses as she digs her claws into the cushion, as she has clearly done several times before.

"Not totally sure this is safe," Rory mutters, hovering behind me, his very own personal human shield. "Pretty sure Matilda would like to gut me like a squirrel."

"A squirrel?" Claudia frowns. "Anyway, no need to worry. Matilda is quite terrifying, but Miles thinks she went for me because I'd been petting a dog. It's dogs she really hates."

Rory whimpers.

"The thing is, Rory is allergic," I say.

"To violent death," Rory says.

"Cats," I say. "They bring him out in hives."

"I'm Australian," Rory says.

"Oh, I had planned to serve cocktails in here," Claudia says, "but not to worry, come through to the kitchen and we can leave Matilda to her throne room."

"Miles is right, you are dazzling, Genie," Claudia says, looking me up and down. "I'd never have the nerve to wear all that color but you really carry it off."

"Thanks, guys," I say, feeling suddenly self-conscious. "Rory picked the clothes out."

"But Genie makes them work," Rory says.

"Ah," Claudia says. "You have very original taste, Rory."

Again, the kitchen is just like mine, except no one has knocked down the wall between it and the front room. There is a small, square, standard-issue table, nicely laid with linen napkins and a posy of fat pink roses in the middle. There's just enough room for us to sit around it and for Claudia to attend to dinner on the hob.

"What are we having?" Rory asks Claudia, going to where she is stirring, to peer over her shoulder. "Smells good."

"Mushroom risotto," Claudia tells him. "Very garlicky and luxurious! With a fresh baby-leaf salad and parmesan dressing."

"Nice," Rory says. "And then what?"

"Oh!" Claudia laughs. "Italian meringue for dessert."

"Right," Rory says. "And then what?"

"We brought some chocolates," I say, handing Miles a packet of more-or-less-unopened After Eights that I got from the One Stop especially. Rory tried one before spending several minutes retching and staring at me with a look of startled betrayal.

"Yeah, we bought them because they are disgusting," Rory says. "I mean, who thought that chocolate, which is a really good thing, should go with toothpaste, which is a really bad thing?"

Miles takes the chocolates and puts them on the side.

"Wine?" he says, picking up a bottle that is waiting in an ice bucket. The price label is still stuck to the side, and that doesn't surprise me. Miles is not the sort of person to have a wine bucket on the off chance.

"Take a seat, take a seat." Claudia bustles, handing four cornflower-blue plates to Miles. "It is ready to serve!"

She seems a bit nervous as she dances around us, spooning risotto onto our plates and garnishing each serving with the leaves. I'd like to think it's because she finds me cool and intimidating, but it's much more likely that she is flat-out desperate to impress Miles. If I were Miles, heck, if I were me, I would be impressed. She looks gorgeous in a pastel-pink dress and the food smells delicious. Finally, Claudia takes her seat and raises her freshly filled wineglass.

"To my new life in Scarborough and new acquaintances, who I hope will soon become dear friends." She glances shyly at Miles. "Very dear friends."

Miles returns her glance with a sweetly encouraging smile.

Our glasses clink, and before I remember to stop Rory from drinking any he's gulped the whole thing down.

"Rory!" I say, laughing nervously. "You are supposed to sip wine."

"Sorry, I was thirsty," he says, smacking his lips like he's just sucked on a lemon. "Huh, that is actually pretty nice."

He slides his glass toward Miles, who looks at me. I shrug and he refills it.

After all, I know I feel the need to get drunk tonight. It would seem churlish not to allow Rory the same outlet, especially with his sworn enemy in the next room. Besides, if he is to learn to live life as a human, he will need to learn to live with a hangover now and again.

And yes, Reader, you are entirely right. I have not thought this through, and I am aware that there are many, many things that could go wrong when your recently human former dog is under the influence. At this point, though, things going wrong is my default setting. In some ways I'd rather just get it all out of the way in one go.

"So, did you guys become friends because you lived next door to each other, or was it the other way round?" Claudia asks as she eats her delicious food with the sort of gusto that's impossible not to admire.

"Bit of both," Miles says, smiling at me. "I met Eugenie on my first day at school. I was getting a bit of flack, new kid on the block and all that. Eugenie stormed over, flattened all my would-be bullies with a few choice words, and sort of took me under her wing. I'll never forget the first time I saw her. There was a no-makeup policy at school, but she had red lipstick on and bright blue hair. She looked like a punk avenging angel."

"Well, Milesington, you were a bit soft for a Hackney boy. Someone had to toughen you up." I smile at him. "I got home after school and my mum said, Go and make friends with the boy next door. He doesn't know anyone. And I was like, Oh god, I've already done my good deed for the day, but that's my mum. Made me go and call for the new kid. And there was Miles."

"So, you've both lived next door to each other since you were at school?" Claudia asks, her eyes widening.

"More or less," I say. "Miles went off to uni for a few years, down south."

"But you came back to Scarborough?" Claudia asked. "Never tempted to move on? Or live in London again?"

"Nope," Miles says. "I know a lot of people think it's important to travel and see the world, and it is, I guess. But this place is home, and home means a lot to me. My people mean a lot to me."

I am his person, or one of them, at least. My heart swells at the thought. Until quite recently that has been enough. I'm sure if I try hard, it could be again.

"And what about you, Genie?" Claudia asks me. "Did you always want to follow in your Nan's footsteps? She said it runs in the family."

"Oh god, no," I splutter into my wineglass. "No, I wanted to be a fashion designer. I've been doing a sort of quest and during that process I've realized that I actually really still want that, more than anything." I glance at Miles. "Almost. But I'm not sure if it's possible now."

"Not now, *yet*," Claudia says, with an emphatic nod. "If something hasn't gone the way I want it to I always add a 'yet' to it. Like, Oh, I haven't passed my driving test—yet. Or, I am not getting the grades I want—yet. Or, I haven't found the job of my dreams—yet. I can cross that one off, though, because I love working at the Rotunda. Then there's: I haven't managed to tell the boy I like that I like him—yet."

"Yet," I say, looking at Miles.

"Yes, yet," Claudia says. "If you really want something, then a lot of the time all it takes is doing it, and doing it again until it works out. And if you add a 'yet' to everything that isn't quite where you want to be, well, then it's still a work in progress. The ending hasn't been decided—yet."

"I actually really like that," I say, surprised.

"Me too," Miles says, smiling warmly at Claudia.

What none of us notices is that while we are all thinking about how very nice Claudia is, a soft fluffy assassin has taken it upon herself to hop off the armchair in the front room and leap up at the door handle almost a dozen times before she manages to open the door just enough to slink through. No one hears the pad of her tiny paws on the hall carpet, or notices when the kitchen door quietly swings open a few inches.

It's not until five seconds later, when the warm, rose-scented air is filled with the sound of Rory's screams, that any of us realizes that Matilda has jumped into the center of the table, knocking the posy of roses over as she launches a vicious full-frontal assault on Rory's face.

"Oh, crap!" I say, as the cat attaches herself to his head like an adorable alien.

"Oh, dear," Miles says.

"Oh no!" Claudia says, leaping up as rose water dribbles off the table edge and onto her skirt.

"I'm being murdered! I'm being . . . Argh!" Rory screams as he leaps out of his seat, grabbing the cat by the tail and trying to yank her off his face. Unfortunately it seems this only results in her digging her claws in deeper, grabbing at substantial tufts of his blond hair with her teeth, and yowling like a banshee with her mouth full.

I'm not sure whose flailing arms send the wine flying, or what sudden movement causes one of the pretty blue plates to smash on the floor, but suddenly I feel like I have a pretty good insight into what it's like to be in a war zone. I'm frozen with indecision as Rory careens into one wall and then another, all the while trying to pry his cat attachment off his face, which only makes her screech and hiss with righteous fury.

"Miles!" Claudia screams. "Do something before the cat has his eye out!"

"Not my eyes, I like my eyes!" Rory screams.

"Right, yes." Miles gets up. "Um. Right, yes, Rory . . . Rory! Stop thrashing about. You're scaring her."

"She's scaring me!" Rory mutters from behind the muffle of Matilda's tummy fur. "And my eyes."

"I know, but if you relax, she will relax," Miles says, very calmly. "Just stay perfectly still and maybe she will get bored."

"I do not feel relaxed, Miles," Rory says. "I feel exactly the opposite of relaxed. I feel unrelaxed."

"Rory, it's okay," I say, reaching for his hand. "Just stay perfectly still and think about Diego. Think about David Attenborough and chocolate biscuits."

"Do the voice," Rory says from behind a great big fluffy belly.

"What voice?" I ask.

"David Attenborough," he says. "Do the voice. Like that time you did when I had to have my anal glands squeezed out."

"Er . . ." I look at Miles and Claudia, lower my voice, get all posh, and go full Sir David. "'In the spring the male penguin will sit on the eggs for several weeks while the female is out at sea . . . Sometimes he will sing Elvis.'"

To be fair I'm not sure if this is genuine intel or the plot to *Happy Feet.*

With a great force of effort, Rory stops thrashing, his fingers squeezing mine.

"More."

"'When Elvis is no longer an option the penguin builds a huge airplane out of parts . . .'"

Is this the plot to *Madagascar* one or two?

"Okay," Miles says. "I am slowly going to make my approach and gently disengage Matilda from your face. Stay calm, try and stay still. Moving will only excite her predator instinct."

"I think her predator instinct is already excited," Rory whispers.

Miles hooks one hand under Matilda's belly, stroking her head and gently murmuring to her. I watch with bated breath as he very carefully takes one weaponized toe at a time off Rory's forehead, disengaging the claws. When I see the wounds begin to bleed I stifle my gasp a beat too late.

"What? Is it bad? Is it very bad?" Rory asks me, squeezing my hand hard.

"Nooooooooo," I lie, staring at the gouges in his forehead. "It's just a few scratches—they will heal in no time."

"The thing is, when she was a kitten she was mauled by a dog, and she has never forgotten it," Miles says, kissing the top of Matilda's head. "It's okay, Matilda, you are perfectly safe."

"I'm glad somebody is," Rory whispers.

"But Rory isn't a dog?" Claudia questions.

"There we are, all done." At last Miles has fully disengaged the cat, who is still stiff with aggression, her four legs stuck out in front of her like a sort of plush Dalek. "I think something about Rory must have reminded her of dogs. Can't think what, though. I'll take her upstairs for a cuddle and lock her in the bedroom to calm down." Miles peers at Rory's face. "Then I'll get some antiseptic to clean up your face."

"Can't you put her in the cage thing? In Genie's car, a couple of streets away?" Rory asks, touching his forehead gingerly. "It's just that I am pretty sure she can pick a lock."

"I don't think she will willingly go in her carrier at the moment," Miles says. "Best not to provoke her."

"Genie." A pale and bloody Rory looks at me through one swollen eye. "Am I going to die?"

"You are not going to die," I say. "Although I'm not sure when you last had a tetanus jab."

"A what?" he quails.

"You are not going to die, Rory, I promise."

Rory does not look convinced.

Miles grabs some catnip out of a drawer and departs with murder cat, and I help Claudia clean up and pour Rory another drink from a fresh bottle.

"This is a disaster," Claudia says, miserable. "This isn't how I planned it at all. I so wanted it to be perfect."

"It *is* perfect," I reassure her. "It still is. At least we had almost finished the first course. And if you like I can go to the corner shop and get more wine."

"No, you're right," Claudia says. "I'm overreacting. It can still be perfect. One day, years from now, we will look back at all this and laugh. And don't worry, I've got loads of wine and a bottle of champagne in the fridge."

"Wow, champagne on a Thursday. I won't know myself."

Miles comes back in with Savlon, cotton wool, and plasters. Sitting down, he begins gently to tend to Rory's injuries.

"Genie, shall we have a girls' glass of wine in the front room while Miles is patching up Rory?" Claudia asks me, nodding at the living room with a suspiciously confidential waggle of her eyebrows.

"Okay?" I reply uncertainly. I have no idea what Claudia and I will have to talk about, but I am very happy to follow the bottle of wine she is carrying.

"Thank you for giving me a pep talk," Claudia says, filling my glass as we sit on the sofa. "I was about to completely lose it and you kind of made me remember this is dinner on a Thursday, the stakes are low. Or at least they should be."

"Oh, you're welcome," I say. "I am familiar with things going terribly wrong all the time. There comes a point when you just learn to roll with it."

Claudia pauses for a moment, as if she is working out how to say something.

"You must think I'm really lame," Claudia says out of the blue.

"What? No? No! You? Lame? No way, siree," I tell her. "No, why would you think that?"

"I'd think I was a lame if I were you," Claudia says. "A needy, desperate-for-friends, lame girl who is trying way too hard to be likable, right?"

"No," I protest, "I am just the opposite of you, that's all. I have lived in one place all my life. I know everything about this town and everyone in it. It must be really hard arriving in a new town, not knowing anyone. If anything, I think you are brave."

"Really? Thanks." Claudia looks up at me with a sideways smile. "I just really want the job to work out, and Scarborough to work out. I thought it would be fine; my family and my mates were like, Are you sure? You won't know anyone and you might hate it. I thought it would be just like going to uni, you know? I'd just meet people. But I've been here two months and I only know the guys at work and you and Rory, and that's just because I basically foisted myself on you because you're Miles's favorite person and Miles is the coolest person I've met so far."

"He said that?" I ask, not realizing I've pressed my palm to my heart until after I've done it.

"He didn't have to," Claudia says, a little wary. "He talks about you all the time."

"Well, anyway," I say. "Clearly you are the coolest person at work. A hot geologist, whatever next?"

Claudia chuckles.

"I know it's so naff, but I'd love if you and I could be friends," she says.

"I think we will be," I tell her. "Scarborough is a great place to live once you get to know it. Miles and I will show you around."

"Are you coming back to finish this dinner?" Miles calls from the other room. "Rory's stopped bleeding. Mostly."

"Coming!" I call back.

"Can I ask you something before we go back in there?" Claudia says, her hand on my arm. "It's just, I sort of tried asking Miles out the other day, but I think I was too subtle because he didn't seem to notice. And I wondered if it's because . . . well, are you and Miles . . . ?" She lets the question hang so heavily I can practically read it in the air. "Because I would never try and get in the middle of anything romantic between you two."

"Romantic! No, we aren't romantic. No romance happening here!" I know I should add one of Claudia's "yet"s to the end of that sentence, and I know if I did that she would back off instantly. But the "yet" doesn't come. I am trying to see a future with me and Miles, and whenever I try and picture it, it's always him and Claudia.

"So you wouldn't mind, then?" Claudia asks.

"Mind what?" I say like an idiot.

"Well, seeing as he didn't seem to get the memo last time, I thought tonight I would formally ask him on a date."

"That would be totally fine," I tell her. Inside I'm screaming like a banshee.

Chapter Twenty-Eight

FIRST AID COMPLETED!" Miles calls again from the kitchen.

Claudia's eyes are wide with excitement.

"Oh my god, I'm going to strike while I'm a bit tipsy and ask him on a date tonight!"

"Like right now, tonight?" I ask her. "In front of me?"

"Yes, while I have the courage." She claps her hands together. "Miles isn't my boyfriend . . . *yet*!"

I'm still trying to digest what Claudia has just told me as I follow her back to the kitchen.

On paper, at least, there couldn't be a better match for Miles than Claudia. She's age appropriate, they like the same things. But clearly Miles and I are meant to be together, right? That's where all this has been leading, hasn't it?

Unless it hasn't.

Unless I've taken life advice from a cheddar-obsessed dog, and all of my feelings for Miles are one-sided after all. And that part of understanding my life's purpose is to let go of the past and forge a new future for myself and Rory.

Fuck's sake, I knew it. I knew this quest stuff was a terrible mistake. I've opened up to my secret feelings and for what? So

Miles can meet the girl of his dreams right under my nose, that's what.

Because it's clear that Miles wants to make a good impression too.

While Claudia and I were bonding in the living room, he turned off the bright overhead kitchen spotlights and lit a series of tea lights instead. The roses are back in their vase, and the colored lights shining in from the garden have turned the poky little room into a flickering seaside grotto of love.

"Oh, Miles," Claudia says, clasping her hands to her bosom. "This is lovely! You've made your kitchen really magical."

"Well," Miles shrugs, "we thought that more subtle lighting might make Rory's injuries rather less . . . obvious." He gestures at Rory, who is sitting with a bottle of wine in one hand and a glass in the other, leaning back against the wall for support. His forehead and cheeks are covered with a series of neatly applied sticking plasters. He is, both figuratively and literally, plastered.

"Oh, you poor darling," I say, putting my arm around Rory as I spot the fastest escape route from the impending meet-cute. "Are you okay? Should we go home and you can cuddle Diego while I feed you ice cream?"

"Don't make me wear the cone of shame again," he tells me, with sudden intense focus. "I can't stand it again!"

"Does it hurt?" Claudia asks, rather perplexed.

"No," Rory says, "it doesn't hurt anymore—not after the fourth glass of wine. The mental anguish will last for a long time—forever, perhaps—but in a way, now that my worst fear has become a reality, I feel a curious kind of inner peace. For there is nothing left to fear now but fear itself."

"Don't mind Rory," I say. "He seems to be really quite intoxicated. I should get him out of your way."

"No, no, please stay," Claudia says as she takes her meringue confection out of the fridge. It does look really good, almost good enough to mitigate the imminent date solicitation situation. Almost. "Pudding will help soak up some of that wine!"

Her voice is high and taut with nerves as she clears off the table and sets the pudding down in the middle with a flourish.

"There's no rush, Claudia," I say pointedly, but it goes over her head.

"Give it," Rory says, beckoning at the dessert.

"First," Claudia says, straightening her shoulders, "I have something to say—"

"Why so much talking? Humans and talking, honestly." Rory groans and I slap him lightly on the wrist.

"Ouch." He scowls at me. "Have I not suffered enough?"

Miles turns to look at Claudia with an expectant smile. You can see how much he likes her written all over his face.

"I expect you've all been wondering what it was that the marvelous Madam Maria had to tell me when I had my reading today?"

To be honest it hadn't crossed my mind, but if I'd had to guess it would have been something about being on the cusp of change, making big life choices, saying yes to opportunity.

"I didn't tell her anything about myself at all; all I told her was that I'd met someone that I really liked. And that I hoped maybe if I asked him out on a date he might say yes. Madam Maria told me, she said, 'You need to ask the question if you want movement in your life. Don't be afraid of asking. The answer will be exactly what you need to find true inner peace and happiness.'"

I mean, that could be asking a pharmacist for laxatives, honestly. Remind me to have a word with Nanna about being a bit more specific with her mystic advice in the future. How many other relationships has she accidentally initiated with this kind of dangerous talk? Then again, as Nanna Maria often tells me, people hear what they want to hear. And all Claudia wants to hear right now is Yes, I will go on a date with you.

"Miles, this is obviously far too much effort to put into asking a boy on a first date, but I have drunk a lot of wine, and I just asked Genie for her blessing and she gave it to me. So with that in mind, please forgive the unforgivable corniness of this situation and say yes to a date with me at the time and place of your choosing."

"You asked Genie for her blessing?" Miles looks at me. I look at my hands.

"She obviously knows you better than anyone, so it seemed right," Claudia says slowly, blushing to the roots of her fair hair. "But now that I'm saying it all out loud I realize that I am coming across like an axe-wielding maniac." She clasps her hands to her face. "Oh god, I'm so sorry . . . what am I thinking? I'll get my coat . . ."

"No, no . . . no, don't be sorry." Miles looks at me again and I make myself return his gaze. There's a question on his face, and somehow I still give the wrong answer. "That's really sweet of you to ask me out . . ."

The three of us sit there, staring at each other in suspended animation. Rory stares at the meringue. Finally, I can't bear it any longer.

"Miles!" I clap my hand on his shoulder. "We can't stand the suspense! Say yes, already!"

"Yes," Miles says. "Yes, I'd love to go on a date with you, Claudia. Thanks for asking."

"Really?" Claudia says, with a flattering smile. "Should I not go home, then?"

"Can we eat pudding now, or what?" Rory asks.

"This is nice," I say with a tiny cheer. "So nice. Really lovely, what a lovely evening. So, so, so nice. You two together at the rock and dinosaur museum. You'll be like Lara Croft and Indiana Jones, going around digging up shit." I pause. "Not literal shit, obviously."

"It's not unheard-of, actually . . ." Claudia says, as if she is about to launch into a talk about fossilized poos and their importance to the understanding of ancient peoples. Rory has other ideas, though.

"Pudding," he says, picking up his spoon and diving right into the center of his dessert. He shovels a load into his mouth. "Pudding good."

Miles just sits there, smiling at Claudia-from-work. She sits down opposite him; her hands reach across the table and take his. They look at one another in the candlelight. My vision becomes a reality.

The family magic is real; it's amazing and wondrous and suddenly I see the whole universe through different eyes, as a place of endless possibility.

Also, it sucks.

"Here." Claudia pushes the whole dessert toward Rory, who accepts the challenge with trademark focus and enthusiasm. "Enjoy, Rory!"

"Yeah, but what about me?" I mutter. "Rory, share, please!"

But just as I reach for my spoon, Rory frowns deeply, looks at me, and then falls forward face-first, right into the pie dish.

"Well, I think that's our cue to go home," I say. "Miles, I'm so sorry, would you mind helping me get him next door? He's a bit of a lump for one."

"Of course, Genie." Miles lets go of Claudia's hands and together we heft Rory into the hall, where I prop him up against a wall, securing him with one hand as I get my coat half on with the other. I pick up the packet of After Eights we brought with us from the side table.

"Do you mind?" I ask Claudia.

"Tonight, Genie, I would give you the moon if I could," she says.

"Chocolate'll do," I say.

A FEW MINUTES later and Rory is lying in the recovery position on the sofa with a sick bowl strategically positioned by his head. Fetching Diego, I tuck him under Rory's arm and cover him with my second-best throw.

"So that happened," Miles says.

"You like her, right?" I ask. "She's perfect for you."

"I like her a lot," Miles says. "But . . ."

"What?" I ask him.

"She asked your permission to ask me out and you said yes."

"Did you want me to say no?" I ask.

He holds my gaze, refusing to let me look away.

"Do you think she thought there was something between me and you?" he asks.

"People do think that sometimes," I say.

"Do you ever think that?" he asks.

I see him and Claudia holding hands across the table, and the way he smiles at her, and how I knew that moment had to happen, that it was inevitable. The only other thing I know for sure is that I want Miles to be happy.

"Nah-ah," I say, with a laugh. "You and me together, like in a romantic way? Imagine!"

"Right," Miles says. "Well, bye, Genie."

Why did that goodbye feel so final?

"Fuuuuuuck," I say to no one once I have shut the door on Miles. Rory snores loudly from the sofa. His leg twitches as if he's dreaming about running across wide-open spaces. I'd better sleep in the armchair, keep an eye on him.

Grabbing my pillows and duvet, I fetch a glass of water for Rory, a bottle of wine and chocolate for me, and commence my long dark vigil of the soul in which I plan to stare at the ceiling and wonder how the hell it came to this.

Chapter Twenty-Nine

GENIE! GENIE! WAKE UP! I'm dying. No, wait—I think it's worse than that. I'm not ready for this! I don't want to go over the rainbow bridge without a tail! I'll be a laughingstock! Genie!"

It's actually Rory's terrible, garlic-laced breath as he shoves his face right in mine that wakes me up a few nauseating seconds before his hoarse cries for help. I don't remember falling asleep. The last thing I remember is lying back in the chair, watching the occasional headlights of a passing car track across the ceiling, when suddenly a switch flicked on in my head, and I knew exactly what I had to do. I must have drifted off soon after that, which feels like it was about ten minutes ago.

Rory is kneeling on the carpet in front of me, his chin on the arm of the chair, with eyes that look much more like they belong to a Saint Bernard than a golden retriever. "Genie, take me to the vet. I'm dying. I hate the vet, but I think this time I need to go. I think that Matilda's claws are venomous and I am poisoned, Genie. I'm poisoned. We must find the antidote before it's too late and I am condemned to cross the rainbow bridge in trousers!"

"Calm down, Rory," I tell him. "For starters, you are not dying, you are just hungover. And secondly, the rainbow bridge is . . .

more of a metaphor that some people use to make themselves feel better when their pets . . . stop living. It's not an actual place."

"Wait . . . ? What?" Rory looks puzzled. "I think you'll find it is an actual place. Three of my friends have crossed over it since I lived here, Genie. I heard their owners talking about it. Oh, wait, no, one of them—Jeff, the bulldog—he bought a farm instead, but I think it's around the same area as the bridge, so that we can all hang out there. Also, what is 'hungover' and is it fatal?"

I decide to let him have the rainbow bridge thing. He's got enough to deal with as it is without us having to get into the ins and outs of the existence of an afterlife. After all, recent, somewhat magical events do make it seem more likely that there might be a strange sort of heaven floating around up there where deities mess with our lives for kicks.

"No, although a hangover sometimes feels like it, it is rarely fatal. It happens after drinking a lot of alcohol—wine, in your instance. Alcohol is a kind of toxin. It doesn't hurt you in moderation, but if you drink a lot of it, it makes you feel . . . well, like you feel."

"Why didn't you tell me?" Rory flops back onto the floor. "Why didn't you tell me that the wine would make me feel like this?"

"I know," I say. "I should have. I'm sorry. Yesterday was a bit overwhelming, even before Matilda tried to kill you and Claudia told me she was going to ask Miles out right in front of my eyes. I took my eye off the ball. That's another thing too much wine will make you do."

"So, I'm definitely not dying?"

"Definitely not," I reassure him. "I'll make you a nice fry-up for breakfast and sweet tea to make up for it, okay?"

"Okay, because now that I'm not dying I need to work out how I feel about all this living."

"What do you mean?" I ask, getting out of the chair to lie down next to him on the carpet.

"I thought I didn't want to die, but now I know I've got another fifty years to go, and I can't even have wine to make it all go fuzzy without feeling like I want to die the next day, I'm not sure that I want to live."

"Welcome to the human condition," I say, rolling over on my side to look at him. "Look, Rory, don't worry. Everything is going to be okay. You are going to get to be a dog again, I promise. I had an epiphany in the night."

"Did it hurt?"

"Yes, actually," I say. "Sort of. Especially the part when I watched Claudia ask Miles out."

"*Out where?* On another picnic?"

"Similar . . ."

"When did that happen?" Rory is amazed. "I mean, that seems like a pretty big deal and I do not remember it at all."

"It happened shortly before you passed out in the pudding."

"Oh, I thought that was a beautiful dream," Rory says. "So, wait. Miles, who you have loved all your life, is going on a date with Claudia, which means"—he looks at me with big sad eyes—"you must feel sad and confused."

"I do," I confess. "But it is what it is and instead of wallowing in self-pity I am just going to be bloody happy anyway even if it kills me."

"Oh kaaaay." Rory sounds doubtful.

"The trouble is, I found a nice safe groove to fit into. It was small and stable and safe," I explain. "I got in the groove and I made it cozy and I've stayed there ever since. I even got a dog to keep me company in my groove."

"Where is this groove?" Rory asks before it dawns on him. "There's not a literal groove, is there?"

"No, it's a metaphor. You *are* learning!" I say "Then all this business with the wish happened.

"I need to face up to the big stuff, the really hard stuff," I say. "And then get back to the person I was meant to me, the person I am. But I'm scared, and I'm going to need you. And Kelly."

"I will help you be brave," Rory says, turning an ominous shade of green. "Out of interest, what are the rules about eating your own vomit when you're human?"

MUM IS SURPRISED and happy to see us as she opens the front door, and then full of giggles as she is immediately engulfed in a huge hug from Rory.

"Granny Rita," he tells her. "I got drunk—it was horrible! I think biscuits will help, though."

"What you need," Kelly says, "is some hair of the dog."

"Tell me about it," Rory says.

I picked Kelly up on the way, waving at her kids as they watched us through the window.

"Thanks for this," I said. "How are things?"

"Better." She nodded. "Like, hard. It's going to be a long road. But now that I know what's wrong, I can help him and we'll get through this together." She twisted in the seat to look at Rory. "Fred's Man Club keeps asking when you are going back, Roar."

"I'll go back when I'm a dog," Rory said.

"Genie." Mum now looks at me in horror as we follow her to the kitchen. "What were you thinking? Getting your dog drunk! You ought to know better at your age."

"You'd think that, and yet results show that I gain zero wisdom over the years," I say. "Anyway, let's call it aversion therapy—he won't do it again in a hurry."

"You poor love," Mum says, planting a kiss on Rory's cheek as she hands him a packet of Hobnobs. "You have as many as you need, and Granny Rita will make you a hot chocolate too."

"Yes, please, thank you, please," Rory says.

"Might I and Kelly get a cup of tea?" I ask her.

"Yes, though you don't deserve it," she says. "Not you, Kelly, you can have two sugars and a Kit Kat."

She tilts her head.

"You look nice in green," she says.

"You bought me this dress," I remind her.

"I know," she says. "It's nice to see you wear it. I suppose you can have a Kit Kat too. Nanna says you've been drawing again. That you are really making some positive changes. I'm so pleased for you, darling."

"Well, I'm trying, actually," I say. "I've realized . . ."

"Yes?" Mum prompts me.

"That maybe . . ."

"Go on," Mum says.

"I have . . ."

"You have . . . ?"

"Issues she needs to address," Kelly adds, putting her arm around my waist. "It's taken a lot for her to come here today, Rita."

"Really?" Mum looks at me keenly.

"Mum . . ." I say and there must be something in my voice,

because she puts down the kettle and crosses to me, putting her hand on my arm.

"What is it, darling?" Her voice is kind and soft—it makes me want to cry.

"I've been thinking about a lot of things recently," I say. "Since Rory, I've been thinking about stuff that I try really hard not to think about, and I think I am ready. To look in the box. You still have it, don't you?"

"Of course I still have it," Mum says. "I would never part with it, my love. But are you sure?"

"Yes, I'm sure. If you, Kelly, and Rory will look with me."

A few minutes later we sit at the dining room table and Mum puts a large, square, pink box on the table. I sit there looking at it, feeling all the muscles tighten in my throat.

"What's in the box?" Rory asks, sitting next to me.

"All the things I bought for my baby," I say. "Things I couldn't let go or look at. So Mum kept them safe for me."

Kelly stands behind me, her hand on my shoulder. Mum sits down on one side of me and Rory draws his chair nearer to mine on the other. He leans against me, shoulder to shoulder, just as he always has.

"I'm here," he says.

"We're all here," Mum says.

Carefully I lift the lid off the box and unwrap the pink tissue paper that keeps the contents safe. The first thing I take out is a soft cream blanket. I hold it to my cheek.

"We had two of these," I tell Rory, looking at Mum, who nods. "I spent ages choosing them, because I'd read that you can't let your baby get too hot or too cold, so I wanted it to be breathable, but also cozy, and for her to feel safe and warm, you know?"

"Yes," Rory says.

"They wrapped her in this after she was born, she was so tiny. I held her," I tell him. "She is buried in the other blanket, just like this. Cozy and warm."

I hold it to my cheek for a moment, closing my eyes as I try to recall the feel of her slight weight in my arms. Carefully I fold the blanket, and setting it aside reach inside the box, taking out a card and opening it to reveal all the evidence I have that she existed in this world.

"Her feet and hands," I say, tracing the contours of the prints with my thumbs. I look at Mum.

"She was real, Mum," I say.

"Oh, yes, darling, yes," Mum murmurs. "Our beautiful little girl. Not a day goes by when I don't think about her. We lost our little granddaughter, and we lost you too, in a way."

But there have been too many days when I pushed every thought of her down and down as far as they would go.

There's a soft white teddy in the box. I take it out and hold it against my chest, and then I reach inside for the last memory. The photograph of me holding her. Eyes wide and dark, uncertain and afraid. That's the person I've been living as all these years.

But when I look at it again, I am amazed at what I see. Amazed at what I could not bring myself to look at for all these years. A young woman, cradling a swaddled baby in her arms, looking at her child. I don't know what I thought this was a photograph of, but now that I look at it again I can see that it's a portrait of love. And it's beautiful.

"Her name was Amelia," I tell Rory.

"She is really sweet," Rory says, his chin on my shoulder.

All these years I've been carrying her in my heart as if her memory was a heavy weight. But I had it all wrong. My love for her will carry me. It will carry me through everything, because I know firsthand that love is instant, it is real, and it never dies. And if that's not magic, then I don't know what is.

"Sweetheart." Mum gets up and puts her arms around me. I turn into her shoulder and begin to cry. Rory leans into me, his weight reassuring, a comfort.

"I'm next to you, Genie," he says. "You're not alone."

"You never were," Mum adds. Suddenly I realize that has always been true.

Chapter Thirty

THE SUN FEELS WARM through the car window as we drive home in silence and I feel drenched in a kind of calm I have not felt for a very long time. For the first time Rory is sitting in the passenger seat next to me. After a while he presses the button that slides down the window and leans his face into the breeze, inhaling deeply, his long blond hair blowing back from his face, his eyes closed. When I keep my eyes on the road and don't look right at him, it's not some dude that I sense sitting next to me but my dog. My Rory. And I miss him so much even when he's right here.

"You were very brave, Genie," Rory says when we get home, me carrying the box of Amelia's things while he helps me out of the car and opens the front door. "You were hurt and scared, but you were brave, and I am very proud of you. Would you like a biscuit? You can have two if you like. I would give you more, but there are only two left because I ate all the others. But I did leave you two. I mean, I licked them, but I did leave them."

"Thank you, Rory. I really appreciate that. But you know what—I'll pass," I say, glancing up at Miles's house.

"What do you think about the other thing Granny Rita said?" Rory asks me as he puts the kettle on. There are some advantages to turning your dog into a human. Training them to make you endless cups of tea is one of them.

"I don't know," I say, reflecting on what Mum suggested before I left. "I'm not sure. I mean, how is it going to help me find my true self? It's a work in progress. It's not like there's a deadline—it could take years. I don't want to run before I can walk. And that is the past. I saw a motivational poster once that said you should never look back."

"Did it have a kitten on it?" Rory asks me.

"Might have," I admit.

"I rest my case," he says. "But anyway, there is a deadline. You want to find yourself and I want to be a dog. And every day I spend in this stupid pink body I can feel a bit of my dog-self crumble away. What if by the time you find yourself you turn me back into a dog that wants to be a man? Or what if my human years and dog years don't match up and it takes you another decade to deal with your stuff, and puff—I go back to being a dead dog? So yeah, I think there is a deadline, Genie, and also that dealing with stuff from your past so that you can move forward is one of the basic principles of therapy, and finally, that you should never accept advice from a kitten."

"You're right," I relent. "You know, you actually could be a good lawyer."

IT HAD BEEN QUITE A WHILE after we had looked in the box, a long time in which I sat on the sofa with Mum's arms around me, my head on her shoulder, before she had said, rather hesitantly, "You know, Aiden manages the restaurant at the Carlton Hotel these days."

"Aiden my ex?" I'd replied, my voice tight and cold at the

mention of his name. "Aiden who studied art and planned on being an anarchist?"

"Yeah, I went for lunch with Lisa from yoga the other day," she'd said. "And there he was, behind the front desk. I was going to turn around and leave but he came after me. Went out of his way to stop me from leaving. He asked me to give him five minutes. He asked me how you were. He said he'd been thinking a lot about how he'd treated you then. Leaving you and never getting in touch after you lost her."

"Right," I'd said. When I tell the story of my past in my head, which I do not do that much in the first place, I always dismiss Aiden as a bit part. I always say it wasn't him that mattered, that it was Amelia. That when he walked out on me I took it with a pinch of salt. That he was meaningless. That's how I like to think about it. That works.

"He asked me to tell you that he is so sorry about the way he treated you then, and the person he used to be. He said he wished he could talk to you, apologize and make amends. I said hell would probably freeze over first."

"You were right," I say. "He's nothing to do with Amelia or me. He didn't even come to the hospital to hold her."

"I know, darling, and that was impossible to understand. But people do change, you know. He's married now, got two kids," Mum had told me. "Both at primary school."

"Good for him," I'd said.

There was a silence in which I could sense Mum running over different variants of the same sentence again and again in her head. Eventually she settled on one. It took courage.

"Actually, I think maybe it would help you to go and see Aiden," Mum had said. "To have closure. I thought it then, when I saw him, but I knew there was no point mentioning it. Now I'm not so sure."

"But I am," I'd said, pulling out of her arms. "There's no point."

"Just listen for a moment," Mum had said. "The way Aiden treated you then, it was wrong. He hurt you, but he hurt himself too. He knows that now, and he wishes he could put it right."

"Well, I'm fresh out of wishes," I say.

"What if you could grant yourself a wish?" Mum asks me. "A wish for you to be free of hurt and regret for good. Because there are some wishes that don't need magic to come true. Just a willing heart and an open mind. So, I'm telling you, because you are my daughter, and I love you: forgiveness will heal *you*."

"I'm not going to see Aiden. I'm not going to make life easier for the man who couldn't bring himself to have anything to do with my baby or tell him that there are no hard feelings, because there are. A lot of them."

"I know, darling," Mum had said. "But it's the hard feelings that you need to let go. Not for his sake, but for yours."

"I DON'T KNOW," I say now. "I know Mum is trying to help, but I just don't know if I can face it."

"I don't know either," Rory says. "I know that I am afraid of that man, from the dark time, before you came to get me. And I know if I saw him now I'd still be afraid of him and angry. When I saw him I was just as scared as I was when I was a little puppy."

"Because dogs always live in the moment, maybe you find it hard to separate the past from the present," I say. "I guess that's not always good."

"It's hard to remember with all this human stuff floating around in my head now, but if I think really hard and I remember what it was like before the wish, and when it was just me and you, I was really happy. Sometimes happy and hungry." He thinks for a minute. "Always hungry, actually. But always happy too, because I felt safe and loved."

"In the end I think that's all that any of us wants," I say. "I know that's what I want."

"I'm going to get Miles," Rory says. "You need a human more experienced in all the complicated stuff."

"No, don't," I say. "He's probably with Claudia and I need to get used to not having him around all the time. I need to sort this out myself."

Rory has left.

FIVE MINUTES LATER he returns with Miles.

"Genie?" Miles says. "Rory said you were ill?"

"Not ill, not exactly—just . . . Miles, I didn't want to bother you, but if I'm honest, I could really do with a friend—one that's been human for more than a week. And as you're here . . ."

"I'm going in the garden to throw stones at Matilda," Rory tells me. "Keep out of your way."

"A man throwing stones at a cat is not a good look," I tell him.

"Oh, but she can have my eye out and it's all hunky dory," he says crossly. "Fine, pigeons, then?"

"Just . . . dig a hole or something."

"Can I put one of each of your shoes in it?"

"Yes," I say, shaking my head at Miles.

"So." Miles sits down on the edge of the armchair, resting his hands on his knees. "How can I help?"

Running my fingers through my hair, I sit and straighten my shoulders, reaching for the pink, square box.

"You know the story," I begin. "You were away at uni when it happened, it was your finals. Kelly rang you. You came back on three trains and sat up all night with me and Kel and Mum, and the next day you went back and took your exams on about an hour's sleep."

"You are ready to talk about Amelia?" he asks, his voice so gentle I want to wrap myself in it.

"I'm ready," I say.

MILES DOESN'T SAY ANYTHING for several minutes.

He has listened while I talked, listened very closely with such close concentration, not looking at me, but with his head tilted toward me, nodding every few words. Now he sits back in his chair and thinks.

"We should go and see Aiden," he says

"Really?" I ask. "You really think so?"

"Rita isn't the sort of woman to suggest something she knows would cause you more harm than good. I don't think she would have mentioned Aiden if you hadn't visited her today and talked about Amelia. I think perhaps she saw an opportunity to help you on your quest."

"But why should I absolve him of any guilt he might feel because of what he did to me?"

"He might feel better if you and he talk, and you say the things you've never had the chance to say before. It might heal him if he is able to look you in the eye and apologize and ask for your forgiveness. But that's not the point, Genie. How Aiden feels isn't your problem. How *you* feel is, and I think Rita is right. I think seeing him will help *you*."

Quite unexpectedly he reaches out and takes my hand in his.

My fingers are cold, his are warm. I lean toward him, longing for more of that warmth.

"You said 'we'?" I ask tentatively.

"Yes," he says. "I'll come with you, of course. That's what friends are for."

We sit there, our fingers entwined and our eyes locked. One tug of his hand, to bring him a little closer, and I could kiss him. I want to kiss him. I want to kiss my best friend Miles more than anything in this world.

"So, when shall we go?" I ask

"Now," he says, letting go of my hand and standing up decisively. "When something scares us it's better to either run at it or run away. Today we are going to run at it."

"Better tell Rory . . ." I say.

"I'll tell him," Miles says. "I think it would be better if it was just you and me for this. I'll find a nice nature documentary for him to watch—something about otters. You go and put on some power lipstick."

"Power lipstick?" I ask him, amused at the phrase coming from him.

"For my mum it was always bright pink," Miles says. "Like the one you wore the other day. She said when she was wearing her power lipstick, quote, "no fucker would dare fuck with her.""

"Your mum was awesome," I say. "Oh god, do I remind you of your mother?" I ask him.

"Not one little bit!" He smiles. That rare, gorgeous smile. "Eugenie Wilson, there is no one in the whole entire world who is even a little bit like you. You are one of a kind."

Chapter Thirty-One

I STAND JUST OUTSIDE the reception area in the grand portico that would have seen the comings and goings of fancy ladies and gentlemen back in the day. Through the modern plate-glass doors that stand between us and the reception desk, I watch Aiden chatting to a customer. Smiling and laughing. Ten years have gone by, and he still looks more or less the same, but I don't recognize him anymore. The cruel, callous version of him that's lived in my imagination has been replaced with this rather short, deferential-looking man who is meticulously dressed, down to his matching tie and pocket handkerchief.

Funny to think that Aiden and I have lived in the same town all these years and never run into each other before. Maybe we were supposed to wait for exactly the right time. Or maybe there is never a right time, and . . .

"Genie." Miles coughs, indicating the growing line of people behind us. "Quite a lot of people would like you to go through the door."

"Oh, sorry!" I call to the queue. "I was just contemplating meeting my ex again after ten years of resentment."

A series of "fair enough" expressions, murmurs, and shrugs bolster me up, and I finally pull open the door. Aiden looks up, with an automatic smile that quickly freezes into a this-is-awkward grimace.

"Genie . . ." He comes out from behind the front desk. "This is unexpected."

"When you ran out on our baby, that was unexpected," I say.

A woman waiting just behind me sucks air in through her teeth, shaking her head at her partner. Apparently, I went right there, right away.

"Trisha," Aiden beckons over a young woman, "please take over for me for a minute, will you?"

He leads us over to an alcove filled with some large potted palms.

"Shall we meet after lunch?" he asks. "There's a café round the corner where they do a nice—"

"No." I shake my head. "My mum and my dog think it's a good idea I come and see you, so I have come to see you, but I am not going to make an appointment to do it. Look, I just want to say that the way you treated me back then, it was shitty. It was shitty and wrong, and it hurt me. A lot. The choices you made damaged me. I've carried the hurt you inflicted on me for a really long time, and you should apologize for that."

"I know." Aiden glances at Miles. "Both of you, come with me—we can talk in the office."

The office is a small, poky, and windowless room with a desk, a chair, and a filing cabinet. There's a photo of two smiling girls Blu-Tacked to it.

"Yours?" I ask him.

"Yeah." He smiles, full of pride, and then takes a deep breath.

"Look, Genie, I don't have an excuse for how I behaved. There are reasons. Maybe because that's the way that my dad treated my mum, and I didn't know better. Maybe because I acted like I knew everything, when really I hadn't got a clue and no one to ask. Maybe because I was scared and full of grief and I didn't want to face how I felt. The baby I wasn't sure I was ready for had died, and part of me felt like I had made that happen. I couldn't deal with it, I didn't know how to. But running away the way I did—it was selfish and small. And since I've had kids, kids I'd die for, it's made me realize I loved Amelia too. I hurt everyone, me included, by not admitting it. I really am sorry, I've been sorry for a long time now, knowing there's nothing I can do to fix it. I'm sorry."

"Thank you for apologizing," I say.

Then the strangest thing happens. I feel a great sense of peace flood through me, and a huge relief. As if the weight I had carried with me for so long has just ebbed away with one simple word. Maybe I sway a little, or look like I might cry. But for the second time that day Miles takes my hand. He squeezes my fingers gently, just to let me know that he is there.

"I feel sorry for the kids we were back then," I say. "We got in far too deep without knowing what we were doing. I accept your apology, and I wish you the best, Aiden."

"Thanks, Genie." He smiles. "What were we like, hey? I thought I was going to lead a revolution and you thought you were going to be a fashion designer and artist. As if!"

"Actually," I say with a sudden realization, "I am still going to be a fashion designer. I'm going to enroll back in college as soon as I get home."

Miles smiles at me as I make the announcement. Just saying it out loud gives me something I haven't felt for a long time: a sense of expectation.

ONCE WE ARE OUTSIDE I wait until we are at my car before I throw my arms around Miles and hug him tightly. One moment passes and I feel him tighten his arms around me. Closing my eyes, I let myself sink against him, and for five beautiful seconds I feel like I've found the place I'm meant to be.

"Genie," he says softly. "I . . ."

"I'm just so glad you were there, Miles. I couldn't have done it without you."

"You could have," he says. "You can do anything you set your mind to, Eugenie Wilson. And I think that maybe, just maybe, you are beginning to see that for yourself."

Just as we are about to leave a busker across the street starts singing "All I Want for Christmas Is You."

"Mate, it's August," I call out to him.

"I know," he calls back. "I just saw you and this song came out of my mouth. Don't know why, but hey, all I want for—"

"Fine, let's go," I tell Miles. I get in the car but he crosses the road and gives the guy a tenner, they talk for a while and shake hands, and then he gets back in the car.

"What was that about?" I ask.

"Saying goodbye," Miles says cryptically. Well, I suppose it is the day for it.

Chapter Thirty-Two

WELL, YOUR AURA has changed color," Nanna Maria says the moment we walk into the shop. She is scrutinizing me with a frankly alarming squint.

"By that do you mean that you talked to Mum?" I ask her. The really weird thing is that when I look at Nanna I see her surrounded in turquoise and gold, shimmering like a sort of full-body halo. Am I seeing an aura? Are auras a thing?

"I did talk to your mother," Nanna Maria admits as she comes over to me and envelops me in a soft hug. "And I want you to know that I am so proud of you, darling. It's hard to do what you did yesterday, deciding to face those difficult times. But also, your aura has changed color. It's looking much healthier, for certain. Nice and pinkish now. Positively peachy. And if I'm not very mistaken, you are coming into your powers with the family magic. I always said you were a late developer."

"I'm not sure I like it," I tell her. "Sometimes it's nice, sometimes it's painful, and a lot of the time I have no idea what's going on."

"That's not the family magic, dear," Nanna says. "That's just being human. As for the magic, it is all of those things too, but you will learn how to interpret what you see. To understand what the universe is showing you."

"Are you sure? Because I barely passed English at school, and if I'm honest it still doesn't seem really real. Even though I know it is."

"It is always harder to believe in the impossible," Nanna says. "That's why they call it faith."

"Will I start talking a load of old cobblers too?" I ask her, with a smile.

"Definitely," Nanna tells me. "And get used to people looking at you like you are rather eccentric."

"Sorry about that, Nanna," I say. She waves my apology away.

"What about Rory?" Nanna Maria says, looking him up and down. "I'd hoped that now that you'd started your spiritual journey to fulfillment that the power of the wish might be broken, but nothing, Rory? No tail down your trousers? No sign of a wet, shiny nose?"

"Nope," Rory says, forlorn. "If anything, I feel a little bit less dog and a little bit more bloke with every day that passes. This morning I woke up thinking about football, and I don't even like football, Nanna Maria. You can't get a whole one in your mouth." Nanna turns her healing hug powers to Rory, who rests his chin on the top of her head. "I'm worried that if I spend much longer in this body I'll stop being able to understand what my friends are saying, and I'll start wanting to do DIY. And then one day . . . one day I might be stuck as a man forever! A man who likes men things, Nanna. And I don't want to be rude, but from listening to every woman who ever talks about men I get the impression that most of them are NOT GREAT."

"Not all men," I say, thinking about Miles again. "Not even most of them. On a case-by-case basis most of them are okay. You're a great man, Rory."

"I DO NOT WANT TO BE A MAN, GENIE." Rory lets go of Nanna Maria and paces away. I have never, ever seen him really angry before. He's right, the man in him is starting to take over the dog.

"I'm sorry." Rory hugs himself tightly. "I don't know where that came from. I scared myself."

"It's okay," I say. "We will figure this out."

"Hmmm," Nanna says, thinking. "There must be something else that is holding you back, Genie—something more you have yet to accept or confront. Or could it be something that Rory needs to do?"

"Rory hasn't got any unfinished business," I say. "Not unless you count my blue heels. He's only eaten one."

"It was an accident," Rory mutters. I ruffle his hair and he musters a smile.

"I don't think there is anything I have left to do," I go on. "I've forgiven Aiden, I've enrolled in a design course starting in October, and I was considering getting a pink . . . like streak put in my hair, an edgy one . . . but other than that, nothing to see here apart from a peachy-auraed girl with not a care in the world."

"There is that thing about being in love with Miles but not telling him because you think it's noble. But how it's noble to not tell a bloke that is in love with you that you are in love with him, I don't know," Rory says.

"Miles has moved on," I say. "I am too late. Accepting that is actually the hardest part of this whole true-purpose thing so far.

But once I'm back at college and making garments again, then I'll be busy, and it will get easier. A person's true purpose is not another person."

"No, but a person's true love might be part of it," Nanna says. "I've never seen two people more right for each other than you and Miles, but I have to admit you do make it hard to work out what's going on. Like two pieces of a puzzle sitting side by side turning in every direction except for the one that would lock them together."

Rory and I look at each other, stunned.

"But . . . but . . ." I splutter. "You've meddled in every little bit of my life from the moment I was born, and yet didn't think to mention that the love of my life lived next door?"

"With a cat," Rory adds.

"*Two things*," Nanna Maria says. "Firstly, when have you ever listened to my advice on anything? And secondly, you can't rush love, Genie, you can't make it happen any sooner than it will. You both have to be ready to turn to one another and fit."

"Well, I'm not going to ruin things for Miles. We're fine as we are."

"You're not fine," Nanna Maria says. "How do you expect there to be a harmonious balance in the universe if you refuse to be honest about your feelings and what they mean to you? All these negative emotions swirling around the psychosphere, it's bad for everyone. Bad for the planet, bad for world peace!"

"I refuse to take responsibility for the state of the world," I say. "I recycle!"

"If you care for that young man at all," Nanna says, wagging her finger at me, "you will tell him that you are in love with him and let him make a choice. Don't deny him that, Genie. It's not fair."

"Oh, okay. I will do that," I say. "Right after I've poked my eyes out with rusty nails."

"I think it's worth a go," Rory says. "You've come so far, be a shame not to finish the last little bit of your quest."

"Being in love with Miles isn't part of my quest," I remind him. "I told you, it's quest-adjacent."

"Darling, if you want to truly free yourself from the emotional chains you have been struggling under, then you must be honest. It might be the only way to release Rory from the wish. And anyway, doesn't Miles deserve the truth?"

"But whyyyyy is it so awkward?" I whine, slumping forward. "Why can't I just hide away from my feelings and the consequences of my actions indefinitely?"

For some reason Nanna Maria mimes zipping her mouth shut as she stares fixedly at me while shaking her head.

"Why do I have to face up to things and deal with them head-on?" I carry on complaining as Rory is slashing his hand under his chin, eyes wide with a silent warning. "I just don't know how I am going to be able to look Miles in the eye and tell him that I . . ."

It dawns on me several seconds too late.

"He's standing behind me, isn't he?"

Nanna Maria and Rory nod in unison.

"Look me in the eye and what?" Miles says.

"That you are the best," I say very slowly as I turn around to look at him. "As a neighbor. And friend. And geologist. You are the best geologist I have ever met. And I've met at least four."

"Really?"

"Really," I say, taking an unconscious step toward him.

"You're the best future fashion student that I have ever met," he says. "But that's not why I am here. I'm here because I think I've got a new lead that might help Rory."

"I got a new lead too," Rory says. "But just after I got it, Genie turned me into a human. And now that I think about it, a lead might be a violation of my human rights."

"Well, anyway," Miles says after a moment. "As you know, I've been traveling around collecting stories of local folklore for a new exhibit at the museum, and today I met a very interesting man. A very interesting man indeed."

"David Attenborough?" Rory asks.

"A druid called Steve," Miles says. "I was talking to him about some of the ancient rites he practices, and he told me that even as recently as his great-grandfather's times, local people would hold rituals in which they became the animal they were hunting or fishing for. Or they'd become the predator that would catch it. Sort of a part-psychological thought experiment and good-fortune ritual where you pay homage to the old gods."

"And part drama-club improv exercise," I add.

"Well, sounds made-up," Nanna Maria says, crossing her arms. My grandmother is amazingly skeptical of other people's strange belief systems.

"'There are more things in heaven and earth, Horatio,'" I tell her.

"What's Horatio the bloodhound got to do with it?" Rory asks.

"So," Miles goes on with extreme good humor and patience, which makes me fall for him a little more, "I told him about a dog I know that had recently been turned into a man, and would one of those rituals help him get back to being a dog?"

"Shouldn't think so," Nanna says, as if she is the authority on druid stuff.

"And he said, yes, he thinks it could," Miles says. "Not a bit fazed by the whole situation, which I thought was a good sign."

"Or a bad one," I suggest, chewing my lip.

"And he offered to perform the ritual with us tonight!" Miles breaks into a smile, and I want to kiss him. Instead, I hop. Don't ask me why, it's something to do other than attempting to kiss a man, okay?

"Tonight!" I exclaim, looking at Rory. "We are performing a ritual tonight?"

"Yes," Miles says, his eyes shining. "At the standing stones in Falsgrave Park. Steve says they will be a great substitute for an actual ancient ritual site. I know they have only been in situ since 2003, but he reckons they will do."

"Well, if they're good enough for drunk teenagers to make out on," I say.

"I don't trust druids," Nanna says, gesturing at her chin. "It's the beards."

"Steve didn't have a beard," Miles said.

"Then is he even a druid?" Nanna asks. Nanna really has a thing about this, but now is not a time for woo industries' professional rivalry.

"Well, it's got to be worth a shot," I tell her. "Right, Rory?"

"Right," Rory says. "Please let us, Nanna. What if I wake up tomorrow and I want to try real ale and collect vinyl? I don't even know what vinyl is."

"Fine, but I'm coming too," Nanna says, relenting a little. "To keep an eye on this hairless druid. Make sure he doesn't try and sacrifice Rory as a blood offering. In the meantime, Miles, Genie has something she'd like to talk to you about."

"Do you?" Miles looks at me, repressing a smile. "What's that, then?"

"Oh well," I bluster, waving my hand as if I can shoo away the very thought of telling Miles how I really feel. "It'll wait until after we've performed the pagan transformation ceremony at midnight in a replica standing-stone circle in the park."

Standard Saturday.

Chapter Thirty-Three

W E HAVE TO WAIT for the moon to fully rise, so it's gone ten by the time we get to the park. The night is bright and clear; the air is still warm with the last lingering heat of the day. It's nice up here, at the top of Falsgrave Park—you really feel like you are in the middle of the countryside, with the tall trees gently waving their long graceful green branches in the breeze, giving us glimpses of the starlit town twinkling below, its own brightly lit firmament. Yeah, it's pretty nice up here, and maybe the whole being-in-unrequited-love thing has made me a bit poetic.

Fortunately, there is the obligatory selection of drunk and horny teenagers already occupying the stone circle, and Steve the druid carrying two bulging bin bags to take the edge off my romantic tendencies. Add Nanna Maria and a very excited Rory to the mix, and all desire I might have to throw myself in Miles's arms and beg him to run away with me is tempered to becoming a mere edge of hysteria. Awks.

"Oi, you lot, scarper," Steve the druid tells the kids, waving his bin bags at them. They respond to his order, his cloak, and his bin bags with the natural skepticism and contempt you'd expect from any healthy young person—with howls of derision.

"Sod off, Gandalf!" one lad shouts.

"Yeah, we're not moving for you, you weirdo," a girl clutching a bottle of cherry-flavored cider and sporting some ripped striped tights tells him. "We were here first. Go and have your old person's sex party somewhere else."

"Very far away," another kid says. "Where we can't see you."

"How dare you! We are not here to have a sex party," Steve says, and privately I think that druids are much less chill than I imagined. However, I've thought about it and I don't want to try talking to the teenagers myself, as they are terrifying as heck. Luckily Rory doesn't have the same misgivings.

"Hi, guys," he says, ambling into the middle of the circle, waving at them with both hands like a children's TV presenter from the seventies, only not evil. "The thing is, we need to use these stones to do an ancient ceremony which will hopefully turn me back into a dog—"

"Oh my god, you're doggers?" one kid splutters, horrified and amused. "I thought you were supposed to do that stuff in cars! Not in a park where children play. We are children, you perv!"

"Doggers?" Rory looks at me and shrugs. "Yeah, I guess we are doggers. And the thing is we really need to do our dogging there tonight." He points at the flat surface of the central stone. "It's happening whether you are here or not. So if you don't want to see any old people dogging, then you probably should move. Otherwise we'll just have to dog round you."

"I'm calling the police on you!" one of the girls yells, as the others scramble to their feet and begin to hurry away. Turns out nothing frightens a teenager like the thought of old people doing it.

"We'd better crack on," I say. "Before we're arrested for . . ." I look at Steve. "No one has to take their clothes off, do they?"

"Once upon a time that would have been the way"—Druid Steve nods seriously—"but you won't catch me doing anything in Scarborough without a vest on. Not even in summer. Not even mystical rituals."

He opens the bulkier of his two bin liners full of things.

"There are, however, ceremonial items to be worn. Firstly, Rory must dress as the animal he is to become."

"I brought my lead," Rory says, fastening it around his neck. I hope the cops don't turn up now. He squeaks his pigeon. "And Diego, and a tennis ball."

"Ideally we would have the skin of a golden retriever for you to wear," Steve says, delving into his bin bag and producing an adult-sized dog onesie in yellow faux fur, which he hands to Rory. "But obviously that would be morally dubious to say the least, and besides, I'm a vegan, so I have substituted any animal products with suitable alternatives."

"It's a me costume!" Rory is delighted as he holds the onesie out to look at. "I love it!"

Miles and I turn our backs as Rory takes off his clothes and puts on the onesie. We can hear him mumbling happily to himself as he zips it up.

"THIS IS WEIRD," I tell Miles.

"It is," Miles says happily. "I must say, Genie, that I have done more interesting and weird things since you turned Rory into a dog than I have done in my entire previous life."

"Really?" I say with a pleased little smile. "Wait, that is a compliment, right?"

"It is," he assures me with a grin. "It really is fun knowing you."

"Now for you two," Steve calls to us, just as the romantic notions are in danger of making themselves known.

"You are a doe," Steve tells me, handing me what looks like the top half of a deer skull complete with antlers, and a hairband to secure it in place. "You strap this on your head and wear this round your shoulders." He hands me a faux fur throw from Dunelm, with the sale label still attached. "Don't worry—I had the antlers 3D-printed. They are surprisingly comfortable to wear."

"Sort of thing you might forget you've got on," I say, attempting to position the antlers with little success.

"Here," Miles says, coming to my aid. Standing before him, I lower my eyes as he secures the band at the nape of my neck, acutely aware of the nearness of him. The scent of his skin and the way his shoulders fill out that anorak. Trust me, no one is more surprised than me by the erotic charge of a portable mackintosh, but the heart wants what the heart wants, and in my case it's showerproof.

Just as he is about to step away I dare to look up at him. For a moment our gazes are connected and I wonder if there has ever been a more ridiculous lovelorn moment in the whole of human history than me, just a girl wearing antlers, standing in front of a boy who is about to put a bird on his head.

"You are the crow," Steve tells Miles, passing him a hat. Miles grins with delight as he puts it on, and my heart skips a beat. Because it is impossible not to fall in love with a man who will willingly wear a black beanie hat with a soft-toy crow, complete with yellow googly eyes, sewn onto it, in a probably doomed bid to return a man to dogkind. But Miles is willing to give it a shot, and that is exactly the quality I look for in a man.

"And you . . ." Steve is about to offer Nanna Maria a cow-shaped fur hat, but the look on her face makes him think better of it. "Actually, no need for you to wear anything. You bring your own mystic power to the circle."

"Indeed I do," Nanna Maria says with more mystery than the situation requires. "Indeed I do."

"If you stand opposite me, Madam Maria," Steve says, regarding my nan with naked admiration that might have something to do with her leopard-print velvet flares, "and Miles and Genie, if you stand opposite each other. Rory, you sit on the central stone, doggy-style."

"Is this where we sacrifice him?" I joke.

"Genie . . ." Rory looks anxious and I break the circle to go and stroke his polyester fur. He really has taken to the onesie, and I can see why. It is comforting.

"Everything's fine," I reassure him. "Mad as a box of frogs but perfectly safe. Now you just concentrate on being a dog. As doggy as you possibly can, okay? We will do the rest."

"I will," Rory says, pulling his hood up. "But I can feel my dogness fading away, Genie. It gets more and more like my rabbit-chasing dream every day—sort of far away and fuzzy."

"You've got this, boy," I say, kissing his forehead.

"Ready?" Steve looks at each of us in turn as I return to my spot, and we nod. Then all of a sudden it does seem that the modern world is very far away. The busy town below us is all at once shrouded in mist, and the row of houses over the road recedes into darkness as if it were never there. Even the orange streetlights flicker and dim. Wispy clouds part to reveal the bright moon above, as Steve the druid begins the ceremony. Rory lifts his face to the stars and howls. It's a deep, long, plaintive cry, and in every note I hear his hope, his longing and despair.

As Steve's chants rise into the air something beautiful happens.

All the stars in the sky grow and luminesce, each one a different color, coming together like a rainbow. Suddenly I can see what has always been there with my own eyes.

Magic is real, magic is everywhere. Magic is possibility, and the dreams that we all have the power to make come true for ourselves.

It's hope and love and kindness flowing through every living thing: people, dogs, the dolphins in the bay, the birds in the trees, even cats. Magic happens every time we protect one another, every time we lend a hand, every time we stand up for hope.

Magic is hope, and hope moves mountains when we believe it can.

Looking up at the kaleidoscope of swirling stars I fling my arms wide open and call out to the whole world.

Magic is real; this life, you and me—we are the proof that the universe is miraculous.

Suddenly I know that every little thing is going to be all right just as long as we never stop believing in the power of hope.

"TRY NOT TO TAKE IT TOO HARD," I tell Rory, my arms around his shoulders a few minutes later. The stars have returned to distant glittering sparkles in the sky, and Rory is still not a dog. "I know it didn't work, but I feel like we're getting close. I really do. I know it's possible now. All this means is that we need to find a different way."

"I don't know what went wrong," Steve says, disappointed. "We did everything right. Perhaps it is because the stones are not ancient . . . or that I misinterpreted the runes . . ."

"Or that it is all nonsense," Nanna Maria says tartly.

"Nanna!" I rebuke her. "I am surprised that you, of all people, are so willing to just dismiss the possibility that some of this might actually be true!"

"I'm sorry," Nanna says, apologetic nevertheless. "The ways of the druids do have much to offer us in the modern world. There's a deep connection to the universe and nature, and aligning man's place within the mystery of creation is something very special and powerful." Nanna looks sadly at Rory, who is hugging his arms around himself, head bowed, leaning into Miles, who has his arm around him. "But I believe that most of the time it is an inherited anthropological wisdom rather than . . . actual magic."

"I would have to concur," Miles says with a nod. "No offense, Steve."

"None taken," Steve replies. "I feel sure it's because the stones were only erected in 2003, mind. Or maybe Rory is too far gone."

"I'm not too far gone, am I?" Rory looks anxiously at me. "Am I too far gone?"

"No . . . no, of course you are not," I say, hating to see him so upset. "I reckon it is the stones being modern. We could take a trip to an ancient henge . . . ? Try again!"

"No point," Nanna says. "You can't mix two types of magic and expect it to work. It's like trying to mix oil with water. No, we need to focus on the things we *know* will reverse the wish."

"I don't want to die!" Rory wails.

"I mean, when it comes to Genie's quest," Nanna says.

"I did that—I've done it a lot," I tell her. "I did a bit just then, and it was brilliant. I feel brilliant, hopeful, and excited. But Rory is still human."

"I do think it might be what you refer to as your 'quest-adjacent stuff,'" Nanna Maria tells me as we arrive at our cars. "I'm so proud of you, Genie. You have come so far, trying to help Rory. You don't have far to go. But the universe likes balance and clarity. Secrets always cause chaos." She looks at Miles with the subtlety of a wrecking ball. "At least try."

"What is there to try?" Miles asks.

"For Genie to speak the contents of her heart to the people that matter the most to her," Nanna Maria says. "Not because those people are the key to her happiness, but because she is. And she cannot be her own key until she finds her courage to be true to herself."

"Sounds awful," Miles says.

And, Reader, that is why I am in love with him.

Chapter Thirty-Four

FOR A MOMENT when I wake up, I wonder if the ritual has worked after all, because there's a golden, hairy animal curled up asleep next to me on the bed. Just for one sleepy instant I feel a rush of joy at having my dog back at my side—my sweet, loyal Rory, always happy to see me. And then I remember: Rory can't bring himself to part with his dog onesie. When we got in last night he'd looked at me and asked if he could keep it on, because it felt like home. We'd sat on the sofa and watched *David Attenborough* for ages and I thought about the disco light stars, snow in August, and how one word can change your life. And I knew what I needed to do.

"At least he's a good man," Rory had said after a long moment. "If I have to be a man I want to be like David Attenborough."

"That's a good goal," I'd said. "Or like my dad, or Miles. But you don't have to give up yet, because I have not given up. Okay? I've decided I am going to talk to Miles. And tell him that I love him, and stuff. Just so he knows that he is loved. Maybe Nanna is right. I'm starting to think she has always been right."

"Genie, I love you," Rory said.

"I love you too, boy," I replied. "And I always will."

And then I'd let him sleep in bed with me. It had seemed fair.

After all, I had ruined his life, when all he had ever done was to make mine better. Even now, when he is hogging most of the bed and snoring.

"Hey, Rory?" I nudge him, but he just hugs Diego the squeaky pigeon even closer until it lets out a high-pitched whistle.

"Are you feeling very bad?" I ask him.

"I feel terrible," Rory says, peering at me from beneath his hood. "Everything hurts, but not like when-you-go-to-the-vet's hurts. It hurts because I feel everything, and think about everything, and I know too much and not enough and I feel sort of helpless, Genie. Not good helpless, like before when you had to take the lid off the peanut butter for me. Bad helpless, like nothing I do matters."

"Oh, Rory," I say. "I think you are almost entirely human now."

"I don't want to be human, Genie," he says, reaching for me. "I want it to stop, please. If we can't change me back, if nothing works to make this go away, will you take me to the vet's, please, and ask them to send me across the bridge?"

"Rory, no!" Rubbing my hands over my face, I sit up in bed. It's now-or-never time.

"It hasn't come to that yet, Rory," I reassure him. "For starters you feel better in that onesie, right? I reckon that's because there is still a lot of you that is dog." Or it's a symptom of the onset of depression, but I decide to gloss over that possibility. I reach for my dressing gown, tying the knot around my waist with a decisive yank.

"I'll go and talk to Miles right now," I say. "I will tell him the contents of my heart, like Nanna Maria said I should, okay? I will say to him, 'Miles,' I will say, 'I am so in love with you. I don't know if you feel the same way—but I need to tell you. I need you to know, even though it terrifies me to death. I need you to know that you are loved by me.'"

"Are you going to say exactly those words, just like that?" Rory asks.

"Yeah, maybe, more or less. Why? Is that okay?"

"Yes, and I know you hate saying your inside feelings out loud, Genie," Rory says. "I get that now more than ever. So . . . thank you. I know you are doing this for me."

"I am doing it for you, because everything that's happened to you is my fault," I say, patting his hood head. "But I'm doing it for me too, Rory. A girl can't spend her whole life in stasis. Sometimes you've got to stick your head above the parapet and get it blown to smithereens like a watermelon."

"You have disturbed me with that image," Rory says, squeezing Diego so hard that he wheezes another squeak. "Want me to come?" Rory's voice is tremulous.

"No, you stay here with Diego. I'll be back soon. If at any point you feel like you are sprouting a tail or something, bark, okay?"

"K," Rory says. "Love you, Genie."

"Love you, Rory."

"Who's a good boy?"

"You are, feller."

He manages a faint smile for me as I close the bedroom door.

It occurs to me as I put on my slippers that I should probably make a bit more of an effort with my physical appearance, considering I'm about to give Miles an unsolicited declaration of love. Except I know that when it comes to Miles it doesn't matter how I look. The way he feels about me won't have anything to do with what I'm wearing or if I'm having a good-hair day. None of that stuff matters to him. So I shove my hair in a scrunchie and wave at the binman as I knock on Miles's front door.

"Early for you," Miles observes as he opens it, his arms full of Matilda, whom he is cradling like a baby, her silly, soppy paws flopping like a bunny rabbit's. I can't help but chuckle at the sight.

"What's so funny?" he asks as I follow him into the kitchen, now with Matilda hitched up on his shoulder peering at me curiously.

"Just how adorable the murder cat can be when she wants to be," I say, unable to resist stroking the silky soft patch over her pink nose with the tip of my finger. "She looks as sweet as a kitten!"

"She is as sweet as a kitten," Miles says, nuzzling his cheek against her cloud of silvery fur. "It's just that she doesn't make a big show of it like a dog does. She knows I'm anxious at the moment, so she's trying to comfort me by being around me more. And she is also trying to get me to give her a second breakfast."

"Who doesn't want a second breakfast," I say, taking a seat at the same table where Claudia asked him on a date a couple of days ago. Matilda hops out of Miles's arms onto the counter, where she paces and purrs as he opens a pouch of gourmet cat food and empties it into a little china dish for her.

"I know you are not a cat person," Miles smiles, stroking Matilda's head as she eats, "but she means the world to me. I don't know what I'd do without her. After Nan died I went to uni, got a degree, and did a postgrad—all the things that Mum wanted me to do—but for all of that time, the whole of it, I didn't have anyone." He pauses for a moment, his eyes on Matilda. "Except for her. I mean, it wasn't like I was bullied or victimized. I knew people. I was in three societies. But I was still alone. Just because I'm me. I know it sounds pathetic, a grown man talking about missing his mum . . ."

"No, it doesn't," I say. "Not at all."

"What I'm trying to say is that being tolerated by a cat is not the same as being loved by a dog. What we have isn't mindless devotion, but it is something special. Something real, because I know if she didn't like me, she'd leave. We take care of each other."

"I can see that," I say. This would be the perfect time to mention that I love him, but somehow I can't quite seem to get the words out.

"Anyway, it's not that I am not a cat person," I tell him. "It's more that I just don't know any cats beyond nodding terms. And Rory has always been really quite skeptical about them as a species, which has influenced my own feelings. But I think, given the opportunity, I could probably be a cat person too. I mean, there isn't a rule that you can only like one kind of pet, is there?"

Having finished her meal, Matilda sits on the worktop and begins to clean her paws, watching me all the while with her cool, yellow gaze.

"At first I thought that Matilda wasn't my kind of person. Then I thought that actually she was really interesting and fun and she became one of my best friends," I say as the cat literally looks down her nose at me. "Now I realize that I actually like her quite a lot, that I've liked her quite a lot, more than quite a lot, for a very long time. Because she is kind and funny and accepting and life without her wouldn't be nearly as fun."

"You are using Matilda as a metaphor to talk about us, aren't you?" Miles says.

"Yes, yes I am." I smile weakly. "I don't think I tell you nearly enough how much you mean to me, and how glad I am to know you."

Miles presents me with a cup of tea, taking a seat opposite me within what some people might call kissing distance.

"I'm really glad to know you too." Miles looks at me for a long time. At least sixteen seconds more than is comfortable, and long enough to make me wish I'd taken a shower after all. Right, come on, Eugenie. It's go time."

"Miles, I have to tell you something . . ."

"Do you remember that Christmas dance that you took me to, your first term at college?"

"Of course," I say. "How could I forget it?"

"Do you still have the dress you made?" he asks.

"Oh yes, I do, the emerald-green avant-garde off-the-shoulder bias cut with the split. I wore it with my pink Doc Martens boots. Yes, I still have it. Though it might not fit me anymore . . ." I smile at the thought of us walking into the dance together. "And I made you a shirt to match, with big billowing sleeves and a pussy bow fifteen years before Harry Styles thought of it. Exactly the same shade of green except it had"—I pause, my eyes widening—"a leopard-print pattern. I made you an emerald-green leopard-print-pattern pussy bow shirt, and you wore it so well."

Miles smiles. "You do remember."

"I remember everything," I say. "Recently I've been thinking about it all the time."

"The band started playing 'All I Want for Christmas Is You,'" Miles says. "The hall was strung with hundreds of colored lights, and we ran outside just as it began to snow . . ."

"And then we . . . we almost kissed," I finish for him. "But Aiden showed up."

"Aiden showed up," Miles said.

"Miles, I wish I'd—"

The doorbell rings sharply, followed by a loud rap on the door.

"We could pretend we aren't in?" Miles suggests as we both freeze.

"Miles! It's me! Claudia! Claudia-from-work!" Claudia calls from the other side of the door. "Thought you might like to go for breakfast?"

"Oh, it's Claudia," I say, so stupidly that I would quite like to stick my head in the toaster.

"Claudia, yes, for lo, it is her," Miles says, not an awful lot less stupidly.

"Probably better let her in!" I grin madly.

"Yes." He nods. "I'm going to do that right now."

Matilda follows him.

The colored lights, the snow, the song: they were all telling me that the kiss that Miles and I never had ten years ago might not be gone. It might just be on a very long pause. Because I know for sure that, for some reason, Miles had that same leopard-print shirt in his bag.

It's only after I hear Miles open the door that I realize I am sitting in his kitchen in my dressing gown. For a second I think about heading out the back door and over the fence, but I am not wearing any pants, which Claudia might find even more troubling were she to catch a glimpse of my nether regions. So I head briskly for the door like nothing is out of the ordinary at all.

"Terribly sorry," I say, like every good British person would in the same situation. "I'll just get out from under your feet."

I gesture toward the front door, which Claudia has left open, and which I can't quite make it through while both of them are standing abreast, so to speak.

"Genie, you are here." Claudia breaks away from Miles, who takes a deep breath in.

"Popped round to borrow a cup of sugar," I tell her, realizing a beat too late the flaw in my plan.

"But you don't seem to be leaving with any sugar?" Claudia laughs, and looks from me to Miles. I look down at my empty hands.

"I've got this really wrong, haven't I," she says, raising her palms to her cheeks. "I thought that there was something between you two, but when you said it was fine to ask Miles out I thought I had imagined it. But now here I am and you can cut the sexual tension here with a knife. Oh god, I'm so mortified."

"No, none of this is your fault, it's all me," I say, stepping forward. And as I do I step on Matilda's tail.

The cat hisses and yowls, shooting off through the open front door.

We hear the screech of brakes and a dull thud.

Chapter Thirty-Five

'M SO SORRY, MATE." The cabdriver stands over Miles as he kneels at Matilda's side. "She just shot out right in front of me. I was only going twenty and I braked right away."

Sinking to the ground next to Miles, I stare at Matilda, who suddenly seems so much smaller. Miles just stares at her, completely frozen. There's no blood but she is completely still. This is awful.

"Is she . . . ?" Claudia stands behind me, speaking through the fingers that are clamped over her mouth. Just then my front door opens and Rory comes out, still onesie clad, and crouches down. For a moment I'm afraid he will laugh to see Matilda so badly hurt, but instead he lays his ear very gently against her tummy and listens.

"She is breathing," he says, "and I can hear a heartbeat. We need to take her to the vet, Genie, quick. From what I can smell she is bleeding. On the inside. Go get her cage and a blanket, Claudia—hurry. Genie, go get your car keys. Now!"

All I can think of as I race into the house, pulling a pair of jeans on before I grab my keys and shove my feet back into my slippers, is Miles, telling me that before Matilda he thought he would always be alone. And the look of love for Matilda.

That cat cannot die.

When I return Miles is sitting in the passenger seat. Matilda is lying in her cage on his lap. His face is blank as he stares down at her. Tears stand in his eyes.

"Miles, I'm so sorry," Claudia says. "I didn't mean for it to happen."

"I know." Miles nods. "Come on, let's go.

"Claudia, want to wait with Rory?" I ask. "We'll call as soon as we know anything."

Claudia nods.

"Right, let's go," I say. A quick glance in my rearview mirror and I see yellow-clad Rory put his arm around Claudia and guide her inside.

RORY HAS CALLED AHEAD so that the vet's is waiting for us as we pull into the car park. A nurse takes Matilda's crate from Miles, asking him questions as we follow her into the waiting room. Miles walks toward the consulting room with the nurse, and then, after a moment, turns to me and holds out his hand. Taking it, I follow him inside.

Rory had been right. The vet tells us that there is internal bleeding, and that she can't be sure how bad the damage done to Matilda is until she operates.

"And you'll call us as soon as you know?" I ask the nurse once again.

"Yes, it will be a long surgery, but as soon as we know how she's doing we will let you know. Try not to worry—she's in really good hands."

"I don't feel like I should leave her," Miles says anxiously, pacing from side to side. "I don't want to leave her, Genie. She might sense that I've gone, and she might be afraid . . . She might need me to be close by so that she has a reason to . . . to make it."

"I know," I say. "It's okay. We will wait. As long as it takes."

He nods and keeps nodding. I can see him turning in on himself, his anxiety climbing and clinging on to him like an ever-winding vine.

I turn to the nurse. "We'll wait outside in the car—is that okay?"

"Of course it is," the nurse says. "We will keep you updated, I promise."

I wind my arm around Miles's shoulders and steer him outside.

"We are close by," I tell him, when we're in the car. "Matilda knows you are here."

"You must think I'm insane," Miles mutters.

"Of course not. Matilda's not just a cat," I say. "She's your family."

Miles looks at me. "Thank you, Genie."

"Hey, Miles," I say, an idea coming to me. "You know your backpack? Inside I saw an old Walkman, once. What do you listen to on that?"

Miles reaches for the bag in the back and brings it out. Unzipping it, he brings out the Walkman.

"It's my mum's," he says, setting it down between our seats. "It had one tape in it: a mixtape. *Marie's Fav Tunes.*" He holds up the headset. "It will be a bit awkward, but would you like to listen with me?"

"I really would," I say. Leaning closer, we each press one of the foam earpieces against our heads, Miles holding the narrow band between us. "I Can See Clearly Now" by Jimmy Cliff begins to play. Reaching across my lap, I find Miles's other hand and take it in mine.

I'm not sure how long we sit side by side, ear to ear, hand in hand in the car park at the vet's. Time doesn't seem to matter. There is just the two of us, waiting, and Marie's resolutely cheerful playlist, full of optimism and love. We watch the white clouds roll over the rooftops, and as we listen I feel like I am starting to get to know the woman that Miles misses so much. Her love for Motown, Northern soul, and the Bee Gees. There's Kate Bush and AC/DC, A-ha and Bon Jovi. I get the impression that she was irrepressible, eclectic, and curious, that she wasn't the sort of woman to make judgments, and that she loved like a lioness. I don't know, but it seems it's all there, in the static-filled gaps between tracks on the tape, almost as if I can listen to her past whispering to me. I'm starting to see that Nan is right about that too. That the voices of the people that we think are out of our reach forever are still there if we only listen.

The last song finishes and the tape clicks to a stop.

Miles lowers the headset, and then ever so slowly lowers his head to rest on my shoulder. I hold my head against his.

The vet comes out of the door in her blue scrubs, walking purposefully toward us. Sitting up, we look at each other and get out of the car.

"Is she . . . ?" Miles starts to ask the question before the vet can say anything.

"She will be fine," she tells Miles. "What a little fighter. She did really well. A close call, for sure, but no major organs damaged. Matilda will need to stay with us for a few days while we keep an eye on her, and she's officially down to eight lives, but she is one tough little cookie."

"Oh, thank god," I breathe, feeling a sob of relief rise in my throat.

"Thank you, vet." Miles hugs the vet unprompted, and she laughs, politely disengaging herself as soon as she can.

"Can I see her?" he asks.

"You can peer through the window and get a glimpse but that's all," she tells him. "Then get your girlfriend to take you home and take care of you, okay?"

"Okay," Miles says. I know it's probably because he's tired and emotional that he doesn't pick up on the innocent mistake, but oh, how nice it would be if that were true.

CLAUDIA IS STANDING in front of my house when we pull up, Rory standing behind her, still dressed as his former self.

She rushes over to greet us as we get out of the car.

"Well, is she going to be okay?" Claudia asks Miles.

"Yes," Miles says, looking at me as if to check. "Yes, the vet said that her recovery will take some time but that she would be okay."

"Oh, thank god," Claudia says, half collapsing in relief. "I am so sorry about all this. About me exploding into your lives like I did . . . somehow I feel this is all my fault."

"It is not your fault," Miles says. "Please don't think that, Claudia."

"I'll go, shall I?" Claudia asks uncertainly. "Call you tomorrow?"

"Actually, Claudia, I wonder if you wouldn't mind coming in for a minute?"

"'Course not!" Claudia says.

"Bye," I say as Miles and Claudia vanish into his house. When I go to open my door, I realize I don't have my key. And I am still in my nightie. I peer through the window and Rory is lying on the sofa, with his headphones on. Listening to K-pop probably.

"Roar!" I bang on the window but he's oblivious. Typical man.

Right, well, the only thing to do is to give Miles and Claudia time to do whatever it is they are doing—god, I hope it's PG-rated—and then ask Miles for my spare key. I sit down on the doorstep and look at my slippers.

Miles's front door opens. I try to blend in with my door.

"So, see you at work tomorrow?" Miles asks Claudia.

"Sure will!" Claudia says. "And listen, Miles, thank you. For being straight with me. A lot of people would have let that drag on and, well, it's okay, you know. I'm kind of glad, actually. I'd rather have a forever friend than a for-now date."

"Thanks, Claudia; for the record I do think you are amazing," Miles says. "All the lads at work fancy you."

"You got that right," she says, almost tripping over my feet. "Oh, hello, Genie. Why are you sitting on your doorstep in your nightie?"

"Locked myself out, classic me," I tell her. "I wasn't, you know, earwigging."

"I know," Claudia says. "Hey, tell Rory I'll see him Tuesday for the K-pop club night?"

"Yeah, I will—are you okay?"

Claudia's smile is a little sad, but her eyes are bright.

"Going to be," she says with a nod. "See you, Genie."

"I'll get your key," Miles says, as Claudia drives off. While he's gone I pace up and down, trying to feel purposeful and determined. This is it, time to complete my quest-adjacent quest at last.

"Here you go." Miles puts the key in the palm of my hand.

"So, you and Claudia, you've decided not to date?" I ask him.

"It's for the best," he says. "Thanks so much for today, Genie. See you later."

Miles lets himself into his house and closes the door without saying another word. Wait, what?

Chapter Thirty-Six

"WHAT'S HAPPENING?" Rory asks as I let myself in.

"Miles and Claudia decided not to date after all and I was about to say, Oh, by the way, I love you, and he just went in his house and shut the door."

"I mean with dinner," Rory says. "I'm starving."

"Rory, tell me what to do?" I plead.

"Call Uber Eats?" he suggests.

"About Miles!" I exclaim.

"Oh, I think only you have the answer to that one," Rory says. "I'll order a pizza while you think about it."

When I close my eyes. I'm back to that moment at the Christmas dance when Miles took my hand, and we stood under the rainbow stairs and felt like two puzzle pieces that had finally found their perfect fit.

"I know what to do," I tell Rory. "It's grand gesture time, boy."

"Are we going on a madcap chase to an airport for some reason?" Rory asks.

"You'll just have to wait and see."

I'M DRESSED and running down the stairs when there's a knock at the door.

"Now that's what I call service," Rory says. "I haven't even ordered the pizza yet because I wasn't sure if we were going to the airport or not. Oh, Genie, you look nice! Are we having a party?"

"It's not the pizza man, you dork," I tell him. I know who it is. I hand him a CD. "Cue this up to track twelve and when I tell you to, press play, okay?"

"I don't even know what this is," Rory says.

"Figure it out, then!"

I open the door and Miles is standing there wearing an emerald-green leopard-print shirt with a pussy bow. It matches my dress perfectly.

"Genie," he says. "I've been carrying this shirt around for . . . well, a long time. I thought . . . I thought one day I'd just put it on and you'd remember, but when you saw it in the rucksack and never mentioned it . . . I thought it was too late. But the thing is—"

"No, wait!" I stop him. "Miles, I have to complete my quest-adjacent quest."

I take his hands in mine.

"Milesington, you were there for me on the most peculiar day of my life, no questions asked. And you were there for me on the saddest." I think for a moment. "You have always been there on the most fun and happiest days too, because a lot of the time it's you that makes them that way. You've always shown me that you care for me, and somehow I didn't really understand how much I care for you until I turned my dog into a man."

"I know and—" Miles tries to interrupt me but I press my finger to his lips. A rather startling move, I'll admit.

"Rory, press play," I call into the living room.

"Hang on!" Rory calls.

"Rory . . . ?"

About fifteen seconds of silence pass by and just when I think I'm going to have to go in there and do it myself, the opening notes to "All I Want for Christmas Is You" fill the summer evening air.

"You are the kindest, nerdiest, sexiest man I have ever known. I am so in love with you that I can't think or breathe or eat until I am sure you know that you mean everything to me. We started something fifteen years ago. If it's okay with you, I'd really like to finish it now."

Stepping out onto the pavement, I take Miles's hands in mine. Standing on my toes, I search his eyes. He smiles. And finally, *finally*, I know what it's like to kiss the man I love.

My arms wind around his neck, his hands pull me close to him, and out of a clear blue sky on a warm August evening, snow begins to slowly fall just for us. The streetlights flicker on in all the colors of the rainbow, and the music from the living room seems to fill the evening as our feet float a good four inches into the air. I know all of this, I see and I feel it, and I know that I am making it happen, because I am happy and because, like every other female in my family line—like *every* woman *everywhere*—I have magic running through my veins.

And at exactly the same time I'm oblivious to it all, because all I can think about is kissing Miles and Miles kissing me.

"Like, so now can we order pizza?" Rory asks. "Like the song's repeated three times already and I think you might be at risk of frostbite."

When Miles and I pull apart we are both grinning just like the stupid kids we used to be.

Miles looks around at the snow. "Genie, how is this possible?"

"Good things are always possible," I tell him. "Look at you. Want to come in for pizza?"

"Not tonight. We've got all the time in the world." Miles shakes his head. "There's no rush. Let's to do it right, like we just met last week."

"I'm some ways, I kind of think we did," I say.

"Good night, Eugenie," he says. "I'll be thinking about that kiss all night. See you tomorrow."

"See you then," I say. We kiss again, more gently this time. Careful and tender, our eyes lock for a long moment before we part again. The snow settles on the pavement outside my door, defying the warmth of the night.

"'Night," I say, closing the door.

Three seconds later there's another knock.

Miles is standing there.

"I forgot to mention," he says. "I'm in love with you too."

I'm walking on air, dancing on sunshine, living on the moon, so it takes me a moment to realize something when I return to the living room to see Rory standing there in his dog onesie.

"Genie," he says. "You've completed the quest, and the quest-adjacent quest, and I am still not a dog. I'm never going to be a dog again, am I?"

Chapter Thirty-Seven

DID EVERYTHING YOU TOLD ME TO," I tell Nanna Maria.

It's been approximately forty-five minutes since I kissed Miles, and it's very hard to be this happy when your dog is this sad and despairing. So I bundled Rory into the car and went to see Nanna.

"And beautifully too," Nanna says, glowing with pride. "Snow in August. It's been a long time since we've had such a powerful soul in the family."

"Yes, and it's so cool, but what about Rory?"

Nana frowns deeply as Rory flings himself onto her pink velvet chaise longue and stares listlessly out the window. "I really thought that would do it."

"So now what?" I ask her. "Rory is getting less doggy by the day. If we can't fix him soon he'll be stuck like this for the next forty years, and he is not keen, Nanna—I mean like *really* not keen."

"I can see that," Nanna Maria says. "He hasn't even touched those custard creams."

"So, what's the plan now?" I ask her. "Is there a rare plant we can source, a coven we can dial up, maybe a wizard with a window?"

Nanna Maria takes me into her bedroom, where I half expect

her to pull down one of her ornaments like a lever and reveal a wall tooled up with eye of newt, a variety of wands, and preloaded crystal balls. Instead she simply sits down on the edge of her bed, legs crossed at the ankles, hands folded neatly in her lap.

"And?" I ask her.

"Eugenie," she says, "it's time for me to be completely honest with you."

"Okaaaay," I say uncertainly.

"I have no idea what to do now."

"But . . . but . . . but . . . but . . ." I'm getting déjà vu.

"I know," Nanna Maria goes on, "I'm so sorry. But I think we have to tell Rory that he's going to stay human."

"But Nana, how can I?" I say. "How can I be so happy, when he will be so sad? I've failed him."

"That's not true, Genie," Rory says, appearing in the doorway. I wonder how long he has been listening.

"You have always made me feel happy and safe, but this last week with you has been the best, despite everything. We've played and talked, and I did disco dancing and ate chocolate. Even though I am scared and confused, you've been there for me."

I hold out my arms and Rory walks into my embrace. After a while Nanna Maria joins in too.

"I am sorry, my darling Rory," Nanna Maria tells him.

"It's not your fault," Rory tells her. "I thought I wouldn't be okay being human. But then I realized that Genie is my magic. She's my wish come true. It will be hard, but I can make it as a man."

"Oh, Rory!" I cry into his shoulder. "I'm so sorry I'm getting your onesie wet, and I'm supposed to be comforting you."

"That's okay," Rory says. "Look, I won't ever completely forget about being a dog. But I know that nearly all the dog bits of me have gone now. So before I have to get a job and a mortgage and figure out my sexuality now that Afghan hounds are off the table, can we have one more doggy day? On the beach tomorrow? Me, you, Miles, Granny Rita, Grandad, and Nanna Maria?"

"Of course we can," I say. "And you know what? You might be almost fully human now, but I have learned how to be more dog because of you. And I promise you that I won't let either of us forget that."

"You are my best friend, Genie," Rory says. "That will never change."

Chapter Thirty-Eight

THE DAY IS WARM, the air still. The sea is quiet and calm.

Miles and I regard each other rather shyly.

"Eugenie," he says, with a small bow.

"Milesington," I reply with a curtsey. I can do that now.

"I was wondering if we might kiss again?" Miles suggests.

"I believe I have room in my schedule right now," I say.

Hesitantly, we approach one another, with slow smiles and tilted heads. I stand up on my tiptoes and our lips almost meet when there was a loud insistent rapping at the window.

"Can we go to the beach now?" Rory asks, his nose pressed flat against the window.

"There's always going to be three of us in this relationship, isn't there," Miles says with a sweet smile.

"No," I tell him. "There's always going to be four. Don't forget about Matilda."

Then we kiss anyway, even with Rory still banging on the window.

IT'S STILL PRETTY EARLY, and the tide is far out. The sea sparkles under the early morning sun, and the firm golden sand is dotted with a few early sun seekers. I scan the beach, seeing families and couples on blankets, towels, and deck chairs, setting up for a day of just being together.

Dogs are allowed at this end of the bay, right down by the spa. Two little terriers run in and out of the waves yapping at each other. Finally, I see a figure that I recognize sitting on a chair that she has brought out from the shop: Nanna Maria, with a large black lace parasol opened over her head, bringing the Victorian Gothic funeral vibe to a day at the beach like only she can. Mum and Dad are lying on towels next to her, holding hands. Dad is reading; Mum's face is hidden under a huge floppy sun hat. Kelly, Dave, and their two are next door, making sandcastles.

"There!" Rory hops with excitement when he spots them, and races across the sand toward them, leaving Miles and me trailing behind.

"Is he going to be all right?" Miles asks as Rory skids to a stop, covering Mum in sand. Mum sits up and hugs him for a long time. I love my mum. Not all mums are like her, endlessly kind and patient. I am one lucky girl.

"I hope he will be," I say, thinking of how Mum cared for me all those years that I wasn't. "All we can do is love him, and help him for as long as it takes, even if it takes forever. That's what love is, I think."

Miles nods. "We'll love him and help him forever."

We stop for a moment, exchanging glances. We are only two kisses in and yet, somehow, I know that when Miles says forever, he really means it. I mean it too.

"Forever," I repeat, kissing him lightly on the cheek. I tell you what, if three kisses get me *this* hot under the collar, then Lord only knows what happens when we finally get some alone time.

"Granny Rita made sausage sandwiches!" Rory says happily as

we join the family, his head in her cooler. "Oh, and cheese cubes! I love cheese cubes. Why does cheese taste better when it's cubed, Genie?"

"One of the mysteries of the universe," I reply.

"And how are you managing?" Mum asks Rory. "Now that it looks likes you'll be man-shaped permanently."

"I'm okay," Rory says, sitting back on his heels and looking toward where the terriers are still cavorting in the waves. "At least I have Genie, and Miles too now that they do the kissing and the butt rubbing. And cheese cubes, and ziplock bags, and chocolate and kebabs and dancing. You know, being human isn't all bad. There's quite a lot to be happy about. I'm surprised you all moan about it so much."

"But you'd still rather be a dog?" Mum asks.

"Yeah," Rory says, with a shrug. "Yeah. But it's okay, Granny Rita, I'll be okay with Genie's help."

"Rory will be just fine," Nanna announces, fanning herself with a red silk painting fan she bought in Spain. "There is one last change yet to come."

"Whatever you say, Nan," I say, giving Mum a look.

"You know what I feel like doing?" Dad says, as he sits up. "I feel like digging a bloody big hole for no particular reason, how about you, Rory?"

"Yeah, Grandpa," Rory says happily. "That's one of my favorite things to do, how did you know?"

"It was that time you dug up my azaleas that gave me a clue," Dad says, as they move off a few feet and set about digging enthusiastically, using their hands as tools.

"Miles." Mum offers Miles a can of pop from her cooler. "I'm so pleased about you and Genie getting together."

"Thanks, Rita, me too," Miles says so naturally that it fills my heart to the very brim with happiness. This is us now. Me and Miles and Rory and Matilda. Weird, odd, and happy to be together. This is us.

"They will be together forever," Nan tells us. "I've seen it written in the stars. At last my Eugenie has found her Miles. And Miles has found his Eugenie. There will be hard times, of course. But these two will never let one another down. I have seen it."

This time I decide that my nan is completely right. She has seen it, after all. And you know what? So have I.

GRADUALLY THE BEACH FILLS UP AND UP, until you can hardly see the gold sand for the brightly colored towels and sandcastles. It feels sort of weird to let Miles see me in my swimming costume before he's seen me in my pants, so I feel rather coy when eventually I relent to Rory's pleas and follow him to the sea for a play. But Miles surprised me by removing his shirt and trousers to reveal some snug-fitting swim shorts. All I do is hope we get some alone time within the next twenty-four hours because, man, Miles is *fine*.

The sea is cold, and then warm, and we three spend several minutes splashing and chucking an inflatable beach ball around, laughing to see how happy it makes Rory. He loves diving under the water, and exploding up out of it to make us shriek.

"I'm going back for cheese cubes," he tells us after a while, grinning broadly. "I can do that now that I am a human. I can have cheese cubes whenever I like."

"Be there in a sec!" I call after him.

I turn to look at Miles, who is glistening with water droplets, and I admire the strength in his shoulders and arms.

"You look very beautiful with fewer clothes on," Miles tells me, inching toward me through the gentle rise and fall of the water. His arms encircle my waist and he draws our bodies close together. I complete us by winding my arms around his neck and cinching my breasts tight against his chest. The heat of his firm body warms me even in the cool sea.

"You look very beautiful too," I say, looking into his eyes.

Our kiss is long and luxurious. I am alert to the touch of his fingertips trailing across my bare back and the press of his thighs against mine.

"I would very much like to be alone with you," Miles whispers into my ear.

"We will be," I say, tilting my head back to smile at him. "And the best thing is we've got all the time in the world to get to know each other as quickly or slowly as we like."

"Yes, but can we start with quickly?" Miles says. "Then perhaps another quickly, and then a very long slowly."

"Yes." I laugh. "I want to try all the speeds."

We are about to kiss again, when there is a commotion on the beach. Looking across I can see a small crowd gathered around, and then catch a glimpse of Rory in the middle of it.

"Fuck's sake!" Even from a few feet out from the shore we can hear the angry growl. I look up and see the awful man that made Rory so scared, his first owner, with his poor pregnant dog cowering and trembling beside him.

"You leave her alone," Rory shouts. Miles and I exchange a glance.

"We better go help," I say.

"Right behind you," Miles says. "Just got to wait to . . . er, cool down a bit."

"YOU TALKING TO ME?" The bloke fronts up to Rory, puffing out his pigeon chest and flexing his wiry biceps, even though Rory towers over him.

"Yes, I am talking to you, Andy," Rory says steadily. "I can't see anyone else around who is kicking their dog."

The crowd that has gathered murmurs in agreement with Rory.

"I saw it too," a woman says. "You should be ashamed."

"I'll be whatever I want to be," the bloke spits back at her. "It's my property." He looks at Rory as if he might recognize him from somewhere. "And how do you know my name, anyways?"

"*She* is a living being," Rory says. "Her name is Mabel, that's what the old lady she lived with called her. She is gentle and kind, and she tried really hard to please you, Andy. You left her locked out when she was in season and now she is having puppies, but you don't feed her enough. She is really poorly, hurt, and afraid because of you, Andy. Because you need to make Mabel feel scared just to make yourself feel strong and important."

"You don't know anything about me," Andy tells Rory, shoving him in his chest with two fingers. "It wouldn't have a home if I hadn't given it one."

I'm about to step in, but Rory holds his hand out to stop me. Miles arrives at my side. We exchange a worried look. I lock my fingers into Miles's. I hope Rory knows we have his back.

"You'd be surprised by what I know," Rory says. "Oh, I know a lot about you, Andy. I know that you received a lifetime ban from owning dogs, after you were caught putting your last dog into fights, even though he never wanted to fight. Even though all he wanted to be was your friend, which you should have appreciated, Andy. Because no one else does."

"What are you, the dog police?" the bloke says, but his bravado is wearing thin.

"Yes," Rory says, and this time he flexes his muscles, broadens his chest to show his power. "Yes, where you are concerned, I am the dog police. I don't want to fight, I don't like fighting, Andy. I am a peaceful guy. But I am pretty sure that if I make one call, we'd find out you are in violation of an order that will cost you a lot of money in fines, and might even see you go inside."

"So . . . what?" Andy looks around, his eyes darting back and forth, searching for a way out of the crowd.

"Give Mabel to me, and I'll let you go," Rory says, holding his hand out for the lead.

"Yeah, give the dog police Mabel and we'll let you go," someone else in the crowd shouts in support. Other people voice their approval of the idea too. Looking around I realize it's not just Rory, me, and Miles that care about Mabel. It's everyone here. Everyone here is ready to stick up for that sweet girl. But it's Rory that's standing his ground.

"You bloody what?" Andy shouts. "What do you think gives you lot the right to tell me how to treat my property?"

"Haven't you heard?" a lady with a baguette in one hand, and a lovely cuddly Doberman on a lead in the other, says. "We are a nation of dog lovers."

"Give Mabel to me, Andy," Rory says, his tone calm but powerful.

Andy looks around, and he finally realizes that he is not leaving the beach with Mabel. Not when all these people are determined to stop him. He hands the lead to Rory and tries to walk away.

"One more thing." Rory's voice stops him in his tracks. "If you ever try and keep any other animal again, and I mean any animal, I will know. And I will come and find you. Are we clear?"

"Fuck's sake. I don't bloody care, more bother than they're worth," Andy says. He tries to leave but Rory steps in front of him.

"Are we clear?" Rory repeats, slowly.

"Fine, yes, we are clear." Andy cowers. "Can I go now . . . Please?"

Rory thinks for a moment.

"No, I have one more thing to say."

"What's that?" Andy asks, eyes down.

"I forgive you, Andy."

"What?" Andy glances at him.

"You had a rescue golden retriever; you made his life a misery. And I want you to know that I forgive you for that. And that you don't frighten me anymore. I realize now that you are nothing to be afraid of, and all of that, it's in the past. It's never going to happen again, because I've changed. And I'm stronger now. Forgiving you isn't about making you feel better, it's about setting myself free from that hurt. And that, Andy, is the best thing about being a human. If you wanted to, you could change too."

"Like I give a fuck what you think."

Shaking his head Rory steps aside and Andy hurries away a few steps before turning back.

"Thanks," Andy says.

The crowd claps and congratulates Rory, moving around him, patting his back, shaking his hand. I lose sight of him for a second and then there he is, crouched down with his arms around Mabel.

"Rory!" Tears fill my eyes as I sink on the sand in front of him, flinging one arm around him and one arm around Mabel. "You were amazing."

Laughing, Miles joins us.

"Seriously, mate, you were so cool," he says, stroking Mabel's head gently. She leans into his hand with her broad head, glad of a kind touch. A tremor of worry trembling down her back.

"You're okay, Mabel," Miles tells her, his voice low and gentle. "You are safe now and so are all your pups. We are going to look after you."

LATER, MUCH LATER, after another trip to the vet to visit Matilda and get Mabel checked over, we are home. All of us, even Matilda, whom the vet let come home since she was doing so well, even if she does hate her murder cone. I'm nervous for a second when I open the front door, but I don't need to be.

Rory walks into the front room; grabbing Diego he takes his seat on the sofa and gives Matilda a long look.

"I suppose you are okay for a cat," he says. She turns her back on him, which I think might be the closest we will ever get to her acknowledging that he's not that bad either. Mabel is hesitant, standing in the doorway looking warily around, but after a few moments Rory gets down from the sofa and sits on the floor. Mabel comes and sits next to him, and he puts his arm around her. Slowly Mabel leans into him and sinks to the floor. This is my new family.

IT'S ALMOST MIDNIGHT when Miles's hand reaches for mine. I turn to look at him.

"Thank you," I say. "For being exactly who you are. For being mine."

"You and me on this sofa, holding hands, is more than I ever thought possible for me. But now I know that anything is possible."

"We could even . . ." I glance at Rory and the sleeping animals. "Go to my bedroom? That is definitely a possibility."

"One I think we should investigate at once," Miles says. As we get up from the sofa, Rory looks up from *Love Island*.

"Time to rub butts?" he asks.

"You go up," I tell Miles. "I'll be one second. I just need to say something to Rory."

"Fine," Rory says once Miles has gone up to my bedroom. "I'll stop talking about butts."

"That's not it," I say, sitting next to him. "I'm so happy, Rory, and I hate that you aren't."

"It's okay, I'm happy you're happy," he says. "And you know, being turned into a human has let me do something I'd have found really hard to as a dog."

"What's that?" I ask him.

"Move on from the things that hurt and frightened me," he says. "So maybe it won't be so bad being human. Eventually."

"But you still wish you were a dog?" I say, leaning my head on his shoulder. An alarm goes off on my watch, and I silence it.

"I really do wish I was a dog again," Rory admits, looking at Mabel as she runs in her dreams.

"Well, whatever happens next," I tell him, "you will always be beautiful you."

We hug each other, and I kiss him on the forehead, and give him one last look before I climb the stairs to where I find Miles standing on the landing.

"Did you get lost?" I ask him.

"Didn't want to go into your room without you," he confesses. "Bit nervous, honestly. Aren't you?"

"Not at all," I tell him after I kiss him. "I've seen this night, and I can tell up front, we are magnificent."

Chapter Thirty-Nine

I WAKE UP to the delicious sensation of Miles's finger slowly trailing down my spine. Rolling over I tumble into his arms, and look at his face, which is attached to his naked body, which is in my bed. Like for real.

"Hello," I say softly. "That wasn't all a dream, then?"

"Very much real," Miles says, smiling. His arms snake around my waist, pulling me even closer against him. Everything is warm, sleepy, super sexy, and just about to be 100 percent blissful when a long squeak comes from outside the door.

"Oh." I sit up.

"Just pretend you haven't heard that," Miles says, trying to pull me back.

"*Squeak. Squeak. Squeak.*" The squeak repeats approximately every one second.

"It *is* a bit of a buzzkill," I tell Miles, wriggling free of his arms. "A squeaky pigeon usually means something important, like unscheduled pooping or imminent starvation."

Climbing out of bed, I pull on a long T-shirt and open my bedroom door.

"It's a committee," I tell Miles. "I think their main demand is breakfast."

Matilda shoots past me, springing up onto the bed, like she wasn't just in a major accident, where she sets about battering Miles with her cone, punishing him for his tardiness with her characteristic ruthlessness.

"Ow! Matilda, sorry!" Miles unpicks her from his face and holds her at arm's length. "Sorry, sorry. I should have known this was all a bit weird for you."

Mabel sits on the landing, looking up at me with big anxious eyes, and then down toward the bottom of the stairs.

The squeaks are now coming from the living room. Mabel taps my bare foot with her paw.

"Can't Rory do it, just this once?" Miles says, climbing out of bed with Matilda tucked under his arm, like a very angry throw cushion.

"Maybe not," I say as Miles joins me at the door. "Not if everything has gone according to plan, that is."

"What are you talking about?" I head down the stairs, Miles and Mabel following me.

"Rory?" When I turn into the living room, a figure is sitting on the sofa, entirely covered by the faux-fur throw. A pigeon squeaks. I'm getting some quite serious déjà vu.

"You okay, boy?" I edge a bit closer, and whip the throw off like it's a Band-Aid.

Rory pounces at me, squeaking Diego madly as he dances around me, jumping up with little leaping twists.

His wagging tail takes out everything in its wake.

"Rory!" I fall onto the sofa and my dog leaps into my arms, covering my face in licks and kisses. "Rory, you're a dog again! Congrats, boy! You're such a good boy! You are *the* OG good boy!"

"Is that the power of our lovemaking?" Miles asks me, laughing with delight.

"Oh my god." I laugh too. "I love you, you dork, but no. I wandered if maybe I might be able to grant Rory a wish now. Didn't want to mention it, in case it didn't work out. But look! It did!"

"This is brilliant, what else can we wish for?" Miles asks, joining us on the sofa with Mabel and Matilda.

"That is for the next ten years or so," I tell him. "We'll just have to make our own happiness between now and then."

"Do you know what?" Miles says. "I don't think that's going to be a problem."

Miles puts one arm around me, one around Mabel, and I hug Rory as tight as I can. I always knew Rory was a good boy, but I never guessed just how much his goodness could change everything.

SO, I TOLD YOU A STORY that might be pretty hard to believe. And that's okay, you don't have to. I can hardly believe it myself and I know it's true. It happened to me, after all.

So, treat it like a fairy tale, or a fable. Take it with a pinch of salt. That's okay.

Maybe it's only when something truly impossible happens to you that you will really start to believe that *anything* is possible.

Acknowledgments

THANK YOU to my brilliant agent, Hattie Grünewald, and my fantastic editor at Avon, Madelyn Blaney. Also to my dear friends Julie Cohen, Kate Harrison, and Angela Clarke. Not to mention, my husband, Adam, and my beloved three dogs, Blossom, Bluebell, and Rufus, for all the material!

About the Author

STELLA HAYWARD lives with her large family and three dogs in the seaside town of Scarborough, Yorkshire, in the United Kingdom.